BY CRAIG DIRKES

# SUCKTOWN,

# ALASKA

## A NOVEL

Switch Press
a capstone imprint

*Sucktown, Alaska* is published by Switch Press

A Capstone Imprint
1710 Roe Crest Dr.
North Mankato, Minnesota 56003

www.mycapstone.com

Library of Congress Cataloging-in-Publication Data
Names: Dirkes, Craig, author.
Title: Sucktown, Alaska / by Craig Dirkes.
Description: North Mankato, Minnesota : Switch Press, a Capstone imprint, [2017] I Summary: When he is kicked out of his first year of college in Anchorage, eighteen-year-old Eddie Ashford promises the university officials to work for one year at the newspaper in Kusko, Alaska, which is a small, depressing town in back-of-beyond, where it requires either a plane or a dog-sled to get around for most of the time—but staying straight is a challenge, especially when he gets caught up in the local marijuana trade.

Identifiers: LCCN 2016046406 I ISBN 9781630790554 (paper over board) I ISBN 9781630790561 (reflowable epub)

Subjects: LCSH: Reporters and reporting—Alaska—Juvenile fiction. I Newspapers—Juvenile fiction. I Marijuana—Juvenile fiction. I Interpersonal relations—Juvenile fiction. I Alaska—Juvenile fiction. I CYAC: Reporters and reporting—Fiction. I Newspapers— Fiction. I Marijuana—Fiction. I Interpersonal relations—Fiction. I Alaska—Fiction.
Classification: LCC PZ7.1.D59 Su 2017 I DDC 813.6 [Fic] —dc23
LC record available at https://lccn.loc.gov/2016046406

Book design: Brann Garvey
Photo credits: cover and page i photo by Robert Dillon; page v photo by Craig Dirkes

Printed in China.
012017        009995S17

In memory of John "Big Papa" Pace.
He was a hard-working, Chicago Bears-loving,
sockeye-slaying loudmouth who put others
before himself.

# WHEN I DAYDREAM

I'm back out there alone, riding on the tail of a dogsled, gliding across the flat, frigid Alaskan tundra, trying to make one last delivery to a guy in a village ten miles from Kusko.

No clouds block the morning sun. The twelve huskies barrel toward the pink horizon atop a desolate, treeless landscape that looks like a vast white sheet. The windless dawn is so quiet, the only sounds I hear are the patter of the dogs' paws on the narrow snow trail and the whooshing runners of the sled. I'm bundled in a thick red hunting coat, black snow pants, and my heaviest boots. The air is cold, near zero. I don't mind.

I spot something ahead in the distance. To my right and far off the trail stands a guy wearing a furry parka, the kind made from animal pelts. Drenched in the rose-colored light, he stands knee-deep in snow and clutches a rifle at his side.

I'm not alarmed. This isn't the first time I've seen a random guy with a gun in the middle of nowhere. I figure he must be out for an early hunt, but I squint to get a better look. I see him raise his rifle. I scan the snow for game animals but see none. I barely have time to process the fact that he's leveling the gun when — BANG! — I hear it.

*Did that dumbass just fire in my direction?* That's my first thought. Then I hear the second shot.

# CHAPTER 1

# WELCOME TO KUSKO

I got my first look at Kusko through the window of a sketchy twenty-passenger commuter plane as it circled above the town.

I sat in the far back, nervous, wiping ice crystals from the bottom half of the window to get a better view of the remote Alaska settlement below. From high above, Kusko looked like a sprawling shantytown, but with snow. My curiosity hummed louder than the propellers of the twin-engine aircraft.

As the plane bounced through strong winds and began its final descent, I rubbed away more ice crystals and caught sight of small houses with heaps of junk piled in back. They dotted the town like sucky versions of suburban homes with swimming pools. The houses appeared to be grouped into three clusters, all wrapped around a town center, situated on the banks of a big, frozen, snow-covered river. Two trucks drove on top of the river ice, looking like ants marching in a sugar trail.

A few rows in front of me, a baby howled, and when his mother tried to shush him, he only howled louder. I looked out the window and tried to ignore him.

Right before we landed, a heavy crosswind sent the plane's wings seesawing up and down. My heart skipped. I clutched the armrests and shut my eyes. *Five seconds until solid ground,* I thought. The plane skidded onto the runway and bounced a few times before it stabilized. I opened my eyes and exhaled. The baby kept howling.

The propellers stopped rotating after the plane halted in front of Kusko Airport. I wiped the top half of the window to get a full view of the building. It looked smaller than the car wash where my dad worked back home — and more rundown than the abandoned gas station across the street from it.

Outside the wind whipped. Snowdrifts had already begun to form on the side of a luggage trolley that was being driven around when we first landed.

Another strong gust rocked the airplane just as my five fellow passengers rose from their seats. The woman carrying the baby lost her balance and had to sit back down. Her baby cried into her chest. I figured his ears hadn't popped. Mine hadn't either. I'd been too preoccupied with curiosity and eagerness to think about manufacturing a yawn.

Other passengers put on their parkas and gathered their things. I stood up, stretched my legs, and collected my backpack from underneath the seat. My other bag was bigger and had to be checked. Back in Anchorage, I'd crammed everything else I owned into my truck, which would be transported to Kusko via cargo plane in about a week. That was the only way in — by plane. No roads connected Kusko to Anchorage, or to anywhere in civilization. That idea — the remoteness of the place — had intrigued me.

"Welcome to Kusko," the pilot announced over the PA.

Now a sharp reality struck me: The fabulous life I'd been living in Anchorage was officially gone. For the next year, there would be no more amazing mountains. No more college. No more awesome house. No more epic parties. No more Taco Bell.

All because I flunked out of college in my first semester.

My dad would kill me if he knew. My mom would roll over in her grave.

I had to redeem myself. I had resolved to do anything I could to make things right. "Anything" turned out to mean Kusko.

\* \* \*

The inside of the airport was just as dingy as the outside. Puke-orange walls. An empty vending machine with cracked glass. Faded nineties poster advertisements from air carriers I doubted existed anymore. The waiting area held clusters of light-blue plastic chairs, cracked and grimy, with stainless-steel ashtrays in the armrests. Three of the ashtrays overflowed with all colors of used chewing gum.

Right away I spotted my new boss — Mr. Dalton Pace, publisher of the *Delta Patriot* newspaper. He stood at the edge of the waiting area. I recognized his smiling face from the paper's website.

Dalton was fifty-something, clean-shaven, and mostly bald, with a dusting of gray stubble covering the sides of his head. He had tired brown eyes and was my height — six feet or so. His smile revealed teeth that were stained yellow, presumably from chew or cigs or both. He wore the same clothes as three other men in the airport lobby — a flannel shirt covered by tan Carhartt overalls. His feet were wrapped in thick leather work boots. He had the chest and arms of a gorilla.

"Are you Eddie?" Dalton asked, walking toward me, extending his hand for a shake. His voice was powerful — a low, gravelly tone that sounded like a cheerful version of a narrator in a horror-movie trailer.

"Better believe it," I said.

We shook hands. I nearly dropped to my knees and yelled mercy from the strength of his grip. His calloused hand was quintessentially Alaskan, with fingers as thick as bratwursts.

"Nice to meet you," he said. "You're a bigger guy than I had in my mind."

I sometimes get that from people whom I've only spoken to on the phone. My voice is a tinge more high-pitched than it should be, leading people to envision me as a noodle-armed twerp. But seeing me in person sets the record straight: six feet tall, a hundred and eighty pounds, blond hair, blue eyes, and stronger than most. Back home in Minnesota, I was a typical Scandinavian boy.

There was no baggage-claim level in the Kusko

Airport — only a greasy-haired guy setting suitcases in the corner. Dalton and I walked across the room to retrieve my checked backpack from a stack of luggage. "I have to admit, part of me thought you'd back out," Dalton said. "A few years ago, I hired a young reporter who landed in town and hopped on the first flight home. Never saw him again."

I laughed long and loud, as if he'd told me a hilarious joke. "What a pansy!"

"I know," Dalton chortled, grabbing the larger of my two backpacks. "Okay, then. A nasty storm is coming and we need to hustle. We'll stop by the office to crank up the heat so the pipes don't freeze, then dash home to feed the dogs. Ready?"

"Yes, sir," I replied, snatching the smaller backpack. "Let's go."

\* \* \*

I followed Dalton outside to the parking lot. The bright sun glistened off snow that swirled on the wind around us. I zipped my red wool hunting coat all the way up, pinching my bare neck in the zipper teeth.

I peered west and saw an apocalyptic wall of gray clouds. *Holy shit,* I thought but didn't say.

"Get used to that," Dalton said, holding down his stocking cap to keep it from blowing away. "The wind gets hundreds of miles to work up its momentum because it's so flat out here."

And flat it was. I gazed toward the Kusko city limits a mile away and saw that wherever the town ended, an empty, horizontal, snowy-white abyss began.

A second later, a wave of blowing snow blocked my view of the city like a white curtain. I could already tell that my Journalism 101 professor in Anchorage, Dr. DeMarban, had been right: Kusko was Alaska without any of the benefits of Alaska.

DeMarban was an old, ink-stained wretch who'd written for practically every newspaper in Alaska at one time or another — including the *Delta Patriot*, back in the seventies. A month ago, in December, he pulled me aside after class to say he had no choice but to fail me. I knew that topic of conversation was coming, and by then I had already started making my plans to get some work experience in Kusko, get some money, and get back to Anchorage.

"Kusko?" DeMarban said. "That's the *last* place you want to be."

He explained that Kusko sat five hundred miles west of Anchorage on flat and empty land, with no mountains to be seen other than the underwhelming Kilbuck range — which he told me you could spot from Kusko only on a clear day. During summer, he said, the town stinks like a compost heap, there are flocks of mosquitoes, and there is more dust than a Sahara sandstorm.

"Bottom line," DeMarban told me, "is that there's a very good reason every book you've read and every movie you've seen about Alaska failed to mentioned Kusko. It's an unromantic shithole."

I didn't believe him. I thought there was no way the place could be *that* bad. Before I'd moved to Alaska in August, I envisioned the entire state as being a big orgy of mountains, humpback whales, and grizzly bears.

For the most part, it was. But Kusko, as I could already see, was a different deal. If DeMarban was right, Kusko was six thousand people voluntarily living in a place flatter than Iowa, windier than Chicago, and dumpier than Detroit — with virtually no escape.

Dumpy town or not, I didn't care much. I viewed the whole thing as an experience.

* * *

Dalton and I climbed into his truck, a rusty blue Ford F-150 with an old topper that must have been red once but had been oxidized pink. My feet crunched on empty pop cans and candy wrappers. The interior stunk like mold.

Dalton turned the ignition and checked his watch. "Let's get moving. About twenty minutes before the storm hits."

During our drive toward the middle of Kusko (on the only stretch of paved road in town, Dalton informed me), I saw that nothing, anywhere, looked new, be it a home, car, fence, shed, or whatever else. If something was made of metal, it was rusting. If it was wood, it was rotting. If it had paint, it was faded and peeling.

"What's up with that?" I asked, pointing toward a cluster of giant red shipping containers that sat near the road, the sort I'd seen on the freight docks in Anchorage. Smoke billowed from pipes protruding from their tops.

"Those are people's homes," Dalton said, fighting the steering wheel against the wind battering the side of his truck. "They insulate the walls, add heaters, cut out doors and windows, and move their families in."

"Really?" I asked, craning to get a better look as we passed the shipping containers. A husky tethered to a pole outside one of the homes lifted its leg and pissed against the tire of a pickup truck.

We drove near the frozen river I'd seen from the plane. It looked even bigger at ground level, perhaps as wide across as two football fields. I could barely see the other side because of the blowing snow.

"That's the Kuskokwim," Dalton said. "Its big brother is the Yukon River, a hundred miles north. Almost every village you'll visit for your stories will be on the Yukon or Kuskokwim. Nothing happens out here without those rivers. The Natives have relied on them for food and transportation for thousands of years."

In Anchorage I'd learned that "Native" was the preferred term Alaskans used for "Eskimo." My college friends who were from Alaska said most Natives didn't get pissed if you called them Eskimos, but most everybody stuck to the script.

We rolled into the center of town. The main drag had a gas station, a restaurant, and a grocery store called Kusko Dry Goods. I spotted more taxicabs than regular cars and trucks.

The grocery store occupied a glorified pole barn. The gas station had two pumps and a dilapidated wooden kiosk where the attendant hid from the wind. The restaurant, Dalton explained, was a former post office building that some Albanian immigrants had purchased and converted into a slop house called

Delta Delicious.

"Watch out for that place," Dalton said. "It'll give you the fuckin' Delta-rrhea."

I was glad he'd cursed. Working at the *Delta Patriot* would be my first real job, and I didn't know the swearing rules at real jobs.

Dalton cranked the steering wheel and fishtailed through a right. "This way to the office."

"Shit, yeah," I said, hoping for a laugh, but getting nothing from Dalton.

On the road in front of us, a group of teenagers wearing coveralls putzed along on three four-wheel ATVs, single file, with rifles hanging on their backs. Dalton honked at them.

"C'mon," he said to himself, checking his watch again. "I got no time for this."

The guys pulled their four-wheelers off to the side. A sudden gust of blowing snow knocked the truck toward the ditch and blocked our view of the four-wheeler closest to us. "Shit!" Dalton said, slamming on the brakes to avoid hitting what he couldn't see.

The wind let up, and the truck stopped, less than ten feet behind the four-wheeler. "Mother!" Dalton said, steering the truck back onto the road.

As Dalton continued past, I noticed a dead caribou bungee-tied to the back of the four-wheeler leading the pack. I thought that was pretty cool. It felt like I'd landed in a cold version of the Wild Wild West.

\* \* \*

Dalton drove fast and kept glancing at the western

sky. His truck skidded a bit on the gravel and ice outside the *Delta Patriot* office, located inside an old Quonset hut — a corrugated steel building that looked like an airplane fuselage cut in half horizontally. I followed Dalton inside and walked into a dim room with two black barber chairs bolted down in front of an oversized, cloudy mirror. The place was empty, and Dalton kept moving without a word.

"Didn't I come here to write news stories?" I asked, again hoping for a laugh.

"Our office is on the other side of that wall," Dalton said, pointing to the far side of the room, near a restroom door. "I share this place with Mikey Colosky, the barber. It works out nice because you can hear everything through the walls. You'll get good story ideas from listening to all the bitching and gossip."

Mikey Colosky must have forgotten to sweep. The floor looked like he'd been sheering a herd of black sheep the night before. I half wondered if he had, considering the place smelled the way a musty barn would if you took away the manure odor and replaced it with hair spray.

"C'mon, Eddie. We need to move," Dalton said.

I followed him through the door to the office, stopped after another step, and beheld bare brown walls. Blotches of rust marked the rounded metal ceiling. One of the four florescent lighting tubes hanging overhead flickered, swinging gently from the wind pummeling the building. There were no windows in the office. The space reminded me of an interrogation room.

Dalton led me to a tan folding table barely strong

enough to support the ancient computer resting on top of it. The old IBM looked bigger than a mainframe.

"This thing run on diesel fuel?" I asked.

"Good one," Dalton replied, jogging to the far side of the room, near his own desk. "That will be your work station."

He opened the door to a utility closet. Inside was a water tank the size of a refrigerator and a small space heater on the floor next to it. Dalton flipped on the space heater.

"Good to go," he said. "The insulation in this closet sucks. When the temperature drops below minus ten, the water freezes. Mikey and I learned that the hard way."

Dalton rummaged through some paperwork on his desk — a real desk, with a decent desktop computer. He seemed to sense my jealousy.

"You'll use my computer for uploading stories and photos to our website, and for emailing big files to the printer for layout," Dalton said. "Your computer is just for writing and emails. Hopefully I can afford to get you a better one soon. For now, money's tight."

I knew Dalton didn't have much in terms of cash flow. He straight up told me so during a phone conversation we'd had a few weeks before I came to Kusko. He still hadn't gotten the *Patriot* resurrected after purchasing it six years ago. He said he needed a reporter willing to work for cheap so he could focus on selling ads.

Dalton didn't have to offer the job twice. After flunking out of college, I was desperate for any job related to journalism. That was my major, or would've been if I'd survived the first semester. When it was clear I was bombing out, my adviser said I would be eligible to reenroll in college after a year, on the condition that I spend the time doing something that proved I was ready to be a college student again. Working as a reporter more than qualified.

As idiotic as I felt for flubbing my first try at college, I kept telling myself that it wasn't the end of the world. Considering I'd turned eighteen over the summer, I'd still be the age of a proper college freshman after my year in Kusko. Going back after a year wouldn't be like in high school, where the flunkies stood out among kids a year or two younger.

In my dad's eyes, however, my botching college *would* be the end of the world. I hadn't told him, and didn't know how or when I could. For all he knew, I was still in Anchorage continuing an exemplary college career as the first Ashford to pursue higher education.

I didn't know how long I could keep Kusko a secret from my dad. At least a few months, I guessed. Thankfully, I didn't have to worry about him coming to Anchorage for a visit anytime soon; he couldn't afford to fly there. To cover my bases online, I had deleted my Facebook account. That was the only place where my dad kept tabs on me.

Deception aside, I was elated to land the reporter job in Kusko. Back in my hometown of Zimmerman, Minnesota, a town not much bigger than Kusko, and in some ways not much cleaner, I started writing sports stories for the local newspaper when I was fifteen. Scoring the *Delta Patriot* gig wasn't a crazy leap.

\* \* \*

Dalton and I hurried out of the office, through the screaming wind, and into his truck. By now the clouds had blocked the late-day sun, and snow had begun to fall. The wall of clouds now lurched along directly overhead. The wind was so strong, I had to use both hands to shut the door.

"We need to feed the dogs and get indoors," Dalton said, cramming a wad of leaf tobacco into his mouth. "My place is a half mile away."

We sped past house after dumpy little house. Some of them could've fit inside my dad's garage, and he's hardly rich. All of them were built a few feet off the ground.

"What's up with the little stilts under the houses?" I asked.

"Permafrost," Dalton answered, spitting into a pop can. "If you built a house right on the tundra, the heat from inside would melt the permafrost underneath, and the place would sink."

We pulled into his driveway. His house was a small blue one-story, like an old lake cabin but without the charm — or the lake.

The neighbor's trash can blew over, fifteen yards to our left. Used tissue and a small plastic grocery bag whipped past the hood of the truck. I was ready to seek shelter in a basement, but in Kusko, there were no basements.

The moment we exited the truck, Dalton's dogs erupted into a blaring chorus of howls, barks, and whines. Their noise prompted every mutt from every other dog yard within earshot to join in. Suddenly, all the dogs within a couple blocks were going crazy. I looked around, listened, and dropped my mouth in amazement. I was surprised I could even hear the other dogs over the shrieking wind.

Dalton smiled over his shoulder and waved for me to follow.

"When one pack starts, all the other ones around have to have their say too," he said, dropping his head to shield his face from snow blowing sideways. "Just wait until my dogs start howling at three a.m. when it's quiet and sound travels better. Dog packs from clear across town will be in on it."

I followed him toward a rundown shed that stood out back in a dog yard that spanned two sides of his home. Each of the fifteen dogs was chained to a metal stake near its wooden doghouse. Each doghouse was filled with straw and surrounded by wooden pallets. Three-foot-high snowdrifts stuck to the west side of every house.

We walked through ankle-high snow, on a path that needed shoveling. The dogs went even crazier when Dalton passed by, bounding into the air and shaking snow off their backs. The clanking of their chains sounded like sleigh bells.

"Why all the pallets?" I shouted over the howling wind.

"So the dogs don't stomp in their own shit all day," Dalton hollered back, veering toward the shed.

Most of the dogs were sandy brown and slightly smaller than an average-sized Labrador. Three white ones stood out from the crowd. The brown dogs looked so similar, I couldn't see how Dalton could tell them apart.

One of the three white dogs had a few gray patches on her back. I walked over to her through the snow. She seemed happier than the rest. It almost looked like she was smiling at me.

"That's Joanie," Dalton said, one hand on the shed doorknob. "Smartest lead dog I've ever owned."

He kicked snow away from the base of the door and opened it. After he went inside, a savage gust of wind slammed the door shut.

I stood just outside the door with my hands over my ears while he retrieved the food. Behind the shed — snowy tundra, tundra, and more tundra. Snowdrifts rolled across the flat landscape like waves on a lake. I doubted any homes rested beyond the hundred-some yards of tundra I could see. Dalton's house must have been planted on the very edge of town.

I looked back toward Dalton's house. He had two next-door neighbors. The house closest to the side dog yard was a dilapidated log cabin. The house on the other side was a nicer home with green paint. Both homes stood twenty yards from Dalton's.

Dalton emerged from the shed with two five-gallon buckets of dog food. "You feed the dogs on the side of the house, and I'll take the ones back here," he ordered, handing me one of the buckets and a metal scoop. "Once the dogs are full, they'll hunker down in their houses and stay warm. We're talking fifty below windchill today. No dog is built for that kind of cold. But they'll be safe now."

\* \* \*

With the work done, Dalton and I unbundled in the entryway. His place looked decent enough for what it was — two bedrooms with a separate kitchen, living room, and dining area. The entire place couldn't have been much bigger than the unfinished basement inside my house back in Minnesota, and our house was no mansion.

I sat down on the living room couch while Dalton got a pot of coffee brewing. I looked outside a bay window facing the tundra. Complete whiteout now. Nothing was visible beyond the doghouse closest to the window.

I didn't know what to make of Kusko. The inside of my head was just as blank as the view outside. I'd been on sensory overload from the moment I walked off the plane, and I hadn't had time to think. *This place'll be cool*, I guessed. *Six thousand people live here. They can't all be wrong.*

Dalton opened the fridge and pulled out a family-sized Tupperware container filled with some sort of brown mush.

"Hungry?" he asked.

"Depends," I said. "What is that?"

"Moose stew. Ever tried it?"

"No. But something tells me that if I'm going to live here, I'd better like that stuff if I don't want to go hungry."

"You catch on fast," Dalton said, chuckling.

He dumped half the container of stew into a pot. While warming it on the stove, he told me how he'd shot a seventy-inch bull moose about a hundred and fifty miles southeast of Kusko, near a town called Dillingham. He flew there every fall to bag a moose. The meat would last him almost an entire year. He poured a bowl for each of us. I sat down across from him at the kitchen table.

"So, Eddie," Dalton said, taking his first bite. "What do you think of bush life so far?"

"Not sure yet," I said, testing the stew with the tip of my tongue. "It's different."

"Bet your ass it's different. Anchorage people are pansy-ass cidiots. Their idea of a genuine Alaskan experience is driving two hours to go combat fishing on the Russian River alongside hundreds of tourists, or camping by the Kenai River in their fancy fifth-wheel trailers. Kusko is the real Alaska, my friend. This'll make a man out of you."

I finished my first bite of stew, then another. A little gamey, but yummy. It tasted almost as good as the beef stew my mom used to make.

"Speaking of genuine Alaskan experiences," I said, "will I get to try mushing?"

"Absolutely," Dalton assured me. "I'll teach you in no time. Soon you'll be running those dogs all by yourself."

CHAPTER 2

# CHEECHAKO

Two hours until deadline. I'd been at the office typing my nards off since seven a.m., writing my third story in four days. That was more stories than I'd ever written in an entire month when I was doing sports back home or pecking away at the University of Anchorage's student newspaper, the *Puffin Press*, in the fall.

I'd published only two stories in the *Puffin Press*. That's it. Two. I'd been assigned four others, but I couldn't manage to turn them in on time. I had more important demands on my time. I could shotgun a beer in less than five seconds, but I couldn't finish a news story in a week.

Dalton sat at his desk, drawing thumbnail sketches of where the advertisements were to be placed on each page of this week's edition of the *Patriot*.

My story was about the U.S. Coast Guard rescuing a father and son who got stranded while hunting caribou twenty miles northeast of Tununak, a village located one hundred fifty miles west of Kusko. I had just gotten off the phone with a Coast Guard spokesman who said the father had activated a personal locator beacon after his snow machine conked out.

When the spokesman said "snow machine," I played along like I knew what he meant. I had no idea. *Is that some kind of ATV I've never seen?*

I figured I'd just write it in. The locals would understand.

"How's the story coming, Eddie?" Dalton asked, sipping coffee.

"Almost done," I said. "Just one thing — what's a snow machine?"

"It's what you tenderfoots from the lower forty-eight call a snowmobile," he said, and laughed.

*K, dick.*

"Thanks," I said. "Any other Alaska terms I ought to know?"

"Cheechako," Dalton replied, still chuckling to himself.

"What's that mean?"

"Look it up."

I didn't have time for that. I needed every minute I could get for the Tununak story. I wanted it to be perfect.

The two other stories I'd already written were about: 1) A non-fatal plane crash near the runway in the village of Red Devil, and 2) A new school lunch program in Kusko, through which all kids in grades K through twelve were being offered locally caught salmon twice a week.

Dalton had put me straight to work the day after I arrived in Kusko, saying we had to crank out an entire edition in just four days — technically, three and a half days, since deadline was every Tuesday at noon.

Beyond pointing me toward the folding table and ancient computer, Dalton hadn't bothered with much training, but he had paused long enough to give me the basics: The *Patriot* circulated in every single village of the Yukon-Kuskokwim Delta — one of the largest deltas on Earth, with twenty-five thousand people living in fifty-six villages scattered across a region the size of Oregon. The printing company shipped five thousand copies to Kusko every week. When the newspapers arrived Wednesday morning, two-thirds of them were divvied up and sent aboard planes to all fifty-six villages. The rest stayed in Kusko, where Dalton set them on a rack at Kusko Dry Goods and inside nine newspaper boxes around town.

My job was to fill the space between the ads, and I was running out of time on the snow machine story.

Dalton's phone rang, and he picked it up before the second ring. "*Delta Patriot*," he said. "Hi, Misty."

I paused at the keyboard.

"Seriously?" Dalton said. "Hold on."

He dropped the phone to his shoulder. "Eddie, what time is it?"

I checked my watch. "Quarter after ten."

He got back on the phone. "My new guy will be there in five minutes."

Dalton dug into his pocket and tossed his keys to me from across the room. "That was Misty Livermont, the court clerk. She has a decent story for you at the courthouse. Drive up there, get the police report, and haul ass back here."

I checked my watch again.

"Get going," Dalton said. "Misty's a Native lady, sits right up front. Looks mean but isn't."

"That's helpful," I said. At first I'd been surprised by the bluntness of Alaskans when it came to describing people as Natives or Eskimos — or whites, for that matter. Back home, the mention of race or color or anything along those lines brought out the cautious side in everybody — everybody, that is, except the elderly and the obnoxious. But in a place like Kusko, where at least half the population was all or part Native, it seemed that word was just another adjective, like short or tall, fat or thin, pretty or plain.

I added, "But I'm not even done with the Tununak story yet."

"I'll finish it while you're gone." Any trace of patience had gone out of Dalton's voice. "Go. Now. Remember, time is money."

I grabbed my coat and bolted out the door.

I fired up Dalton's truck and flipped on the headlights. I still wasn't completely used to it being dark after ten a.m. I felt like I should be feeling hungry for breakfast, not lunch.

I stepped on the gas, because when Dalton said time was money, he meant it. On my first day, he had explained that for every hour we were late sending stories and photos to the printing company in Anchorage, he was out two hundred dollars. The copy editors, layout artists, and printing press operators who worked at the printer got paid not only for the time they spent producing the *Patriot*, but also the time they wasted waiting for us to send them content.

Two minutes later, I pulled up to what apparently passed for a courthouse in a place like Kusko. The rundown building was the size of a small-town bank. Sky blue paint flaked off the wood siding.

I left the truck running and dashed inside, where behind the front counter stood a Native woman who wore a hard-nosed expression and a red sweater with wildflowers knitted across the front. She held up a piece of paper.

"You must be Misty," I said. "I'm Eddie from the *Patriot*."

"Here," she replied, handing me the paper. "We just logged this in to the blotter. I figured Dalton would want to fit it in this week."

Dalton had already typed up a half-page of police-blotter entries for the back page of this week's paper. Each entry included one sentence about a crime somebody was either charged with or convicted of, and the blotter was intended to include every crime committed in the YK Delta. Dalton had the power to transform any of the entries into a full-blown story — including the one I held in my hand.

"Thanks," I said with my head down, scanning the document. I couldn't believe what I was reading. I glanced back at Misty and added, "Crazy story."

"Get used to it," Misty said with a smirk. "Out here, drunk people do stupid shit all over the place."

I laughed — not just because her comment was funny, but because it sounded even funnier coming out of the mouth of a woman who looked like she belonged in a church basement knitting more sweaters like the one she had on.

* * *

Twelve minutes until deadline. I typed so fast I was practically sweating.

"How you coming, Eddie?" Dalton asked, typing just as feverishly. "Don't overthink it. The story doesn't need to be flashy."

"Almost there," I said.

"You got a headline in mind?"

"Pilot Station man crashes and burns."

"Nice," Dalton said.

He had offered to write the last-minute story, but I insisted that I could handle it. I wanted to prove I could deliver under pressure, although I wasn't entirely sure I could.

My story opened like this:

PILOT STATION, Alaska — State Troopers arrested a 22-year-old male resident of this Yukon River village after he got drunk and rammed his four-wheel ATV into the only gas pump in town. The pump burst into flames, and the fire spread to a nearby house.

I made a quick call to get a couple quotes from the owner of the gas station and cranked out the story faster than I'd ever done before. I concluded with a line about how the town's three hundred fifty residents would be without a fuel source for several days, shouted "Done!", and pressed the return key extra hard to flaunt my accomplishment.

"What time is it?" I asked.

"Ten to twelve," Dalton said. "Email me the story, and that'll be a wrap."

I sat back and watched as he scanned the story. I took a sip of coffee, but spat it back into the mug. I'd been so busy, I hadn't touched it in almost an hour, hadn't known it went cold.

"Nice job," Dalton said without looking at me. "I think you'll do just fine here."

"Thanks," I replied, prouder of myself than I let on. "So, what now? Am I done for the day?"

After four days of nonstop work, I was exhausted and wanted to chill, but Dalton said he wanted to show me how to upload all the stories and photos to the *Patriot*'s website, which he explained had to be done by three p.m. every Tuesday.

"So we'll still be here awhile," he said. "And after we finish here, you get to go home and clean up dog shit in the yard while I cook us dinner. *Then* you'll be done."

That was not the news I wanted to hear.

"I guess child labor laws don't apply to eighteen-year-olds," I said. It was a joke, kind of. The blank look on Dalton's face told me he wasn't sure whether I was serious.

"No, they don't," he said.

Suddenly, the mood felt serious.

"I'm just goofing," I said, trying to diffuse the tension. "I mean, I won't lie. I'm gassed after the last few days, but I can soldier on."

"Correct answer," Dalton said. "Welcome to the real world."

# CHAPTER 3

# HIGH THERE, FINN

I put on my boots in the entryway of Dalton's house while he got to work cooking moose stew in the kitchen. I had just finished a ten-hour day at the office. My watch said six o'clock now, and outside the sky was pitch black.

"Food should be ready after you finish outside," Dalton said.

I flipped a switch that turned on floodlights for the dog yards. While slipping on my mittens, I stepped outside the front door and grabbed a black garbage bag from a box on the top step and a spade that rested against the house.

After little more than a week of living in Kusko, this was my fifth time cleaning the dog yard. Dalton's fifteen mutts were shit factories, dropping two or three loads per day. Scooping up their turds required a solid hour of work every forty-eight hours. The work was nasty at best, but made worse because some dogs apparently liked to take dumps in their food dishes. One upside: the cold diluted the odor.

I started in the back. Joanie had shat on the flat roof of her house, and the frozen poop was rock solid. I chipped away but couldn't dislodge it all. Joanie sat on her haunches watching me, wagging her tail, and smiling.

I never imagined that cleaning the dog yard would be so much work. When Dalton first contacted me about working at the *Patriot*, I had glossed over the part of his email that talked about the dogs. He wrote:

Hello, Eddie,

I'm Dalton Pace, owner and publisher of the *Delta Patriot* newspaper in Kusko. Thanks for emailing the stories you wrote for your hometown and college newspapers. I see promise in your work. You could have what it takes to be a real journalist. Would you consider moving out here to be a reporter? The work experience would be invaluable.

Invaluable, and adventurous. You'd get to fly to Native villages to cover stories.

Although I couldn't pay you much, you could live with me for free. I'd ask that you stay at least a year and also help take care of my sled dogs.

Please give me a call so I can explain in detail.

Sincerely,

Dalton

It took me more than a half hour to clean the backyard, shivering in the cold with a neck-warmer pulled up over my mouth. Best I could tell, Kusko was slightly colder than Minnesota, and noticeably colder than Anchorage, where the ocean air kept things in check.

As I lumbered through the snow to the side yard, I noticed that all three houses across the street had snow machines and four-wheelers, but no cars or trucks, parked in their driveways. Five minutes later a taxi stopped in front of the dilapidated log cabin next door, and from the cab emerged a young guy in a red down jacket, high-tops, and black athletic pants with two white stripes down the sides. He looked like he'd just finished playing basketball.

I stopped working and eyed him from the side yard. I assumed the guy was a neighbor Dalton had told me about, a kid named Finn Wassily. If I'd seen Finn's house back in Minnesota, I would've assumed it was a hunting shack — and not much of one.

"What's up, dude?" he hollered, waving from near his front door.

After pulling the neck warmer down from my mouth, I said, "Not much. Just cleaning dog shit and being cold."

Finn only nodded, so I added, "I'm Eddie, your new neighbor."

"Cool, brother," he replied.

He turned to head inside, then stopped and glanced back at me, as I stood there with a red nose and a bag of dog shit in my hand. He smirked, shook his head slightly, and said, "Why not stop over when you're done?"

"Sure, man," I said. I was relieved to talk to somebody my own age. Other than Dalton and old

Misty at the courthouse, the only people I'd interacted with during the past week were at Kusko City Hall. On Monday Dalton introduced me to some city council members so that I'd feel more comfortable covering their meetings. I'd never written that kind of story before and felt stupid, like I had something to hide. If pressed, I still couldn't explain what the word "ordinance" meant.

I didn't feel any more intelligent about the other stories I was writing, either. Kusko was a different world. Every other story was about somebody dying, getting hurt, or trying to survive some mishap. If not those things, then the story had something to do with wildlife.

The two stories I'd written earlier that day were: 1) Vehicle travel prohibited on the Kuskokwim between the villages of Aniak and Chuathbaluk due to dangerous ice conditions, and 2) A decline in the musk ox population on Nunivak Island, located a hundred miles west of Kusko.

Before Finn disappeared inside, I called out, "Actually, can I come over now? I need a break."

He waved for me to follow, so I left the dog yard, tailed Finn inside, and took off my coat. The interior of his little house looked less ramshackle than the outside, but not by much. In the living room, I counted six strands of duct tape covering cracks in the logs, which to me seemed like a pretty weak effort to keep out the cold. Finn's oversized box TV and the lava lamp next to it were plugged into an electrical outlet that dangled by its wires out of the wall. His kitchen appliances looked ancient — like they were about to blow — and the pots and pans hanging above the stove were caked with brown and black perma-grease. The furniture seemed nice enough, though. A huge black sectional sofa faced the TV and occupied much of the floor space. In front of the couch rested an antique wooden chest.

Finn looked full-blooded Native, as far as I could guess. He was a bit shorter than me, with a slim build and black hair clipped too short to style. His brown eyes looked like they'd seen a lot.

We both sat down at the kitchen table, looked at each other, and endured some awkward silence before I deployed my standard Alaska ice-breaker. "Did you grow up here?" I asked.

"St. Mary's," he said. "Hundred twenty miles north on the Yukon River."

"Nice," I said, though I had no idea whether St. Mary's was nice or a complete shithole.

Finn explained he was eighteen and had moved to Kusko the previous June, right after graduating from high school. He said he was related to half the people in St. Mary's and needed to get out.

"Plus," he added, "there are no jobs in St. Mary's whatsoever. In Kusko, at least there's *some* work."

He continued, "So, what's your deal? What's a young gussuk like you doing out here?"

"What's a gussuk?" I asked.

"That's Yup'ik for white boy."

"What's Yup'ik?"

Finn explained that Yup'ik was the Native tribe that occupied southwest Alaska. He broke down all the other big tribes — the Inupiats, who lived north of the Arctic Circle; the Aleuts, who lived in the extreme southwest in that long string of islands that look like a mastodon tusk; and more. It seemed like most of my conversations turned into Kusko tutorials.

"There are some other big tribes," Finn said. "But us in the YK Delta, we're Yup'ik."

Finn grabbed us two Mountain Dews from the fridge, and I had to tell him my story. I kept it short, but I told the truth — how I'd moved to Alaska for college, bombed out of school, and moved to Kusko to redeem myself.

"That sucks," he said. "What happened with school?"

"All my classes started at eight or nine a.m., but the parties didn't end until four a.m.," I said. "I couldn't get used to going on less than five hours of sleep."

"Too much fun in Anchorage, eh?" Finn said.

"Beyond awesome," I said.

"Really?" he said. "Do tell."

I gave him the longer story, which started with my friend R.J., a hockey player who was on scholarship in Anchorage. I'd tagged along with him in coming to Alaska, and through a wealthy husband and wife who were hockey boosters, R.J. and I ended up with what had to be the sickest college pad in Alaska. For next to nothing, the couple rented us a two-bedroom apartment in the basement of one of their homes, basically a giant log palace in the wilderness. The structure was stupefying. It was a towering A-frame flanked by two additions that were large enough to be decent homes themselves. Although our apartment wasn't extravagant, the rest of the home was a rich person's idea of rustic glory — moose-antler chandelier, flannel couches, antique gun racks, twenty-foot-tall stone fireplace, and a full-body mount of a thousand-pound grizzly bear in the center of the main room.

"No shit?" Finn asked when I mentioned the stuffed grizzly.

"It gets better," I explained.

The south-facing cabin was built on the side of a mountain, at the edge of a rock-ribbed, ninety-foot cliff. Our apartment door led to a cobblestone patio the size of a tennis court, a space that doubled as the official launching pad for members of the Anchorage Hang Gliding Club. Mountains towered all around, and our closest neighbor was a full half mile away. The nearest town was Eagle River, ten miles from the UA campus. We called the place Chateau Eagle River.

"The owners were never around," I said. "We threw parties four or five nights a week. One time, some honeys from the gymnastics team did balance beam exercises on the back of the stuffed bear. They were up there with beers in hand and didn't spill a drop."

"Damn!" said Finn, wide-eyed.

I thought about R.J. then and wondered what he was up to back at the Chateau. He was kind of a strange-looking guy, with shoulder-length hockey hair that was feathered down the middle, a chipped front tooth, and a body shaped like a beer keg. But he was a kick-ass hockey player, and despite his appearance, he'd fiddled ten times the beans I ever did.

Finn grabbed a glass from his cupboard, opened his freezer, and pulled out a liter of cheap-looking vodka.

"Want any?" he asked, pouring the vodka and some Mountain Dew into his glass.

I thought about Dalton next door, my new boss and landlord. He was probably wondering where I'd disappeared to.

"No, but have at it," I said. "Drinking would kind of defeat the purpose of why I moved to Kusko. I need to take it easy until I get my shit together."

"Out of curiosity," I added, "how'd you get the booze?"

Finn pulled out his cell phone, tapped on it, and handed it to me. "Check it out," he said.

I saw five or six phone numbers organized into a category called "Sauce."

"Those guys are all bootleggers," he said. "Each number connects me to — "

"Bootleggers?" I asked, astonished.

I was in for another Kusko tutorial. Finn explained how the local liquor market worked. He said Kusko was a "damp" community, meaning it was legal to have alcohol in town, but illegal to sell it. Even the mouthwash and vanilla extract at Kusko Dry Goods were kept behind the counter. The airport had a special kiosk for alcohol shipments from Anchorage. The local authorities allowed people to purchase a certain amount of liquor per month. If you wanted more but ran out, or forgot to place an order, or exceeded your monthly limit, or were underage, you called one of the numbers on Finn's phone.

"Before ten p.m., a liter of vodka costs seventy-five bucks," Finn said. "After that, it goes up by seventy-five every two hours. The drunker people get, the more they're willing to pay. And that's just in Kusko. Village prices are fifty percent higher, sometimes double."

Finn said alcohol was flat-out illegal in villages, which blew my mind. I thought liquor bans existed only in history books in America.

"That's why Kusko is such a shit show every weekend," Finn said. "All the villagers come here to get drunk."

I was standing up to leave when someone rapped on Finn's door. My first thought was that Dalton had finally gone out looking for me, but when Finn glanced out the window next to the door, he laughed a little and whispered, "These two again."

He opened the door, and with a whoosh of cold air entered two girls about my age. Maybe still in high school, I guessed. Maybe not.

Finn took their coats. One of the girls had blond hair, a stud in her nose, and a hoop through the right side of her lower lip. The other had long, straight black hair and perfect skin, definitely the better looking of the two. Both wore skinny jeans with bulky, earth-toned hippie sweaters.

"What's up, girls?" Finn asked. He plopped himself down on the black couch and motioned for the ladies to join him. I stood near the table with a dumb grin on my face.

As the girls made their way to the couch, the cuter one stopped and pointed at me. "Who do we have here?" she asked.

Finn told them my name and introduced them as Bristy, the dark-haired one, and her friend, Hope.

The girls sat down on either side of Finn, and

eyeing me, Hope said, "So, like, is Eddie cool?"

"I'm pretty sure," Finn answered.

"Good," Hope said. "Let's get down to business."

Finn opened the top of the wooden chest and pulled out an electronic scale and a freezer bag filled with a pretty significant volume of pot.

*Holy balls,* I thought, trying to keep a straight face. *Is this happening?*

I'd been around plenty of weed in my day. I almost never smoked the stuff, but lots of my high school friends did, often roasting fatties while they went ice fishing. Zimmerman was on the northern-most fringes of the Twin Cities suburbs. The place was borderline rural, which meant every guy in my high school was a hard-ass who lived on a farm, played football, played hockey, fixed pickup trucks, hunted, fished, or did all of the above. And when they did those things, they liked to do some of them with a buzz. Between bongs, bowls, dugouts, red hairs, and skunky smells, I knew how everything worked.

Still, I couldn't believe how open Finn was being about selling drugs a half hour after we'd just met — and knowing that I worked at the paper and that the publisher of the paper lived right next door.

*Play it cool,* I told myself.

Finn reached into the sack of weed and pulled out a couple of nugs. "You lovely ladies want an eighth this time, right?"

"Yep," Bristy said. Next to her, Hope checked her phone. I'd been told Kusko was the only place in the YK Delta with cell phone service. Villagers had to use landlines.

Bristy added, "This stuff better be better than the last bag you sold us."

"Suck it, nerd," Finn said. "That stuff was fine. You only think it was bunk because you two smoke too much. You've built a tolerance."

Finn put the buds on the scale and sprinkled some loose stuff on top, like a deli worker adding a few more shells of pasta. He lifted up the scale and dumped the smoke into a sandwich baggie. "One eighth, right on the nuts," he said, handing the baggie to Bristy.

Finn's weed was the first I'd spotted in Alaska. Nobody ever had any at the parties R.J. and I threw because almost all of the people at them were athletes on scholarship. They stuck to booze.

Bristy snatched the baggie, walked past me, and sat down at the kitchen table. She was even cuter up close. "Wanna smoke up?" she asked.

"Nah, I'm good," I said. "But can I smell it?"

"Whatever's clever," she said, then handed me the bag.

I lifted it to my nose and inhaled a whiff. It smelled like bubble gum lodged up a skunk's butt. I figured it had to be way more potent than the ditch weed my friends used to burn back home. *Way* more.

"Wow," I said. "If I smoked even one hit of this, I'd be higher than a giraffe's ass."

The girls laughed.

"What's your story, Eddie?" Bristy asked.

"Yeah," Hope said. "Who the hell are you?"

The girls laughed again.

I told them everything I'd just told Finn about why I was in Kusko, how I planned to go back to school, and how I wanted to party but shouldn't.

"I bet you miss your parents," Bristy said. "Being so far away, I mean."

"I miss my dad and brother." I paused. "If my mom were still alive, I'd want to call her all the time too."

Everyone got quiet.

It'd been years since my mom died, yet I still hadn't discovered a way to say so without making people feel awkward. "Don't worry, guys. It happened a long time ago."

"Sorry to hear that," Bristy said. "We know a girl who lost her mom in a plane crash last summer. Her dad survived but he's in a wheelchair now."

"That's rough," I said.

She continued, "And this other guy we know in school — he's a junior, but we still have gym class with him because our school's juniors and seniors have gym together — his dad just died of something, but I can't remember what. Hope and I used to rip on the kid because he has a lisp. We'd always tell him to say 'sophisticated sausages.' But we don't rip on him anymore because we feel so sorry for him."

"I can definitely relate," I said.

"We know this other girl — well, she graduated last year and moved to Seattle for college, and I don't know if she'll be coming back to Kusko, so I don't know if we can still say we *know* her anymore. So I guess it's more like we *knew* this one other girl. But anyway, her mom died of — "

"Stop, Bristy. Just stop," Hope said. "We gotta go."

"Hope's parents are away," Bristy said. "We're gonna go to her place and spark up. Nice meeting you,

Eddie. It's a small town, so I'm sure we'll bump into you again. I bet we'll end up seeing you an average of five or six times per month at the grocery store, or maybe over here at Finn's place, or maybe at — "

"Shut it, Bristy," Hope said. She stood up and gave Finn some money; then they were gone.

The room went quiet, except for the wind whistling through some wall cracks Finn had yet to cover with duct tape.

Finn seemed to sense I was uncomfortable about the transaction I'd just witnessed. He stared at the floor and took in a deep breath.

"I don't sell a lot," he said. "Just enough for some extra cash. And I hardly ever smoke."

"No worries," I said. "But aren't you scared of getting busted?"

"Not really. I rarely have more than an ounce in my possession; you're only looking at jail time if you get pinched with more than that. The truth is, my job slinging luggage at the airport doesn't pay enough for me to survive. I'm just doing what I have to do right now."

"What about your future?"

"I haven't thought that far ahead."

Finn stood up and headed to the bathroom. I needed to get home and finish cleaning the dog yard. And I wanted to get to bed early — my truck was supposed to arrive at the airport at seven a.m.

I nodded and said, "I gotta get back."

I was happy to have made my first friend in Kusko, drug dealer or not.

CHAPTER 4

# REUNITED!

Somewhere inside the jumbo cargo plane in front of me, a sharp metal something lacerated the side of my beloved truck. The shrill scratching sound reverberated off the high ceiling beams, rusty steel walls, and oil-stained concrete of the cavernous airplane hangar. Heaters the size of refrigerators were bolted to every corner of the ceiling, but the hot air they blew did little against the frigid air gushing through the monstrous opening to the runway.

I stood at a customer service counter tucked into one corner of the building. The metal-on-metal noise made me drop the pen I was using to fill out the receiving paperwork.

"Hey!" I said to the scuzzy warehouse guy across the counter from me. "That's my truck!"

He turned around and looked at the cargo plane as workers off-loaded pallets of nonperishable foods, which I assumed were destined for village grocery stores and Kusko Dry Goods.

"I don't see a truck," the guy replied apathetically. "That sound could be anything."

"Wrong," I said. "A father knows."

The truck was my baby: a 1982 Toyota Land Cruiser FJ40 4x4. The FJ was a rare sight and a classic — a small SUV that resembled a Jeep Wrangler, with two doors and a short wheelbase. Mine was red with a three-inch lift, beefy thirty-three-inch tires, a brush guard in front, and a roof rack up top.

Seconds later, the FJ rolled down the loading ramp at the rear of the aircraft. One of the cargo workers was at the wheel and looked happy to be there. I jogged to the truck and circled it while it was still in motion. Sure enough, a wavy foot-long scratch scarred the middle of the passenger door.

The driver got out and joined me on the side of the vehicle. He took off his green mesh trucker hat and scratched his head, seeming unsure of how to console me. "That'll buff out," he said.

"No, it won't," I said, thumbing the scratch, recalling the car-detailing expertise of my dad, who'd managed a car wash for twenty-plus years. "If you can feel a scratch with your fingernail, wax won't do squat. It'll need paint."

Pissed as I was, I let it go. The excitement of being reunited with my truck overpowered my anger. The truck felt like a little piece of home.

The FJ used to belong to my grandpa, Gustaf, who bought it a decade before I was born. Every summer, he drove the FJ from his country home in Milaca to my house in Zimmerman, with the hardtop off, to take me walleye fishing an hour north on Mille Lacs Lake.

The FJ finally crapped out when I was in ninth grade. My grandpa sold the rims and tires, hoisted the truck onto some blocks, threw a tarp over it, and retired it to his pole barn.

Unbeknownst to me, my dad and my brother, Max, had spent the past summer restoring the truck so that they could give it to me as a graduation gift.

They sprung it on me while I was eating tater tot hotdish on a hot summer night in early August. As I sat with my dad at the dinner table, I heard the rumbling of an unfamiliar vehicle in our driveway. "Put this on over your eyes," my dad said, pulling a blue bandana from his back pocket.

I looked down at the entryway of our split-level home and saw Max peek his head through the front door. "C'mon, Eddie," he said. "Take off your bib and put on that blindfold already."

I wrapped the bandana around my head. My dad clutched my arm and led me from the kitchen table to the driveway. "What's going on?" I asked, standing barefoot on the blacktop in front of our yellow cookie-cutter suburban home.

"Max and I are proud of you," my dad said. "We hope that chasing your dreams will be more fun driving this."

I took off the blindfold, and there was the FJ, looking better than ever. Although it was a cloudy evening, I could have sworn a single ray of sunshine beamed down on her. I sprinted to the truck and started dry-humping a front fender. Dad and Max laughed.

I stepped back and looked the FJ up and down. "Seriously?" I asked. "Grandpa parted with this? Did you two fix it up? Are you *kidding* me?"

"It's all yours, little squirt," Max said, patting me on the back. "Super, super-huge pussy or not, we love you."

Max was a full-time auto mechanic at Zimmerman Auto Salvage. He told me that he'd worked on the truck an hour or more every weekday for two months, after my dad dropped a couple grand for a used engine and other parts. My dad had been saving the money for almost a year. Thankfully, he didn't have to pay to have the truck repainted. Hank Gunderson from Hank's Auto Salon owed him a favor.

I corralled my dad and Max together for a group hug. "Thanks, guys," I said. "I love you both."

After I let go, Max wound up and slapped the back of my head, hard, like I was a bratty kid about to do something wrong.

"Dammit, Max!" I yelped.

"Whatever you do," he said, "don't ever let this truck out of your sight. Dad and I dumped a lot of time and money into this beast. You hear?"

"Loud and clear," I said.

I turned the key in the truck's ignition, listened to it rumble, and backed out of the driveway to do some victory laps along Zimmerman's main drag. Two weeks later, R.J. and I drove it thirty-three hundred miles to Anchorage.

In December, I told Dalton that backstory about my truck while we were hashing out the details of my employment. I insisted that I couldn't come to Kusko without the FJ.

He agreed to ship the truck to and from Anchorage, on two conditions: I had to stay for the entire year I promised, and I had to accept a wage of ten dollars per hour instead of twelve.

I didn't have a choice in the matter. I flat-out *could not* be without my truck.

And the money thing didn't bother me. Compared to being a poor college student, I'd be living large on ten bucks an hour.

\* \* \*

I hopped into the truck inside the airplane hangar, near the customer service counter. Just as I dropped it into gear, I noticed a pallet of newspapers between the cargo plane and me.

I rolled down my window. "Hey!" I said to the same scuzzy warehouse guy, pointing at the pallet. "Are those papers the *Delta Patriot*?"

"Yep," he said.

"Mind if I grab one? I work there."

"Go ahead."

I got out of the FJ, dashed over, and snatched a copy. Two of my stories decorated the front page — one about a lady who barely survived falling through the ice near the village of Grayling, the other about how local authorities were searching for a suspect who shot out the tires of a four-wheeler driven by a guy en route to the nearby village of Kwethluk.

I felt damned awesome after seeing my name under the headlines. I wanted to reinstate my Facebook account and post a selfie, with a cheesy-ass duck face, holding the *Patriot*.

I was a real journalist, for a real newspaper. I wished I didn't have to hide it from my dad. I wished my mom were alive to see.

I tossed the paper onto the front seat of the FJ, pulled out my phone, and sent this text to my father: "Got an A on my paper."

A minute later, he responded: "Proud."

# CHAPTER 5

# HOT. H-O-T. HOT.

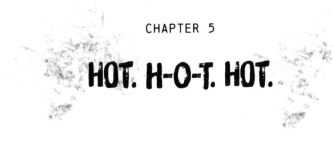

Dalton stormed into the office in a huff. He was a half hour late in returning from the morning paper route because his truck wouldn't start in our driveway, even after we tried to jump it. He'd forgotten to plug in the engine block heater the night before. I lent him the FJ and took a cab in.

"The papers barely fit in the back of your little buggy," Dalton said, shaking off the cold. He hung his coat on the back of his desk chair and flipped on his computer. Five spitters — three pop cans and two plastic water bottles — littered the top of his desk. I rarely saw him without a fat gob of leaf tobacco in his mouth. He was worse than a baseball player.

"It's not a buggy," I said. "It's the sweetest ride this side of — "

Dalton cut me off. "Eight days," he said and sighed while staring at his computer screen. "I haven't sold a new ad in eight damn business days. I gotta get cranking."

Dalton spent five or more hours a day making sales calls to businesses in Anchorage, Fairbanks, and sometimes Seattle. He targeted gun and outdoors companies, bulk grocery suppliers, and other businesses that sold stuff rural Alaskans needed. Although Kusko Dry Goods' weekly two-page ad made Dalton enough money to cover the paper's expenses, he needed to sell many more ads to earn a living. And lately, he wasn't getting the job done.

"Maybe you should try selling ads to more businesses in Kusko," I suggested.

"Pointless," Dalton replied. "They all say the same thing: 'I don't need to advertise. Everyone in town knows where I am and what I sell.'"

Dalton's financial issues were starting to bug me. After three weeks of living in Kusko, I still hadn't traveled to a village to cover a news story. I thought one upside to the job would be getting out to the villages. But it wasn't until *after* I'd arrived in Kusko that Dalton said January through May is his slowest time of year, when he's too poor to pay for village flights. I felt cheated.

I sipped the last of my morning coffee. I stood up from my desk and shitty computer to pour more from the antique-looking coffee percolator plugged in next to the fax machine. Dalton's favorite mug sat on the little table. Black letters on the white mug read: coffee makes me poop.

"Can I pour you some?" I asked, holding up his mug. "Our meeting is about to start."

"You just wait, Eddie," Dalton said, peeking over his computer at me but ignoring my question. "This summer, I'll sell so many ads that the *Patriot* will be twenty-four pages instead of twelve. They say this year's dividend might break two thousand. That's enough money for folks to put thirty percent down on a new four-wheeler or sixty-horse outboard. Every power-sports dealer in Anchorage and Fairbanks is going to advertise with us."

I'd heard about the "dividend" from a guy I knew back in Anchorage, a UA hockey player born and raised in Alaska, but it sounded too good to be true.

"People really *do* get money just for living here?" I asked.

"Every fall," Dalton began, snatching the cup of coffee that I had poured for him, "Alaska residents get a fat check from the state's oil fund. The amount is different each year, but can hit two thousand per person. Come late summer, businesses across the state will ramp up their marketing efforts to get people excited about buying their products when the dividend checks get cut in the fall. It's a feeding frenzy for selling ads."

"Will I get a check?" I asked, sitting back down at my desk.

"You haven't lived in Alaska long enough," Dalton said. "You'll get your first one a year from now, in 2011."

"That blows," I said.

I wanted a dividend check now. I could already tell my paychecks wouldn't go far in Kusko. Walk into Kusko Dry Goods with fifty bucks, and you'd walk out with nothing more than eggs, bread, milk, a dozen packs of ramen noodles, and some wilted produce.

Not to mention, gas cost almost seven dollars a gallon. When I saw the prices in Kusko, I worried I'd be just as cash-strapped as I was in college.

"Ready to meet?" Dalton asked.

We were scheduled for our weekly editorial meeting. Every Wednesday, after Dalton returned from delivering the paper, we'd discuss story ideas for the next edition of the *Patriot*.

"Let's talk at my desk," I requested, wanting to avoid a front-row seat to Dalton's tobacco-spit mess.

Dalton wheeled his chair over the tattered brown carpet and sat down across from me. "What stories you got for this week?" he asked.

"So far, nothing too juicy. One is about a proposal for a new walking path in Kusko, another about changes to the spring hunting regulations, and drunk-guy-does-stupid-shit in Hooper Bay. That's it so far."

Dalton thought for a second. "I have one more for you. A senior girl at Kusko High School just won an academic award for a special spelling bee she started up. Go interview her."

"Done," I confirmed. "Am I allowed to use the word 'dork' in the headline?"

"No." Dalton smiled. "Be nice, and get a photo."

* * *

The next afternoon, I drove the FJ to Kusko High to interview the spelling bee girl.

A blizzard had dumped on the city the night before. Sheets of slippery, compressed snow covered the dirt roads. I counted two cabs in the ditch.

Kusko, I had learned, was the unofficial taxicab capital of America, with one cab for every seventy or so people. Each ride cost a flat five dollars per person. Between high fuel prices and the cost of shipping a car or truck from Anchorage, owning a vehicle was a luxury few people could afford. It made more sense to pay for cab rides than to own your own vehicle.

Now that my truck had arrived, I was learning that fact the hard way. I could already tell that keeping it going would burn a big chunk of my paychecks. Worse, I couldn't drive the thing anywhere special in the first place — just one stretch of asphalt to and from the airport and a maze of dirt roads snaking through the neighborhoods. All told, having the FJ in Kusko was like owning a Porsche but never driving it outside of a cul-de-sac.

I pulled up to the high school and parked in a visitor space. The building had green metal siding and looked slightly larger than the Zimmerman Rec Center back home. A billboard-sized mural of a sockeye salmon covered the exterior of the gymnasium. Parked below the mural were about two dozen snow machines and four-wheelers that students had driven to school.

I dug into my jacket pocket for my phone to check the time. I had missed a text my dad sent over an hour ago. It read: "Why did you delete your Fbook account?"

*About time he asked,* I thought.

I'd suspended the account almost two months ago. I responded to my dad with a bullshit line I'd been waiting to use ever since: "I was wasting too much time on it. Need to focus on classes/studies."

I slung my backpack over my shoulder and headed inside. A moment later, the sound of my snow-covered boots squeaking on the floor echoed through the main hallway. Brightly colored murals of hallmark Alaskan scenes plastered the concrete walls — bears catching jumping salmon at the top of a waterfall, a breaching humpback whale, a mama moose and her calf wading in a lake below a mountain.

I entered the principal's office and encountered a receptionist with bad teeth and a polyester pantsuit straight out of the seventies. I asked her about the girl who won the award for starting a spelling bee.

"You go see Taylor Sifsof. Hold on," she said from behind the counter. Kusko was full of Albanian immigrants, many of whom drove the cabs in town. Why they all chose to move to Kusko, I did not know. I'd thought they were Russians when I first arrived, but Dalton had straightened me out.

The woman dialed the classroom, spoke two sentences, hung up, and spoke to me again. "Taylor in classroom studying while rest of students at lunch. You go to classroom. Room 107, just around corner."

Part of me was anxious to find out what a rural Alaskan nerd looked like. I doubted she'd have many zits, since eating salmon was supposed to be good for the skin. Her other Poindexterian features were anybody's guess. I left the office, walked past empty classrooms, and tapped on the door to Room 107. The door opened.

Ho. Lee. Shit.

Standing there might have been the hottest girl I'd seen. Ever. Anywhere. On TV, in person, in a magazine, in a movie, on a billboard. My ding dong went from zero to boner faster than a car's airbag can deploy. I untucked my red flannel shirt to hide it.

The girl looked exotic. I couldn't pinpoint her lineage. Whatever she was, it amounted to a luscious mishmash of every female physical characteristic I held dear. Tall? *Check.* Long, straight blond hair? *Check.* Olive skin? *Check.* Pouty lips? *Check.* Hint of a buttchin? *Check.* Big bombs? *Che* — actually, I couldn't tell. The light-blue sweater she wore was too bulky. But with how perfect the rest of her was, it was fair to assume she was hiding a nice rack of sleeper boobs under there.

"Hello," she said with a smile. Her voice was raspy. I loved raspy.

I looked into her cornflower-blue eyes and paused. She didn't have a lazy eye or a sleepy eye, but something was off. It almost seemed like she was looking at someone behind me.

"I'm Eddie," I said nervously.

Girls of Taylor's stifling hotness always made me jumpy. I became self-conscious immediately, wondering which Eddie I should be to impress her. Overly nice, churchy Eddie? *Maybe, because chicks dig sensitive guys.* Subdued, mysterious Eddie? *Maybe, because chicks dig the strong, silent type.* The real Eddie? *Maybe, because the slightly arrogant yet fun-loving Eddie that is me has a decent enough track record.*

I cleared my throat. "I hear you won an award for a spelling bee or something?"

"I did!" she said. "But, wait now. I've never seen you in town. Who are you with? Are you here to, like, crown me Queen Nerd of the YK Delta?"

"No," I said, laughing. "I'm the new reporter at the *Delta Patriot*. My boss said I should write a story about you."

Her face lit up. "Wonderful!" she said. "The more exposure we can get for this program, the better."

Taylor turned around and walked toward her desk in the front row, where she'd been reading a textbook. She wore tight blue jeans.

Perky pooper? *Check.*

I sat down at the teacher's desk and pulled my reporter notebook from my backpack. "Everyone else is at lunch, right?"

"Yep," Taylor said. "They'll be back in fifteen minutes. We'll need to make this quick."

"Shouldn't you be at lunch too?"

"I have too much work. I ate at my desk."

Once again, it seemed like Taylor was looking at someone behind me. I turned around and saw nothing but a whiteboard with smudges of red marker that hadn't been erased well enough.

"So," I began, "what's up with the spelling bee?"

"It's not just any spelling bee — it's a *Native* spelling bee," she said. "Yup'ik and other Native languages are in danger of dying out after the next generation or two. Creating this spelling bee is my own little way of trying to keep the Yup'ik language alive."

"Are you fluent?"

"I probably know a couple hundred words. But my dad can speak it. He grew up in the village of Anvik. He's half Native, half Italian."

Again I focused on her right eye. Its iris was slightly wider than the left one, and that eye didn't seem to track correctly. It lagged, not obviously or dramatically, but enough to spot.

"What about your mom?"

"She's a full-blooded Swede and can't speak Yup'ik. She emigrated here twenty years ago. Both my folks are teachers at the junior high."

That explained Taylor's exotic beauty. Throw a Native, Italian, and Swede into a blender, and you get a tall glass of gorgeous her.

Taylor went on to say there are Native immersion schools across Alaska. She'd been working with the University of Anchorage's language center to develop curriculum for each school to organize a spelling bee for their own particular Native language — of which there are about twenty in Alaska. Ten of the schools signed on and would hold their own Native spelling bee in the spring for kids in elementary school and junior high.

"Basically," Taylor said, "the spelling bee idea started with me, and now the University of Anchorage is taking it across the finish line. I won their 2010 Award for Young Innovators in Cultural Education."

I congratulated her while looking into her right eye. I switched to her left eye and asked how she came up with the idea.

"I love my culture and wanted to do something to help preserve it," Taylor said matter-of-factly.

"And?" I couldn't tell if she was being sincere or sarcastic.

"And that's it," Taylor said. "I love Kusko. I love its people. Not being fluent in a Native language wasn't going to stop me from starting the spelling bee.

Do people who volunteer at pet shelters have to own a pet?"

I checked the time. The other kids would be walking in at any moment.

"Got time for a quick photo?" I asked, standing up from the teacher's desk and pulling my camera from my backpack.

"Sure," Taylor said and rose from her own desk.

"Where do you want me?"

*Anywhere I can have you,* I thought, but what I said was, "How about over by the windows. We'll use the natural light."

I felt like I was quickly becoming a decent little photographer. Dalton gave me a digital SLR to use, with a wide-angle lens. I'd shot a few things for stories, and I'd been practicing around town. My photos were turning out pretty nice. Prior to landing in Kusko, I had never photographed much of anything, and I only shot with my phone.

I popped off a few frames of Taylor.

"Can I see?" she asked.

I let her look at the photos on the camera's digital display.

"I like these!" Taylor said. "Can you send me one?"

Bingo. That was just the in I needed. Now I could email the photo, she'd reply with a thank you, and I could respond with something irresistibly clever. Side bonus: I now had photographic evidence that the hottest girl alive lived in the middle of nowhere. After ten minutes of knowing her, I was already blind to her weird eye.

"Yep, I'll email you," I said, all laid back, trying to disguise my excitement. "I might send some follow-up questions for the story too. I'll see how it goes."

She jotted her email address on my notebook. Then she smiled, looked at me, and asked, "What about you, Eddie? Where you from?"

Good *God* did I love how she said my name.

"Minnesota. I came up to Anchorage for college, then to Kusko to work at the *Patriot* for a year."

*Or forever, if you end up wanting to raise our babies here.*

"Cool that you're a writer," Taylor said. "I like to write too. I've been keeping a journal forever."

She handed me my notebook, and I told her, "Great to meet you."

"You too," Taylor said, sitting back down at her desk.

I began walking out the door, dodging incoming students. I stopped, turned around, and walked back to Taylor.

"Did you forget something?" she asked, looking up at me.

"Do you know what 'cheechako' means? My boss said I should look it up."

Taylor chuckled. "Everyone in Alaska knows that word."

"Everyone but me, apparently."

"It means a newcomer to Alaska who doesn't know his head from his ass about life here."

# CHAPTER 6

# READY, SET, HIKE

Dalton and I shuffled around in the back dog yard, ankle-deep in snow, corralling eight dogs for my first solo mushing trek. We had knocked off work early to take advantage of the windless day, bright sunshine, and twenty-degree warmth. I wore my favorite red hunting coat and a pair of black snow pants he'd lent me.

"Before long, you'll graduate to a regular twelve-dog team," Dalton said, holding a brown dog named Boris between his knees, fitting a harness around the pooch's neck. He lifted Boris's right front leg and slid it through a hoop connected to the neckpiece, then the left leg.

The lead dogs, Joanie and Biff, were already harnessed and attached to the aluminum sled at the front of the gangline. They stood near the shed at the foot of a snow trail. An ice hook on a ten-foot rope anchored the sled so the two dogs couldn't take off.

"I'm pumped for this," I said.

I took my time getting Aggie, another brown dog, fitted correctly. Once I secured her harness, I grabbed her by the collar and pulled her over near Dalton, who was busy attaching Boris to the gangline. Boris and Aggie were swing dogs, meaning they stood second in line behind the lead dogs.

"Suck it, nerd!" Finn hollered from somewhere next door.

I looked around and spotted him behind his living room window. He'd cracked it open just enough to hurl his favorite insult at me. I took off my glove and flicked him off.

"Wanna hang later?" he hollered.

I'd been stopping over at his house to play Madden football.

"If I'm still alive after this," I yelled.

"Have fun," Finn said before closing the window.

A few minutes later, Dalton and I finished harnessing the four remaining dogs — Lunchbox, Diesel, Lenny, and Kuba — and attaching them to the gangline. Ready to rock.

I hopped on the back of the sled while Dalton circled around behind me. The dogs knew it was go time and barked out of their skulls. Some were so excited that they ran in place, kicking up snow but going nowhere; they looked like muscle cars doing brake stands. The sled jerked forward a few inches every time two or more of the dogs lunged in unison.

"Get on the brake," Dalton instructed.

I pressed my right foot, hard, onto the brake, a square-foot rubber pad with sharp metal spikes on the bottom. The brake, positioned between the footrests, plunged deep into the snow.

Dalton dislodged the ice hook, ran toward me, and tossed the hook and rope into the front of the sled. I pressed my foot onto the brake even harder, but it still wasn't enough to keep the dogs completely at bay. They dragged the sled and me along the trail, at the pace of a speed walker.

Dalton jogged behind me to give me some final instructions. "Hold on tight," he said. "The second you release the brake, you're going to fly."

I swiveled my head around and watched Dalton pumping his arms, running clumsily in his snow boots, trying to keep up.

"How far should I go?" I asked him.

"About eight miles," he said. "Four miles ahead, this trail will connect to another trail that leads to the village of Napakiak. Turn around where the two trails intersect. Yell 'Joanie, home!' and she'll swing the team around."

"What if I get lost?"

"Impossible," Dalton said, louder, as the distance between us grew. "Joanie always knows the way home."

"What if I wipe?"

He didn't answer.

"Dalton! What if I wipe?"

"You won't!"

*Well that's reassuring*, I thought.

"Okay then!" I said. "Here I go!"

I let off the brake. The dogs took off. My head snapped back, and I went off-balance. The burst of speed created a windchill on my face. I held the handlebars tightly and stabilized myself. I looked back and waved at Dalton, now more than fifty yards away. He waved with both hands.

I turned back to the trail of hard-packed snow ahead. Riding the sled triggered the same exhilaration and freedom I'd felt the first time I successfully rode a bike without training wheels, or drove my dad's old Ford truck, solo, on my sixteenth birthday.

The dogs and I glided along at a steady speed of perhaps fifteen miles per hour. The gentle, repetitive pitter-patter of their paws on the snow sounded like they were dancing on velvet.

I decided to test the brakes, just to get the feel. "Whoa!" I shouted, pressing my foot onto the rubber brake pad. I gripped the handlebars solidly as the back of the sled wagged back and forth like a car skidding on ice. Twenty yards later, the sled stabilized as the team came to a complete stop.

Joanie, at the front of the team, looked back at me, curious about the holdup. "Hike!" I commanded, instructing her to accelerate.

Joanie snapped her head back to the trail and hit the gas. The other dogs followed suit. Less than ten seconds later, they hit full stride.

I gazed to my right, to my left, and straight ahead. I saw nothing but blue sky and flat, vacant, snowy-white tundra in every direction. I supposed that if I didn't have the dogs and lost my bearings out here, it'd be more disorienting than getting lost in outer space.

A moment later I looked back in the direction of the house and Kusko city limits. I saw neither. In two minutes, I had gone from being at home to being in the absolute middle of nowhere.

\* \* \*

A few miles into the trip, I realized that for the first time since I moved to Alaska, I could hear myself think. The dogs, the silence, the serenity, and the sunshine were detoxifying, cleansing all the mucky bullshit that had built up inside my head.

Thinking clearly had been almost impossible in Anchorage because of all the parties, the sleeping in, the parties, the skipped classes, and the parties. My head always hurt. To numb the pain and beat the stress, I partied more. That led to more headaches and more parties.

I hadn't been able to think much in Kusko, either. After little more than a month of living there, the place was turning out to be similarly mind-numbing, but in a different way. Almost every day was the same: go to work, go home, clean dog shit, watch TV or read, repeat. It was a waste, not an Alaskan adventure. I could do that stuff anywhere. Plus, I was piss-poor. And I didn't need my truck here after all. And I barely knew anybody.

And Taylor. I wasn't getting anywhere with her. We'd been in touch a few times after I emailed her the picture, but none of her responses provided much promise. I wanted to see her, but without a bona fide hint from her, I didn't have the balls to ask.

I thought about her most recent email:

Eddie,

Whatever. There's no way walleye tastes better than salmon. Get it straight, cheechako.
Kidding. Your stories about Minnesota are cool. I'd love to take a trip there someday . . . or anywhere, really. I've never traveled farther than Anchorage. That's why I've been applying to colleges outside of Alaska, but I don't know if I'd ever go. I love Kusko. That probably sounds weird.
It's late. Just wanted to touch base.

Taylor

Bor-ing. All her emails were like that — short and friendly but kind of lame — and not exactly flirty. And she took days to respond. Was she only writing me to be nice? Or did she just suck at writing a decent email?
Doubtful, considering how smart she was. Taylor said in another email that the race for 2010 valedictorian of Kusko High School was down to her and some other dude, and that her cultural-education award would probably be the clincher.
But if Taylor didn't dig me, then why bother writing me in the first place? Why keep it going?
Who knows. The odds favored her not liking me. She was way too smart, and way too hot.

\* \* \*

I snapped out of my pity party when the dogs kicked up a flock of a dozen ptarmigan twenty yards ahead. The little white game birds looked like oversized doves. I didn't see them coming because they were so well camouflaged.

The drumming of their wings spooked Biff, who slowed for a moment before realizing Joanie, running to his right, hadn't let up. I watched the birds fly against the blue sky, then lost them when they dipped down against the snow.

We continued motoring along the four-foot-wide snow trail. Behind me, the cluttered imprint of the sled's skis and the dogs' paws stretched all the way to the horizon. Far to my left, a red fox stood out against the snow, near the only tuft of bushes I'd seen in several minutes. He sat on his haunches, licking a front paw, watching the world go by.

The peaceful surroundings chilled me out. Prior to this solo mushing trip, when I wasn't thinking clearly, all those negative thoughts about Kusko, Taylor, and bungling my first stab at college would have gotten the better of me.

Not anymore. I felt energized now. *Good things are coming*, I thought.

I wasn't ready to hate Kusko. Soon the weather would warm. Fishing would start. I'd fly to villages to cover stories. Finn was supposed to take me ptarmigan hunting. And now I could mush by myself whenever I wanted.

*Suck it up, pussy*, I thought. *Life is about to get better.*

The trail started veering left. It intersected with another trail at a spot that looked like a roundabout. This had to be the place Dalton mentioned.

"Joanie, home!" I shouted.

Joanie led the team onto the roundabout. We circled around a loop as big as a baseball diamond. A minute later we were back on the trail to home.

"Hike!" I yelled.

\* \* \*

By the time I saw rooftops along the horizon, the dogs seemed gassed, panting heavily and scuttling at a pace that barely qualified as running. A few minutes later we came within sight of the dog yard, about a hundred feet ahead. The dogs slowed to an uninspired trot; then they sped up again. The sled jerked, and I almost lost my grip.

"Whoa!" I commanded the team.

But we kept going like that — jerking ahead and halting. From what I could see, Joanie and Biff were having a power struggle. Biff, at the front of the team on the left, kept trying to run full bore; Joanie, at the front on the right, held back to decelerate. This confused the rest of the dogs. Half of them followed Biff's lead; the rest, Joanie's.

"Whoa, Biff!" I shouted.

I saw what he saw. Rosebud had gotten loose in the dog yard. She stood at the edge of the property, barking, just a short ways ahead. She had been in heat all week. *Shit*, I thought. *Biff wants to get laid.*

Biff's lead was winning out. The team and I were coming in too hot. I pounded my right foot on the brake. We sped past the shed on a collision course with Rosebud's doghouse, straight in front of us. Rosebud bounced on the roof of her house and barked like mad.

Biff and Joanie pulled up inches short of Rosebud's house. Boris and Aggie halted behind them, followed by Lenny and Kuba. But Lunchbox and Diesel — the wheel dogs, running last in line — couldn't stop in time. They smacked into Lenny and Kuba from behind. The four dogs tumbled to the ground, tangled in the gangline, snarling and biting at each other.

I jumped off the sled and got in the middle of the ruckus. Popping his jaws, Lenny stood on top of Kuba, who was defenseless with his front legs snarled in the mess.

"No, Lenny! NO!" I smacked him on the nose, and he let out a squeal and cowered.

Next to me Diesel and Lunchbox played a game of chicken, growling diabolically to test if the other had the minerals to make a move. I had to be more careful with them because Diesel was basically a wild animal. Beyond letting me harness him or attach him to the gangline, he only took orders from the pack leader — Dalton, who was nowhere to be found, of course.

"Easy guys," I said, keeping a steady eye on Diesel while I unhooked Lunchbox from the gangline. Lenny and Kuba stood calmly behind me.

I took Lunchbox by the collar and led him a few feet away, after which Diesel stopped growling. Situation diffused. My blood stopped pumping. I took a deep breath and looked around to see if anybody saw what happened. I felt humiliated, like I'd crashed a car in my own driveway.

My eyes shifted to the front of the team. There, at the front of the gangline, was Biff, gleefully humping Rosebud.

*Son of a bitch*, I thought.

I couldn't let go of Lunchbox so I dragged him over near Biff and Rosebud, hoping to pull them apart. Biff was on Rosebud and in jackhammer mode. Holding Lunchbox's collar with my right hand, I reached my left arm underneath Biff's neck and yanked on him, but it did no good. I couldn't get them apart.

"Dalton!" I yelled, hoping he'd hear me from inside the house and come bail me out. "Help!"

No response.

I left the lovers, led Lunchbox to his doghouse, and hooked him to his chain. I hustled to unhook the other dogs and get them back to their houses. By the time I got back to Biff and Rosebud, Biff had dismounted Rosebud, but the two dogs were still attached. He had stretched his back leg over her backside so that they were facing opposite directions, ass to ass.

I grabbed Biff's collar, but before I could move him, I heard an unfamiliar voice say, "Leave them alone!"

I turned around and saw Nicolai Vawter, the pastor who lived next door, walking toward me and wearing only a bath towel around his waist and mukluk boots up to his knees. We'd waved at each other in passing but had never spoken.

"They'll be stuck together for a while," he said. Nicolai was tall for a Native. He had short gray hair, skinny arms, and a sizable spare tire. His gut jiggled with every step he took through the snow. "The male is releasing prostatic fluid."

What could I say to that? I just nodded.

"Pulling them apart could hurt him," Nicolai added.

"What?" I ended up shouting, half because I didn't really understand and half because it didn't compute that Nicolai was practically naked outside in the cold.

"Prostatic fluid," he said. "It takes a while to discharge. That's the issue."

Biff stood there, facing the tundra, looking like he could go for a cigarette. I nodded, sighed, and searched for something to say to the half-naked pastor in the cold sunshine.

"Aren't you freezing?" I asked.

"I won't be for long," he replied, pointing toward a structure that looked like a miniature log cabin. "I'm about to take a steam bath. You're welcome to join me — when things are settled out here."

Dalton emerged on a narrow snow path on Nicolai's side of our house. The two men waved at each other as Nicolai headed into his steam bath. Dalton strutted up to me, smiling.

"Where were you?" I asked, annoyance clear in my voice.

"Watching from inside, laughing my ass off," he said.

"Why didn't you come help?"

"I wanted to see if you could handle the situation," he replied. "And you did."

\* \* \*

I stood in front of Nicolai's steam bath, wearing my snow boots, boxers, and a T-shirt, holding a wadded-up bath towel. I shivered and considered whether I was up for this. I was curious about Eskimo steam baths, but I knew about one local custom that made me nervous: in a steam bath everyone went nude. Young, old, guy, girl, your weird uncle Ned — didn't matter. If you steamed, you steamed naked. It was part of YK Delta culture. Finn had explained it to me. He said he steamed naked with his grandma all the time, and it wasn't even weird. I, on the other hand, was reluctant to steam with Nicolai. When it comes to nudity and young males, clergy don't exactly have the greatest track record.

Every fifth house in Kusko had a steam bath in the backyard. Outside Nicolai's I stalled, taking a good look at the log structure. It seemed a century old, made from logs that were practically petrified and fused together by old, cracked mud.

Finally I entered a small vestibule big enough for two people to crouch down and disrobe. I stripped off my clothes and dumped them in the corner with my towel. I crawled through a small hinged opening that looked like an overgrown pet door.

The inside of the steam bath was hotter than Death Valley and darker than a Tim Burton movie. I couldn't see a thing. I didn't want to feel my way around for fear of accidentally clutching a handful of Nicolai's balls.

"Where am I at, Nicolai?" I asked, on my hands and knees.

"Shuffle to your right and take a seat."

I dripped with sweat before I could even sit down. Grit and grime loosened from every pour of my body.

As my eyes adjusted I could see the vague silhouette of Nicolai's body straight across from me, but I couldn't see his face. Between us, a wood-burning stove with a pile of stones stacked on top of it kicked out dry waves of heat and a dim bit of light. Next to the stove rested a five-gallon bucket of water and a plastic mug. Nicolai dipped the mug into the bucket and poured water on the rocks. The water crackled into a blistering cloud of steam that filled the room and my lungs.

"Damn!" I yelped.

"I joined the steam club a few years ago and couldn't be happier," the naked man said.

"There's a club?"

Nicolai chuckled and launched into an explanation of how he'd been referring to the ranks of Kuskoites who'd quit showering altogether and steamed instead. He told me he saved water and felt cleaner than after a shower. Considering the sheet of sweat slicking my skin already, I couldn't quite imagine feeling clean when it was all over.

Then we were silent — silent and naked and sweating. I wasn't sure what to say next. I still wasn't totally used to being talked to and treated like an adult. I'd been doing a pretty good job at projecting confidence when I was interviewing people for the *Patriot*, but just beneath the surface, I often felt like a moron talking to anybody over age thirty. They knew about things like water bills, mortgages, and politics. The only grownup thing I could talk about was news writing — and maybe hunting. Outside of that, I was knowledgeable only about boobs and music and how poor I was and my FJ, and funny shit from college and high school.

"Cool steam bath." That was the conversational gold I finally came up with. "I mean, cool like it's good. You build it?"

"Nope," Nicolai said, competing with the sound of water fizzling on the rocks. "This thing was built long before my house was. It's probably been here more than a century. I've made some improvements, though."

After another sweaty lull in our conversation, he said, "How do you like Kusko so far?"

Considering he was a pastor, I didn't want to lie. My dad took Max and me to church sometimes, and some of the stuff stuck.

"I don't love it, but I don't hate it, either. I had it pretty good in Anchorage. But I'm trying to suck it up. I've been telling myself that in twenty years, I'll look back on all of this and smile."

"That's the attitude," Nicolai said, his eyes closed as he spoke.

By now my eyes had adjusted to the low light. I imagined my pupils were as big as hockey pucks.

"What about you?" I asked.

"I've been in Kusko almost five years. I spent most of my life in the villages."

"Do you have family in town?"

"Everybody who's from the YK Delta has family everywhere out here."

Nicolai explained he was a divorced father of one. He'd moved to Kusko to become pastor of Kusko Moravian Church, a Protestant denomination.

"There are a lot of bad things in the YK Delta," Nicolai said. "I want to be part of the solution."

He wasn't kidding about the "bad things." On top of what I'd been reading in the police blotter, I'd learned that rural Alaska had some of the highest rates of violent crime in all of America. An Alaska state trooper told me that nugget when I interviewed him for a story about some dickhead in the village of Aniak who roughed up his five-year-old daughter and sent her to the hospital with bruises everywhere and a broken arm.

Nicolai scooted closer to the fire and reached for a small dish filled with soapy water and a sponge. He grabbed the sponge and began cleaning himself with it.

"Do you know anything about Dalton?" I asked. "I live with the guy, but he never talks about himself. He won't talk about his past, other than the fact that he's from here."

"I know that they used to live in Fairbanks, where Dalton worked for the newspaper. I'm guessing he moved back here after he and his wife split up. That's all I got."

"I didn't know he'd been married," I replied.

"He was married years ago. But he couldn't get his wife pregnant and they separated," the pastor said. "That's just what I heard, anyway."

Nicolai dropped the sponge at my feet. I dipped it in the soapy water and started scrubbing my arms and shoulders.

After a moment of silence, I asked, "Why is stuff so messed up out here?"

"Stuff is messed up everywhere."

"But how could stuff be *so* messed up?"

"I don't know, Eddie," Nicolai said. "What I do know is that people run into problems when they get fooled into thinking that what is wrong is what is right. Then there are other people who do know what is right, but they don't have the sack to do it. In the end, it all comes back."

Yes, I was impressed by a pastor who used the word "sack."

## CHAPTER 7

# DON'T PRINT THAT

Fifteen minutes until deadline. I had just finished my final story. Only the headline remained. I stared at the computer screen, stumped.

"Hustle, Eddie," Dalton ordered, putting on his jacket. "I can't leave until your story is done. What's the holdup?"

"The headline," I said.

"What have you got so far?"

"'Mayor shifts from green to brown.'"

Dalton scratched his chin and thought. "Add the word 'surprise' at the beginning, with an exclamation point. That'll make it seem like a bigger deal than it is."

The night before, I'd stayed at the Kusko City Council meeting until ten o'clock, praying they'd finally address something newsworthy. The only halfway interesting tidbit came when Kusko's mayor, Marty McCambly, insisted that Kusko City Hall be painted brown instead of green, the color he and the council had previously agreed upon as part of a remodeling project scheduled to begin two months from now, in May.

"Genius," I said. "That one word will make the story Pulitzer Prize material."

"Okay then, smart-ass," Dalton said, standing near the door. "I'm out to help Lon Bokey butcher meat. Send your story to the printer, then get on my computer and start uploading web content."

Dalton was on his way to help his buddy cut up two caribou he'd shot twenty miles north of Kusko. Although the caribou season was closed to many Alaska residents in our area, an extended season remained open to people who depended on the meat to live.

After Dalton left, I stayed at my desk a few extra minutes to write an email to Taylor. I stared at the email she'd sent the night before, while I was trapped in the city council meeting. Her note mentioned the passing of my mom, which I'd been forced to tell her about when she'd asked about my family.

"Living without a mom must be utter hell," she wrote. "I'm so sorry, Eddie. No words."

She went on to write happier things, such as the improved odds of her being named valedictorian. "The other guy in the mix is a clumsy wimp who can't run a 5K in less than thirty minutes," she wrote. "If he can't by May, he won't get an A in his gym class. That'll give me the edge in GPA."

Taylor's assumption was correct: living without a mom was hell.

My mom's name was Rose, and she died of cancer when I was twelve. Talking about her death was virtually impossible before I became a teenager. I was too young to handle my emotions. One time, I coldcocked a kid for taking my pencil without asking. Other times, I woke up crying in the middle of the night . . . which still happened now and then.

I still feel extra terrible for my dad. He always busted his ass for our family, managing a car wash by day and working three evening bartending shifts per week at the Zimmerman VFW. After my mom died, he had to pick up two more bar shifts to make up for my mom's part-time income at the local hair salon, called Zimm Trim. He was always too busy to give me the attention I needed while I was grieving; I had to cook most of my meals myself. Although he spent time with Max and me every chance he could, he was stuck between a rock and a hard place. If the bills didn't get paid, we'd lose our house.

I started typing what must have been my tenth email to Taylor in six weeks. I was sick of writing to her. I wanted to see her face.

I responded with this:

Taylor,

Thanks for saying that. It's been a while since my mom died, and some days it sucks just as huge as the day we lost her. But life goes on, I guess.

Cool about valedictorian. If that other dude starts running the 5K fast enough, I'd be happy take out his knees for you. Just let me know.

On a different note, my fingers are cramping. Writing emails to you on top of writing stories all day is too much. Wanna just hang out sometime?

Eddie

\* \* \*

The next day Dalton was running an hour late to our weekly editorial meeting. Normally it took him two hours to do the paper route. Now it was almost eleven o'clock.

I sat at my desk, farting around online. I had already checked my personal email account four times, hoping Taylor had responded with a yes to my invitation.

Then the door from Mikey Colosky's barber shop burst open. Dalton stood in the door frame, tapping his right foot on the floor, looking irritated. He held a bundle of newspapers under his arm and pulled out a copy. He walked a few steps closer and tossed the newspaper onto my desk.

"Page five," he said. "Bottom story."

I spread the paper onto my desk and flipped to page five. The story opened like this:

## Surprise! Mayor Shits from Green to Brown

By Eddie Ashford
Staff Writer / Delta Patriot
KUSKO, Alaska — Mayor Marty McCambly shocked Kusko City Council members Monday by demanding that Kusko City Hall be painted brown. In a February meeting,

McCambly and council members agreed the building would be painted green as part of a remodeling project scheduled for this spring.

Dalton glowered at me as I read the story all the way through and scanned it a second time. I couldn't find any errors.

"What's the problem?" I asked. "Is 'shocked' too strong of a word? I thought it might be, but I had to spice things up somehow. If that's the issue, then that's on you — you read the story and cleared it."

Dalton frowned. "I cleared the story before it had a headline."

"Yeah, and then I wrote the exact headline you told me," I said, pointing at it.

"Read the headline out loud," Dalton said.

I cleared my throat. "Surprise! Mayor shits — "

I couldn't believe my eyes.

"NO!" I blurted, wincing like I'd just watched a train hit a school bus.

In a way, my blunder was just as big of a train wreck. Not only did the headline say "shit," it included the color brown. On top of that, readers who liked to eat kale or were familiar with changing baby diapers would get an added chuckle over the color green.

"This is not happening," I said, mortified.

"Yep, it's happening," Dalton said, still hovering over me. "I've had a lot of explaining to do around town this morning. That's what's taken me so long to get back here."

"Does Mayor McCambly know?"

"He's the first person I talked to. He laughed. You're lucky he has a sense of humor."

I sighed long and loud. "Now what?"

"You don't ever do that again, that's what," Dalton said. "You'll read all your stories and headlines backward, three times, before they get to me; you'd be amazed at how many typos you'll find reading backward."

"Shouldn't the proofers at the printer have caught it?"

"Yes," Dalton said. "I'll call them later today. I need to know every last hole in my net."

I started freaking, worrying I'd be fired. What would happen then? Would Dalton be off the hook paying the return shipping for my truck? How would I afford a plane ticket back to Anchorage? Where would I live in Kusko?

Dalton walked to the utility closet, opened the door, and flipped on the space heater. The daytime low was supposed to flirt with ten below, abnormally cold for early March.

While he did that, I dug into my coat pocket for my phone and sent R.J. this text: "My room still open?"

He responded: "Always. But why? Bush life getting to you already? Is your pussy aching?"

Me: "No. I'm fine. Just checking. Drink one for me tonight."

Him: "Word."

Dalton sat down at his desk and flipped through his Rolodex, visibly agitated by two pages that were stuck together.

I wanted assurance that I was safe, that mistakes happen. "Please tell me this isn't the worst mistake one of your reporters has made. Is it?"

"It's up there," Dalton said. "Years ago, a girl wrote a story about a literacy program at Kusko Elementary and misspelled 'literacy' in the headline."

Dalton smiled. I laughed, to reinforce his lighter mood.

"What about lately?" I pressed, hoping for a more recent example that proved accidents were common.

"What about your last reporter?"

Dalton stopped smiling. He flipped more pages of his Rolodex. He didn't want to respond.

"Well?" I asked.

Dalton stopped flipping and looked square at me. "I can't remember. You're the first reporter I've had out here since last summer."

My heart sank into my stomach. *I'm all he could find,* I thought.

Dalton pretended he didn't say what he'd just said. "Ready for our meeting?" he asked.

Internally, I reeled, but I faked a smile and said, "Look, Dalton — "

"I know you're sorry, Eddie," Dalton said. "You're not the only one at fault. The mistake was everyone's."

"Thanks," I said, wheeling my chair to his desk. "I really am trying my best at this job."

"I know you are. And you're doing fine." Dalton did not smile in return. "We just need to be more careful."

"Right," I said. "More careful."

Dalton sighed and said, "Okay then, Eddie. What stories you got for this week?"

# CHAPTER 8

# MY CRIB

There was a God. Ms. Taylor Sifsof, the hottest girl north, south, east, or west of anywhere, had accepted my invitation to hang out, and now she sat in a tattered yellow armchair in my bedroom. Orange light from the antique oil lamp on my nightstand flickered onto her face.

She smelled like honey and looked hotter than what I remembered. She wore tight black jeans and a red V-neck sweater that left nothing to the imagination. Her long blond hair spilled down her shoulders and rested on her chest — the amazing bounty of her chest. My brother would've called it a real jiggle farm, but he was stupid like that. It looked perfect, though. They looked perfect. I barely noticed Taylor's wandering eye.

"Fifteen for two," Taylor said, smirking.

We were playing cribbage, which R.J. and I had converted into our favorite drinking game during my semester in Anchorage. With each space Taylor pegged ahead of me, I imagined the swig of cheap beer I'd have been gulping if I'd been playing against R.J. But I couldn't have that kind of fun in Kusko, certainly not with Taylor.

The cribbage board, which Dalton had whittled out of driftwood from the riverbank, rested on the nightstand between Taylor and me. I sat on my bed.

It was eight o'clock at night, and Dalton wasn't around. He'd agreed to skedaddle for a while. Taylor and I had been playing for more than an hour, caught up in conversation, bullshitting like long-lost friends. With her around, I paid special attention to my special area. My dork was far too unpredictable, just begging to embarrass me. I worried it wasn't a question of if I'd pop a stiffy, but when.

We finished laying down our four-card hands. "Last card for one," I said, advancing one of my two blue pegs. "What you got?"

"Two aces, a two, and a three," she said. "That's a double-run for eight."

It was my crib, and she still beat me by fifteen spaces. I had yet to win a game.

"That's three wins in a row," Taylor said. "I thought you said you could play."

"I can. I'm just unlucky tonight."

"You're more than that. You're an embarrassment."

"Whatever," I said, shuffling the cards for another game, loving every insult she could throw at me.

Taylor sat up straight and stretched her back. I pretended not to notice her honkerburgers.

"Speaking of embarrassments," Taylor continued,

"what's your all-time most embarrassing moment?"

*It's coming up any second now, when I pull wood,* I thought, sitting on the edge of my lumpy twin-size mattress. She sat three feet from me. My bed and the armchair took up most of the room. I didn't have a closet or dresser. I had to fold and fit all my clothes into two semi-rusted metal filing cabinets.

I heard a beep. "Hold that thought," Taylor said, checking her phone.

I pulled out my own phone and sent a text to R.J.: "Dude. Hottest chick ever. In my room. Right now."

He responded immediately: "Lies. You're in Kusko. Unlike the girl in your room, the one in mine is real."

Me: "Bite shit. You partying?"

Him: "Gong show."

Taylor put away her phone, as did I. "Most embarrassing moment?" I began. "Gym class my sophomore year, every day at one o'clock."

"Really?" Taylor said.

*Crap,* I thought. I'd opened my mouth without thinking. Time to backpedal.

"Yeah, that was . . . um . . . not gym. I mean . . . it was speech class. I hate giving speeches, and I had to do a five-minute informational speech on the causes and effects of chlamydia — "

"Bullshit!" Taylor said. I had hesitated too long, and she knew it. "Tell the truth."

I explained how when gym class ended, all the guys were required to hit the showers. It was mandatory. No getting around it. And I still hadn't finished puberty. It became a ritual for those a-holes to point at my you-know-what and call it the name of a famous bald man.

They came up with a new name every day.

Taylor laughed and said, "Like what?"

"Kobe Bryant. Vin Diesel. Dwayne Johnson. And I'll never forget George Foreman, because that name eventually morphed to George Foreskin. It was *so* humiliating."

She laughed so hard she couldn't say what she wanted to say. Finally, she pointed toward my crotch. "What about Daddy Warbucks?"

"Whatever!" I replied.

Taylor laughed at her own joke until she finally sighed, shook her head, and collected herself.

"Making fun of you is fun," she said. "Besides your sucking at cribbage and being a late bloomer, how else can I rip on you?"

She looked at the caribou hide hanging on my wall and cocked her head. The beige walls of my room were mostly bare, other than the hide pinned above my bed and a University of Anchorage hockey poster on the door. Finn gave me the hide as a gift, saying I had to have *something* in my room to make it look Alaskan. Taylor did not look impressed.

"That bull wasn't even three hundred pounds," Taylor said. "That's puny. Caribou around here are the biggest in Alaska; bulls from the Mulchatna herd can hit five hundred pounds."

"How do you know it wasn't a female?" I countered.

"Caribou cows are way smaller than the bulls."

She stepped up onto my bed, peeled part of the caribou from the wall, and grabbed a strip of hide near what would have been the animal's belly.

"Because of this," she said. "It's the penis sheath.

And unlike you, it looks like he actually had some hair down there."

Another well-executed cheap shot. Taylor balanced shit-talking and femininity with grace. I loved it.

I did the same kind of thing, but in the opposite direction. I'd been dialing things back considerably. If I talked to her like I did Finn or R.J. or even Dalton, or most other guys I knew, there was a chance I could scare her off. Every time I said something coarse, I strategically offset it with something sweet. I internally pre-screened every question I asked and every response I gave with the scrutiny of a politician. I couldn't afford to slip up. Not with how hot she was.

Taylor sat back down on the armchair. "So, I still don't understand how you ended up in Kusko."

I'd been dreading that topic. Given Taylor's smarts, I felt inferior. I'd feel even more inadequate once she knew I flunked out of college. But I dodged it by showing her one of the two stories I'd written in the *Puffin Press*. I thought the story might counteract the dumbassery of my college fail.

"I'll tell you in a second," I said, setting the cards aside to retrieve a copy of the *Puffin Press* from under my nightstand. "But first, check this out."

She opened the paper and read the story, which opened like this:

## Physics Prof Parades Penis in Public

By Eddie Ashford
Staff Writer / Puffin Press
ANCHORAGE, Alaska — A local physics professor has debunked a popular scientific theory by proving that what

goes up doesn't necessarily come down.

Alaska Technical College professor Matt Filipenko was convicted of misdemeanor indecent exposure Friday following an Oct. 25 incident in which the 47-year-old paraded around a downtown block party flashing his penis.

The story also included a photo of the guy smiling ear-to-ear, holding his dong like it was a winning Powerball ticket. I'd used my phone to shoot the photo from his waist up, but it was clear where his hands were.

Hysterical laughter from Taylor. "Oh my!" she said. "How on earth did you come up with this?"

I explained how I was at the block party and watched the whole thing go down.

"That's *so* gross," Taylor said. "But how come you're not still in college?"

She wasn't going to let it slide.

"I got kicked out," I said.

Taylor's face went grim. "I don't understand. You're such a good writer."

"Thanks, but I'm not even sure about *that* anymore," I said, recalling my headline gaffe. "Did you see this week's *Patriot*?"

Taylor cracked a smile. "I didn't want to bring it up."

"I've heard enough about it this week," I said. "All I really know is that I never *meant* to flunk out of college. It just happened. I got caught up in having too much fun."

"But how did you end up here?"

I explained everything about working at the *Patriot* for a year to prove to the university's admissions officials that I was ready to be a college student again. "I'm doing what I need to do to make things right," I said. "No more partying for this guy."

"Good," Taylor said. "I mean, good for you."

I doubted Taylor partied, but I asked anyway.

"Nope," she said. "I have too much going for me."

"Oh, right," I said, feeling like a blue-ribbon dipshit for being a poster child of teenage irresponsibility.

"Plus," she continued, "both my parents are teachers in Kusko. If I got into trouble, that would reflect poorly on them and what they're trying to accomplish. Lots of their students come to class exhausted because their parents were up all night getting fucked up. It's so sad."

The mood had grown too sullen. I needed to switch it back to happy. Before the gloomy talk started, I'd even contemplated going in for a kiss. I wasn't so sure anymore.

"I'm excited to get back into school," I said. "I'm the first Ashford to attend college. I can't blow it this time."

"I'm sure you'll do great," Taylor said.

I couldn't tell if she was just humoring me. Had I blown it? Or did she like me? It seemed like Taylor and I shared a periodic table's worth of chemistry. Or was I wrong? *It could go either way,* I thought.

Taylor's phone beeped again. She pulled it from her pocket and looked at the screen.

"My friends are on their way to pick me up," she said, typing a message.

Slowly, I rose from my bed. "Yeah, I suppose," I said, like an old-timer getting ready to leave a family reunion.

She'd taken a cab over. Whomever she was texting, it wouldn't take them more than a few minutes to arrive, even if they were on the far side of town. This was Kusko, after all.

Taylor finished texting and bent over to slip on her black leather shoes. In doing so, the top of her shirt opened up enough to give me a glimpse down her sweater, where her monstrous and heroic set of guns stressed her pink lace bra.

Boner. A big one. I doubled over to mask it.

"You okay?" Taylor asked, standing up again.

"Yeah, just a cramp," I groaned, grabbing at my hamstring. "I think I've been sitting too long."

If I stood up, I'd have looked like I was trying to shoplift summer sausage.

"I'm okay, really," I assured her, still doubled over, now pretending to stretch. "This happens all the time."

She looked at her phone and said, "In that case, I'm going to use the restroom before my friends get here."

"Cool."

While Taylor did her business, someone knocked on the front door. My dink deflated faster than the time my brother walked in on me with the swimsuit edition of *Sports Illustrated* open to a pic of Brooklyn Decker.

I opened the front door and there, outside and up to their ankles in snow with a rusty old Suburban idling behind them, stood Bristy and Hope.

When they saw me, their mouths dropped in perfect surprise. Bristy pulled the hood of her parka off her head, astonished. "Eddie? You live *next door* to Finn?"

I didn't understand why they were freaking. "Um, yeah," I said happily. "What's up, ladies?"

Hope looked almost frantic. "Holy shit, Eddie. You haven't met us yet."

"What? Why?"

"Because you saw us at Finn's house. Taylor will know why we were over there," Bristy said. "And she can't know we smoke weed."

"Because of her parents?" I asked.

When I heard Taylor coming up behind me, I stepped toward Bristy, shook her hand, and said, "I'm Eddie."

"Hi, I'm Bristy. This is my friend Hope."

Taylor was pulling on her coat as she stopped beside me. "I see you've met my two best friends," Taylor said, smiling. "I'd love for us to sit around and talk, but if Bristy opens her mouth, we could be here for another couple hours."

"No worries," I said. "All good."

Taylor hugged me and said, "Thanks, Eddie. I had a lot of fun."

Instead of concentrating on Taylor and her honey smell and her big squishy chest pressing against mine, I glanced at Bristy and Hope and bulged my eyes. Hope pretended to wipe sweat from her brow.

"I had fun too," I told Taylor, releasing her. "Maybe we could all hang out sometime?"

"Totally," Taylor said. "I've got a busy few weeks ahead, but maybe after that."

"Cool," I said.

Of course, that wasn't cool. Taylor wanting to hang out in a few *days* would have been cool. A few weeks? Who says that? Who's that busy?

# CHAPTER 9

# LITTLE PEOPLE

The ptarmigan had no clue they were being stalked.

Finn and I army-crawled up the side of a knoll half covered with snow. Wet, spongy tundra canvased the rest of the landscape.

The miles of tundra we'd traversed with the dog team was flat, but this particular area looked something like an arctic golf course, with rolling mounds of earth flowing across an area the size of several soccer fields. The mixture of white snow and brown tundra looked like an ocean of rocky road ice cream.

Clouds hung overhead, locking in the warmth of the unseasonably mild April day.

"Where there's one bird, there's more," Finn whispered, crawling to my right, clutching a semiautomatic .22 rifle with a black synthetic stock. He had spotted the bird near some waist-high bushes while sitting in the dogsled as I drove.

The dog team waited forty yards behind us,

anchored by an ice hook. The knoll blocked the ptarmigans' view of the dogs, who were lying down and resting quietly.

My elbows and knees, soaking wet, sank into the mushy earth as I slithered along next to Finn. He stopped us just before we reached the top of the little hill and handed me his rifle.

Finn tapped my shoulder. "After you shoot the first one, keep blazing," he whispered. "If the birds are clumped together, you should be able to tag two more before the rest fly away."

I crawled four feet forward to the crest of the mound. Thirty yards in front of me, a flock of about ten ptarmigan strutted about, pecking at the ground, weaving in and out of the bushes. Enough snow had melted that the white birds stuck out like sore thumbs anywhere the brown tundra was exposed. Finn had told me the birds' feathers would turn that same color in a few weeks, meaning this was a good time to be hunting.

I clicked off the safety and aimed through the iron sight. I bore down on the bird closest to us; three more birds stood just behind it, near the bushes.

"Give 'er hell," Finn said.

I pulled the trigger. The gun made a sound like a firecracker exploding in a pop can.

Direct hit on the first bird. I knew it was a clean shot through its chest, because it keeled over faster than a fat man having a heart attack.

The other birds didn't fly away. I took aim again, capitalizing on their slow reaction time. I shot twice and missed. The next shot connected. Second bird down. On the fifth shot, the gun jammed.

"Shit," I said, handing the gun to Finn.

He pulled the action open and shut, open and shut, trying to dislodge a bullet stuck in the receiver. I turned my attention to the flock and noticed the birds still hadn't flown away. A couple of them hovered around the two I'd just killed, and were like, "What happened to John and Martha?"

"What the hell?" I whispered. "Check it out. All the other birds are still hanging around."

Finn squinted at the flock. "Dude!" he said, cracking a smile. "They're drunk!"

"What?"

Finn continued, "Like, hammered. They must have eaten fermented berries. I've seen this before. Those birds aren't flying anywhere." Finn finished with the gun, adding bullets to the ten-round clip. "Watch this."

He locked the clip back into place and proceeded to dust four more birds, uttering his favorite insult after every kill: *BANG! Suck it, nerd. BANG! Suck it, nerd. BANG! Suck it, nerd. BANG! Suck it, nerd.*

We stood up. A couple birds that had escaped into the bushes flew away, clumsily, like bush pilots who'd pounded a few too many.

We walked down the knoll to retrieve the birds. They littered the ground in a ten-yard circle.

I grabbed one and studied it. The bird looked similar to the ruffed grouse I used to hunt with my dad and grandpa.

Finn held up the first bird I'd shot. "Look at this fatty," he said. "Tonight we'll slow-cook him and the others in cream of mushroom soup. Nice shooting, Eddie."

Finn and I tossed all six birds into the front of the sled, and I walked off to dislodge the ice hook.

"Hold up," Finn said. "Time to celebrate."

I doubled back and joined him at the front of the dog team, near Biff and Joanie. Finn pulled a dugout and lighter from the inside breast pocket of his green wool hunting coat. He slid the top off the little wooden container. A one-hitter sprung up. He snatched the one-hitter and poked at the weed inside the dugout.

"Finally ready to smoke up with me?" Finn asked, offering the one-hitter and lighter.

Finn tried to get me to smoke most times we hung out, but I always declined. Now that I'd killed my first ptarmigan, he'd probably use the accomplishment as leverage to try to push me over the edge. I'd figured out that Finn had lied when I first met him, when he said he didn't smoke that much. Dude smoked a lot. He barely drank, though.

"I don't know, Finn," I said, kneeling down to pet Joanie, who licked my face. "Like I told you, I've only smoked twice, and the second time I got real paranoid. Being out here in the middle of nowhere would probably make me tweak worse."

Finn frowned. "Don't be a pansy," he said. "You just plugged your first ptarmigan. It's party time."

Part of me wanted to get high to take my mind off my problems. In the past month, I'd been feeling more and more pessimistic about Kusko — and my entire life situation in general. The thought of moving all the way back to Minnesota had even crossed my mind. Between botching college and the bleakness of Kusko, it was Alaska: 2, Eddie: 0.

"If I smoke that stuff," I said, standing back up, "you promise not to screw with me?"

Finn crossed his heart.

"Okay, then," I said, accepting the lighter and one-hitter. "But just one pull."

I held the small pipe to my mouth, lit the business end, and inhaled. The smoke felt like hot thumbtacks pricking at my throat and lungs.

"Hold it in as long as you can," Finn said.

I exhaled in barking coughs. Smoke streamed out of me like it was coming off a forest fire.

"Atta boy," Finn said, chuckling. "You don't cough, you don't get off."

He took the pipe from me, smoked the two remaining hits, and poked a fresh one for himself.

"Well?" Finn asked, lighting the freshly packed one-hitter. "You baked or what?"

After I'd finished coughing, I took inventory of how my mind and body felt. Nothing seemed out of the ordinary, other than a hint of guilt. "I can't tell," I said.

"Well, it looks like your dog is," Finn said, nodding toward Joanie. "She must have gotten a contact high."

I looked down at Joanie. She peered up at me, smiling, curling her lips back and baring all her teeth.

"Dude!" I shouted, pointing at her. "Joanie's smiling!"

"I know," Finn said, snickering. "You've told me she does that."

"Yeah," I said, laughing even harder. "But, like, she's a dog, and she's *smiling*!"

My reaction got Joanie so excited she smiled even

harder, wagging her tail and shaking her butt with her eyes closed.

I almost pissed my pants. Joanie smiling was the funniest thing I'd ever seen. I lost control of my body and fell to the ground in front of her. "This dog is fucking *smiling*!" I whooped, grabbing her by the jowls and getting right in her face.

She opened her eyes and looked into mine. "Joanie!" I said. "You're a dog who knows how to freaking *smile*! You're the shit!"

She licked my face and kept on smiling.

"Guess that answers *my* question," Finn mumbled. "Get your ass up, Eddie. Act like you've been here before."

"Damn that dog's funny," I said, composing myself. "I swear — without her and the other dogs, I'd probably be losing my shit in Kusko."

"Losing your shit?" Finn asked, returning the weed to his jacket pocket. "What're you talking about?"

"I've been having second thoughts about Kusko," I said. "Hell, about Alaska in general."

Then I rattled off my laundry list of issues — failing in college, my lame life in Kusko, the truck situation, my empty bank account, the prospect of being stranded if I made more monstrous fuckups at the paper and Dalton decided to fire me. (Other than my shit/shift typo, he didn't have a lot of reasons to be unhappy with me, but, still, I had a sincere fear of screwing up, getting fired, and being trapped.)

"In Alaska, everything I touch turns to shit," I said. "Now that I've smoked with you, I'll probably go on to become a drug addict."

Finn pulled the weed back out of his jacket, raised an eyebrow, and smiled. He shoved the weed back into his pocket and said, "What about Taylor? Are you still talking to her? That chick's a smoke show. If you can get past her weird eye, that is."

"She's a smoke show either way," I said. "I'm angling to hang out with her, Bristy, and Hope sometime in the next couple weeks."

"I wish I could join you guys," Finn said.

"I know," I said. "Sucks that Bristy and Hope pretend not to know you."

"Yeah, but whatever. I know plenty of other people," Finn said. He thought for a second. "What if Taylor digs you? Would that make you like Kusko?"

"Maybe, but I don't know," I said. "This place is a full-on sucktown."

Finn laughed halfheartedly.

I felt like I'd insulted him. "Sorry, Finn. I know Kusko is your home. I'm not saying I'm too good for the place. I just — "

I spotted something out of the corner of my eye, fifty yards away. I went silent and stared in the direction of some bushes at the foot of another knoll.

"What?" Finn asked.

"Something small and dark," I said. "I don't know what the hell it is, but it's in there."

Finn studied the bushes I pointed to. "Did it run fast?"

"Yes."

"Really fast?"

"Superman fast."

"Fuck, Eddie." Finn clutched my shoulder. "It's the little people. We need to get out of here. Now. There might be more of them."

I looked at him, confused. "Little people?"

"Yes, the fucking little people," Finn said, almost knocking me to the ground as he ran past to dislodge the ice hook in back of the sled. "There's no time to explain."

Finn threw the hook and rope into the sled and got in, kicking away dead birds to clear himself a spot. "Drive!"

"What?" I jogged toward the back of the sled. "Which direction?"

"Doesn't matter! Just go!"

I jumped onto the sled. "Hike!" I commanded the team. The dogs took off. I jerked my head in every direction, trying to spot a little person.

"Faster!" Finn said, riding in the front of the sled with the gun in his lap, his eyes locked onto the bushes in question.

"Dammit, Finn! What are the little people?"

He turned toward me, holding the sides of the sled. He looked afraid. "They're little bastards, a foot or two tall. They live out here on the tundra, underground. They hurt people."

*Good God*, I thought. *How do they hurt people? Do they have weapons? What kinds of weapons? Spears? Bows and arrows? Do they bite? Are they rabid? If I get bitten by something rabid, how long until foam starts coming out of my mouth? Once the foam sets in, will my mouth always be foamy, or will that just happen when I'm mad?*

"EDDIE!" Finn screamed, hanging his body off the sled so that he could see behind me. "DON'T TURN AROUND! ONE OF THOSE FUCKERS IS RIGHT ON US!"

"HIKE!" I bellowed at the team. "GODDAMMIT, HIKE!"

The dogs ran like they had jet packs strapped to their backs.

I started crying, but I held my eyes closed. "GET THE GUN READY, FINN!"

No answer.

"FOR THE LOVE OF GOD, FINN — WHY HAVEN'T YOU FIRED YET?"

I opened my eyes and saw Finn, sitting there, wearing a smile wider than Joanie's.

"That thing was a rabbit, you stoner," he said, shaking his head. "Got you."

# CHAPTER 10

# DEAD END

I had to wash the FJ quickly. Dalton said if we ran out of water before the next delivery in three days, he'd dock me fifty bucks to pay for half of an emergency delivery. I couldn't afford that.

I attached a green garden hose to the spigot jutting out from the house near the front door. I didn't have time to hit the truck with soap and a sponge — just a good once-over with water to rinse away the worst of the dust and dirt that had accumulated ever since I moved to Kusko.

The sun shone brightly at nine o'clock at night. On this last Saturday of April, the sun wouldn't set until close to eleven p.m. After that, you could still read a newspaper outside almost all night because the sun never dipped too far below the horizon.

I turned on the water and jammed my thumb into the hose to create pressure. As I sprayed a clump of mud off the driver's-side front fender, I heard a woman's voice yell from across the street, "What's her name?"

I looked to my right and saw our neighbor, Peggy Paniptchuck — a Native lady in her fifties with short black mom-hair and a stiff-legged walk. She had just exited a cab, arriving home after her shift working at the airport.

I didn't know if she meant my truck or what. But considering she liked to give me shit all the time, she probably meant something else. I was pretty sure she had a crush on me.

"The FJ doesn't have a name," I said with a smile.

Peggy ambled across the street toward me. "That's not what I mean. You haven't washed that truck since you got here. You must be trying to impress a girl."

*How'd she know?* I thought.

Peggy approached as I doused the spare tire mounted to the back of the FJ. "Guilty as charged," I said with my back to her, rushing to finish washing the truck.

She chuckled, patted my ass, and said, "Don't fuck it up."

When I turned around, she was already hobbling back to her house. "That's all you wanted to say?" I asked, laughing.

"Yep," she replied.

\* \* \*

Gravel crunched beneath the tires of the FJ as I pulled into the driveway at Taylor's place. I parked near the house, hopped out, and looked around.

Taylor and her parents lived in Kusko's newest housing development, across the road from the Kuskokwim River. I counted ten boats — eight aluminum flat-bottoms, two wooden skiffs — speeding across the lazy, dirty brown water. The ice had broken up a few days before, giving everyone a sharp case of spring fever. Just like in Minnesota, folks had been champing at the bit to put away their coats and shovels, turn off their furnaces, and live life the way it was meant to be lived — outside.

The homes in Taylor's neighborhood were about the only modern ones in town. They were nothing spectacular, with their tan vinyl siding and red or green trim, but in Kusko they looked luxurious.

Tinfoil covered a second-level window of the house next door. Dalton had told me people sensitive to light did that from April to August so they could sleep.

I walked up to Taylor's door and knocked. Her house was one of the two-bedroom homes, with a newer steam bath in back.

I heard laughing inside. Taylor opened the door, in stitches.

"Oh my gosh, Eddie," she said, giggling as she leaned to give me a half-hug hello. "You have to try this. It's the funniest thing ever."

"Okay?" I said.

Taylor wore gray leggings and a tight white tank top. The tank top acted as a megaphone for her boobies as they shouted, "Look at us! We're right here! Now that you've looked once, look again!" I looked and looked again and hoped I wouldn't get caught.

I followed Taylor inside, where everything looked

spotless and the whole place smelled like vanilla. Family photos plastered the crimson walls. One photo showed Taylor, probably a couple years earlier, sitting on top of a big bull moose that, judging by the blood on the snow, was a fresh kill. She looked like a toddler riding a Clydesdale. In one of our first conversations, Taylor had told me that her dad started taking her hunting with him when she was twelve years old. She shot her first ptarmigan that year and downed her first caribou at age fourteen. In another photo, Taylor and her mom hugged and smiled on top of a mountain at sunset. Both wore spandex from top to bottom and looked like they'd just run to the summit. Taylor's mom was beautiful (for a mom), with short blond hair and a sleek, thin build.

From the hallway I heard voices and laughter. Taylor led me into the living room, where Bristy and Hope sat at opposite ends of a brown couch. Bristy had her bare feet up, and Hope, who also had on a tank top (thank you, spring) but with baggy blue jeans, slouched against the armrest. They both wore dumb smiles.

"You remember these two," Taylor said.

I nodded and smiled at Bristy and Hope, and they started giggling just like Taylor had been.

"I wondered when I'd see you two again," I said, pretending like the only time I'd ever met them was the night at my house. I sat down on a red easy chair across from Bristy and Hope while Taylor plopped down at the dining table, which stood behind the sofa and between the living room and open kitchen. "What's so funny?"

"You probably won't think it's funny," Bristy said, having barely composed herself. "Name a state or country, plus a random object."

"What do you mean?" I asked.

Hope said, "Like Kentucky steak sauce, or Chilean toilet plunger."

Taylor exploded in laughter at the mention of the Chilean thing. She repeatedly slapped the kitchen table with her hand, like she couldn't take it anymore.

I stared up at the ceiling and thought for a second. I looked back down at the girls. "Irish ice auger?"

They all cracked up. Hope laughed so hard that snot dripped out her nose. Bristy got tears in her eyes.

"What is this?" I said, laughing too, but not really knowing why.

"They're fictitious sex acts," Hope said. "Like, 'Taylor Kentucky steak sauced him,' or, 'Eddie gave her the old Irish ice auger.'"

"Hilarious!" I said.

"Yeah, well you won't be laughing after I give you the old Turkish pump handle!" Taylor replied.

*Whatever that is, please do it to me,* I thought.

More laughter from everyone. It seemed like they were all high, but I knew that wasn't likely with Taylor around.

"Or the Arabian pickle slicer!" Hope said, kicking her legs like a wounded animal.

*Maybe she really is high,* I thought.

Bristy screamed, "And don't forget about the Peruvian condom!"

Everyone stopped laughing.

Hope snapped out of her convulsions. "You're

doing it wrong, dumbass. A condom is already something sexual. The object has to be something nonsexual for it to be funny."

We all laughed again, this time at Bristy's expense. She wasn't amused. "Whatever, douche-mongers. I still think it's funny. You guys think *you're* so funny? The only thing that's funny is how — "

"Stop talking," Hope said, cutting Bristy off before she could begin another one of her pointless rants about nothing.

After we settled down, I asked Taylor about the Native spelling bee.

"I forgot — when's it scheduled in Kusko? I should probably write a little story about it."

"Next Friday, in the multipurpose room at Kusko Elementary," Taylor said. "I'm super excited. A few other schools around Alaska have already held their competitions. The lady from the UA language center said they all went perfectly. The winning word in the town of Barrow was 'akargik.' That's the Inupiat word for ptarmigan."

That reminded me of something.

"I know this is random, but do any of you know anything about the little people?"

The girls laughed.

"We all have stories," Bristy said. "But let's get out of here."

"Yeah," Taylor said, rising from the kitchen table. "It's too nice out to be inside. I heard Joey Bragg is going wakeboarding tonight. Let's go watch."

*Wakeboarding?* I thought. *What's so special about wakeboarding?*

\* \* \*

The girls put on sweatshirts before I followed them out. I wore a long-sleeved camo T-shirt, blue jeans, and my camo baseball cap flipped backward. It must have been fifty-five degrees outside. But after the long cold winter, it felt more like seventy-five.

I kicked a rock as we marched across the gravel road to the Kuskokwim. I purposely walked behind the girls so I could gawk at Taylor's backside without getting busted. Hints of pink highlighted the partly cloudy sky above us. Another bitchin' part about the long days in Alaska: the sunsets lasted for hours.

"So then," I said, "what about the little people?"

In front of me, Bristy said, "They're mythical little creatures who live underground on the tundra. My grandpa loved talking about them when I was younger. Anytime anything went wrong, he always blamed it on them."

"Same with my grandma," Hope said, turning around to explain. "Whenever she heard noises or lost things, she said, 'Damned little people.'"

Taylor took the lead as we followed her onto a narrow trail through a patch of dead grass. Just ahead of us, five boats glided across the Kuskokwim.

"Which one of those boats is Joey's?" I asked. "And who is he, anyway?"

"He goes to high school with us," Taylor said ahead of me, stepping onto the sandy shoreline. "But he doesn't have a boat."

The rest of us joined Taylor on the shoreline. Bristy pointed to an area fifty yards to our right, near what looked like a boat launch. "There he is," she said.

Through a cloud of gnats backlit by the sunshine, I saw a dude our age off-loading dogs from the back of an old white pickup truck. Taylor ran toward him and left us behind. I wondered, jealously, why she seemed so excited to see him.

I hung back with Bristy and Hope and walked in between them. Once Taylor was out of earshot, I asked the girls, "Are you two high?"

Bristy's eyes went wide. She punched me in the arm and said, "Don't even say that!"

"What about that night?" I asked, keeping an eye on Taylor to see what would happen when she reached Joey. "Why can't Taylor know you guys smoke weed?"

Hope tongued the hoop through her lip and gave me a hard look. "Basically," she said, "Taylor doesn't have room in her life for any extra bullshit. She doesn't want to be associated with friends who party, because her parents are teachers. It's a small town and word travels. She caught us smoking weed a year ago and practically disowned us."

"Well, you're both acting high," I said. "The Chilean whatever wasn't that funny."

"Drop it, Eddie," Bristy said. "And don't go saying anything to Taylor. Even though she's probably freaking about nothing, we don't want to get into trouble with her. We've been best friends since kindergarten."

Then, thirty yards ahead, Taylor jumped up into the air and reached for Joey. He caught her and swung her around in a circle, like a military husband reunited with his wife.

My first knee-jerk thought: *I'd like to kick that kid's ass right now.*

Joey, wearing a black sleeveless T-shirt, looked like a more muscular version of Finn, and he was probably stronger than me because I'd barely worked out since I moved to Kusko. There was no gym other than the one in the high school. All I'd been able to do was pushups, and some curls with a five-gallon bucket of water.

I saw red, and I knew Bristy and Hope could tell.

Hope grabbed my hand to get my attention. "He's her second cousin, you fucking spaz."

*Phew,* I thought. *Thank God.*

"I couldn't care less," I said.

"Whatever, Eddie," Bristy said.

I walked through a crowd of eight sled dogs, brushing my knees against their sides. I inadvertently stomped on a gangline resting beneath the dogs' feet just as Joey tossed a tangled pile of harnesses onto the ground.

Taylor took a step back so that I could shake Joey's hand. "What gives?" I asked him. "Dry-land mushing on the beach is a cool idea, but where's the sled?"

Joey smiled. "I'm not mushing. I'm wakeboarding."

*Now I get it,* I thought. *That's badass.*

Joey pulled a wet suit from the bed of his truck and changed into it behind the driver's-side door, shielding himself from the girls, who stood on the outskirts of the dogs.

The girls got to work harnessing the dogs, without being asked. "Thanks for the help," Joey said, watching them through the door window as he changed.

I grabbed the dog closest to me — a mocha-colored mutt with black patches — and began fitting his harness. I was impressed not only that the girls knew how to harness dogs, but that they were so good at it — especially Hope, who was doing it faster than me.

"You know how to do this?" I asked them.

"We're Alaskans, dumbass," Hope said.

I laughed, but nobody else did.

A minute later, Joey spread the gangline onto the beach, ten feet from the mucky brown water. The girls and I attached the dogs to the gangline while Joey hooked a long rope onto the back of it. He grabbed the rope and the wakeboard and hiked down the shoreline until the rope was taut, thirty feet behind the team. The girls and I knelt down and petted the dogs to occupy them.

Joey waded twenty feet into the water, waist-deep, hauling the rope handle and wakeboard with him. He half hollered, "Someone needs to drive my truck and trail us down the beach."

"I will," Taylor replied.

Joey sunk into the water up to his shoulders to fit the wakeboard onto his feet, the rope handle floating just in front of his face. He grabbed the rope handle and balanced himself in the water, lying back slightly, with the tip of the wakeboard peeking above the river's surface.

"Hike!" Joey shouted.

The dogs lunged forward, fighting against the weight of Joey and the resistance of the wakeboard plowing through the water. Ten seconds later, the dogs hit full stride and Joey was upright. The girls and I whooped and cheered as Joey sailed past us, the dogs kicking up sand as they barreled down the shoreline.

With one hand holding the rope, Joey waved and

shouted, "Drive, Taylor!"

She hustled to the truck, started it, and backed onto the beach. She peeled away toward Joey, who was now more than a hundred yards upriver. She drove with her left elbow hanging out the window, like a farmer driving down a country road.

The other girls and I stood alone on the beach. "That is *so* effing cool," I said. "How far can he go?"

"The beach ends after a half mile or so," Hope said.

With Taylor gone, I finally had time to get to the bottom of some things.

"So," I said as Bristy and Hope began skipping rocks onto the water. "I know Taylor can't know you two smoke weed, but does she know Finn?"

"She knows who he is and what he does," Hope said. "Everybody in our school knows what he does."

"Do you think she'd be pissed if she knew I hung out with him?"

"Probably not," Bristy said.

I wondered, *"Probably not" because Taylor didn't like me as more than a friend and didn't care what I did?*

Only one way to find out.

"Ladies," I began, "I just need to come right out and ask this. Does Taylor like me? Like, *like me* like me?"

Bristy and Hope dropped their rocks and looked at each other gravely, like I'd just asked a question they didn't want to answer. They stayed silent, apparently hoping the other would be the first to speak.

Finally, Hope did the honors. "Sorry, Eddie. Don't waste your time. She doesn't — "

"Stop," I said, cutting Hope off. I could feel all the blood drain from my face. I didn't want to know why. At all. Every word of Hope's explanation would be more painful than the last. Nothing is more demoralizing than finding out the girl you like doesn't like you back. Nothing.

*I was right after all*, I thought. *Taylor is too smart and too hot for me. Out of my league.*

"I have to go," I said. "Tell Taylor I forgot about something I have to do."

"But, Eddie — " Bristy said.

"I don't want to hear it."

I turned toward Taylor's house and started walking. I wanted to run.

\* \* \*

I peeled out of Taylor's driveway and started driving around in the orangey twilight, not knowing where I was headed. I drove the dirt roads through neighborhood after crappy little neighborhood, in a daze. My body was so numb, I couldn't feel my right hand when I grabbed the stick to switch gears. I kept driving, and driving, and driving, for who knows how long, as thousands of tiny rocks pinged against the FJ's undercarriage.

I drove onto what I thought was a new road, but then I recognized the kids riding their bikes as the same group I'd seen a few minutes before. *I was just on this road*, I thought.

I continued driving, searching for a road I hadn't already traveled. I couldn't find one. I couldn't just roll on down some country highway, the way I could back home. The town felt like a hideous song, stuck on repeat. I couldn't go anyplace new.

Finally a dirt road I'd followed just ended. No street sign warned me of a dead end or a washout or anything. I jammed on the brakes. My head almost hit the steering wheel when the FJ's front tires sank into doughy tundra. I'd arrived at the edge of a vast expanse of nothingness. So vast, I could practically see the curve of the Earth. I shifted into reverse and accelerated but didn't move. The FJ was stuck.

I couldn't drop the vehicle into four-wheel drive without locking the front hubs. When I got out to do it, I became paralyzed by the world around me. The faint sound of a dog pack howling on the other side of town filled the cool, calm night air. The sky was on fire. A small flock of white tundra swans flew so close overhead, I could hear their wings whooshing. The scene would have stupefied anyone.

At that moment, I should have appreciated the beauty and tranquility of the world around me. For the rest of my life, I might never again experience the peacefulness and purity of the dazzling sights and sounds before me. Yet I felt only loneliness and isolation. I felt like I was all by myself, lost at sea, clinging to a scrap of driftwood.

I turned my head east, toward the empty abyss of tundra. Along the horizon, I could barely make out the profile of the highest peaks of the Kilbuck Mountains. Somewhere beyond those mountains, five hundred miles away, my friends were having fun in Anchorage.

They were there, and I was here. In Kusko. For another eight months. Broke. With no chance at Taylor. Completely alone.

"Kusko sucks," I said out loud, to no one. "I want out of here."

# CHAPTER 11

# TRY SOME BEAVER

I sat at my desk Monday morning, unmotivated as a stubborn mule. Dalton sat at his, wearing his tan Carhartt overalls, trying to close an ad deal with a new Polaris dealership in Anchorage.

"Don't wait another month," Dalton said to the business owner on the phone. "Get into people's heads now, before your competitors start running their dividend ads."

Dalton kept talking, and I kept sulking. I was supposed to be writing a story about a break-in at Kusko Clinic, a small family practice on the east side of town. On Saturday night, one or more hoodlums had busted open the back door and swiped five thousand dollars' worth of Valium, OxyContin, and other prescription meds.

Instead of writing the story, I perused travel search engines for flights to Anchorage, and visited Yute Cargo's website to calculate shipping costs to get my truck back there. The combined cost for both was north of thirty-five hundred dollars, which I knew I couldn't come close to ever being able to afford. But it was fun to dream.

Dalton said into the phone, "Thanks again, I'll get you into the next issue," and hung up.

"Did you hear that, Eddie?" Dalton asked excitedly. "I just scored a four-month contract of half-page ads. They'll run every week until the dividend rolls out."

*Whoopee,* I thought.

"Awesome," I said, trying to act happy. "Does that mean — "

"It means we'll bump up to sixteen pages for the foreseeable future. So you'll need to crank out a few more stories every week."

I didn't hesitate a millisecond before asking, "Can you pay me more?"

Dalton appeared too thrilled by his sale to be annoyed by my question.

"Now I can afford to start flying you to villages," he said. "You can shoot all the photos you want to fill up the extra pages — as long as the photos are good, of course."

After five months in Kusko, I'd finally get to experience the adventure of traveling to some of the farthest reaches of the planet, of visiting parts of Alaska few people ever got to see. Maybe I should've been excited, but I sure didn't feel excited. I felt cranky and sour. I still felt trapped. I wanted to be done with Kusko.

The text Taylor sent me the night before only reinforced my misery. Bristy and Hope had told her about our conversation — how they told me I had no shot and how I took off.

"I never meant to lead you on," Taylor wrote.

I responded, "No worries. Good luck with the spelling bee."

She sent me a frowning emoticon followed by, "I'd like to talk to you."

I didn't want to have the let's-be-friends convo. "I'm good," I wrote. "See you around."

I deleted our text thread, and Taylor's number, from my phone as Dalton stood up from his desk to leave.

"I need to run some errands," he said. "Try to finish that story by noon, then I'll take you to lunch."

"At Delta Delicious?"

"They have a new lunch menu. I hear it's not bad."

* * *

"Done yet?" Dalton asked, walking through the door and onward to his desk.

I was still bogged down in the story. It was supposed to be six hundred words and include a photo, which together would fill half a page. I had barely written three hundred words and still hadn't shot the pic.

I shook my head and stared at my computer screen, trying to think up an excuse. When he asked why not, I lied and told him I'd gone to Kusko Clinic to shoot the photo of the busted door, which ate up some time. I crossed my fingers, hoping he wouldn't ask to see the photos.

Dalton sat at his desk, checking his email. "Got another story for you," he said. "Sheriff Buzz Berger just emailed me a nice lead."

"What's the deal?"

"Big marijuana bust in the village of Tuntutuliak, forty miles southwest of here."

Dalton forwarded me the email. The sheriff detailed the events of the bust and made note of the fact that marijuana prices in villages had never been higher, leading dealers to take risks they normally wouldn't take. At the end of the email, he added, "Don't print that part about the fuckin' prices, though. I don't want to tempt any more dealers. Security at Kusko Airport is shitty enough as it is."

I'd seen Buzz at the courthouse but had never met him formally. In writing he sounded unprofessional.

Dalton sat up from his desk. "Let's go eat," he said. "Just make sure you finish the marijuana and clinic stories before deadline tomorrow."

I hopped into Dalton's truck and we headed to Delta Delicious.

During the drive, I couldn't stop thinking about the weed story. It had given me an idea.

Granted, it was a crazy idea. But given the depths of my agony, crazy seemed like a step upward.

\* \* \*

I pulled up to my place at around eight o'clock. I'd spent all afternoon and early evening willing myself to write the two stories Dalton had assigned, shooting a photo of the busted door at Kusko Clinic after he left the office. I barely finished the clinic piece and would have to get up extra early to pound out the weed story. Writing while depressed isn't easy.

I looked over at Finn's house and saw a rusty old pickup in his driveway. I decided to wait a minute. I didn't want to show up unannounced and make his customer jumpy.

I pulled out my phone, intending to kill a little time by sending a text to R.J. But I saw that my dad had texted me earlier. He'd written: "When do your finals start?"

I didn't know how to respond. Part of me wanted to come clean about bombing out and moving to Kusko. It's not like throwing a pissed-off father into the overflowing river of shit I'd created could make the river rise any higher. I'd already screwed myself hard enough.

I stared at my phone. "Two weeks," I wrote. "Burning the midnight oil. Studying hard."

I got out of the FJ and walked to Finn's house as the rusty pickup in his driveway backed out. I made an effort not to look at the driver, and when I knocked on Finn's door, he opened right away.

"What up?" he said with a grin. He wore a camouflage smock, and the smell of cooking meat poured out around him. "Come on in, brother. Try some beaver. I just finished slow-roasting a meaty one I trapped."

"Thanks, but no thanks," I replied.

"Don't knock it, man," he said. "Beaver is rich and oily but real tasty. I think you'd like it."

He led me in and motioned for me to sit down at the kitchen table. From the kitchen counter he grabbed a plastic plate that supported a heap of beaver meat the size of a full rack of ribs, then took a seat across the table. He used a fork and knife to cut hunks of meat clinging to the dead animal's spine. I watched him take a huge forkful, shove it into his mouth, and chew, chew, chew.

"I have to ask something," I said. "Did you sell weed to that dude who just left?"

He nodded as he scooped in another forkful.

"How much?" I asked, then waited for him to swallow.

"An eighth," he finally said.

"How much did you charge?"

"Seventy-five bucks. But this is really good stuff. Normally it'd be sixty."

Finn stood up and walked to the slow cooker on his kitchen counter. He used a ladle to scoop carrots and onions onto his plate. He sat back down.

"So," I continued, "what would you charge for an ounce of the sixty-dollar stuff you normally sell?"

Finn said around four hundred for an ounce. When I asked how much an ounce would sell for in the villages, he said double or more.

"So," I said, "in theory, you could sell an ounce in a village for nine hundred?"

"Yeah, I guess. But I don't have the balls to — " He paused. I saw the light bulb turn on. "Wait a minute, Eddie. I see where you're going with this. I don't know, man. That's a slippery slope."

"Dude, I'm about to be flying to a different village almost every week," I said. "Dalton finally has money to start sending me. Airport security won't think to check my bags because they know I'm a reporter."

That was true. Everyone knew flight security was

lax in the YK Delta — and most everywhere in rural Alaska. What Sheriff Berger had said in his email only confirmed that fact. The main thing you had to worry about was getting past Kusko security. After that, you were basically home free in whatever village. Although village public safety officers — known as VPSOs (every village employed one) — would drive out to the runway and greet the passengers of every airplane that landed, they only checked the bags of folks who looked like they might be smuggling something. None of the villages had funding for sophisticated security measures.

"I really need some money," I explained. "I've got to get the hell out of here."

"Since when do you want to leave Kusko so bad?" Finn asked.

"Since Saturday," I said. "Taylor denied me."

"Ouch," Finn said, scooping another mouthful of beaver.

"That's not all," I said. "There's all this other bullshit that's been building up, and all I do lately is work and pick up dog shit and work and pick up dog shit and work and watch you eat beaver."

Finn laughed as he chewed.

"I mean, I'm eighteen," I continued. "I can't take this anymore."

He nodded, and I kept on talking. I explained why I couldn't just up and leave: I didn't have time for a second job to pay for a flight and shipping my truck, I couldn't sell my beloved truck, and my dad was too poor to help me — which he probably wouldn't do even if he had the money, just to teach me a lesson.

"But if I sell some weed," I said, "I could be back in Anchorage in just a few months. I could pay my way out of here and reenroll in college — or move back to Minnesota."

"You want to sneak pot onto an airplane, but you're afraid to try beaver meat?" Finn said.

I rolled my eyes and stood up to get myself some beaver meat. I forked a leg the size of a chicken breast and dropped it onto a plastic plate. I hacked off some meat with a knife and took a bite. It tasted like an overly rich and ultragreasy rump roast. Not bad.

I continued my previous line of questions. "So, how much would I have to pay for an ounce through whoever you get it from?"

"Probably three hundred." Finn didn't even look at me. He just spoke flatly and cut up the remaining beaver on his plate.

"So I could buy it for three hundred, charge nine hundred, and net six hundred?"

"Sounds about right."

I thought about the numbers I'd crunched on Yute Cargo's website earlier in the day. Shipping my truck to Anchorage would cost around three grand — a fee that, in retrospect, underscored just how badly Dalton had needed a reporter when he hired me. He was willing to pay three thousand dollars to ship a truck he knew I wouldn't really need. I thought I'd been lucky to land the job; turns out he was seriously desperate.

I did the math in my head: three thousand divided by six hundred is five. Five marijuana deals if I moved an ounce each time. I could do that before the end of summer.

"What do you say, Finn?"

He took another bite of beaver. He chewed slowly, then took a second bite.

I knew he was buying time, and I wasn't in the mood. "Well?"

"Yeah, bro," Finn said. "I'll hook you up. But you better know what you're doing."

# CHAPTER 12

# GLOWING FiSH

The buzz of my electric razor woke up Dalton through the paper-thin bathroom walls. That didn't surprise me. Drop even the faintest, cutest little girl-fart in there, and the whole house would hear it.

Dalton stirred in his bedroom across the narrow hallway. "The hell?" he muttered to himself, half asleep in his bed, annoyed that I'd ruined his last half hour of shuteye. A minute later, he clunked around in the kitchen, brewing a pot of coffee. "Eddie, want any of this?"

"Sure," I replied, still shaving. "Sorry about the noise."

"Yeah, well what's taking so long? You barely get a five o'clock shadow."

True. But I wasn't shaving my face. I was shaving my ass. Puberty might've arrived late, but it left me with an exceptionally hairy ass, a fact known by just a handful of people, including five girls in Zimmerman and two girls in Anchorage.

"I'm shaving my pubes," I said, figuring Dalton would assume I meant my bush.

"Remind me to never use your shaver," he said.

I stood naked in the shower, on top of a pile of my own short-n-curlies. I'd cut down the trees but still had stumps to grind. I lathered with shaving cream and used a proper razor to glide through the stubble. Once finished, I turned on the water for a quick shower.

"Make it fast," Dalton said through the wall. "We're almost out of water."

This was another Sucktown reality I'd come to know: only a third of Kusko homes had piped water. The rest of us had water tanks — three-hundred-gallon tanks were typical — that the city filled once a week. Run out, and an emergency refill set you back an extra hundred bucks.

I finished showering in less than thirty seconds, dried off, and got dressed in my bedroom. I put on a green T-shirt underneath baggy, blue-jean overalls. After almost five months in Kusko, I'd conformed to the local male fashion trend of wearing overalls more days than not. When in Rome.

Dalton had a cup of hot coffee waiting for me on the kitchen table. He watched the news while seated on his couch — a maroon L-shaped sectional with a musky odor just shy of offensive. Every other piece of furniture in the house looked like it'd been discarded by a secondhand store. The home itself was decent, but the furnishings were not.

I sat down at the table and sipped the coffee. I only had time for half a cup because I needed to be at Finn's house so he could drive me to the airport.

"Where you headed today?" Dalton asked.

"Unalakleet."

Dalton's coffee almost blew out his nose.

"Unalakleet?" he blurted. "What the hell for? You do realize Unalakleet isn't in the YK Delta, right? The *Patriot* isn't even sold in that village — it's fifty miles out of range."

Dalton had worked out a deal with Yute Express, the YK Delta's largest passenger airline. He paid a flat two thousand dollars that allowed me to travel standby to almost any village in western Alaska, up to two times per month, through October.

"I know Unalakleet is too far north," I said, smiling coyly, knowing he'd love my explanation. "But I've got a juicy lead. Everyone in Alaska is going to want to read this story."

"What's the story?"

"Glowing fish."

"What do you mean, *glowing fish*?"

"I mean, the king salmon are lighting up like freaking glow sticks. Finn told me about it. He knows a guy who's seen it with his own eyes."

The kings had just started running. Generally speaking, Alaska's salmon runs work like this: kings in late May and June, reds in July, silvers in August. Finn had explained all that too.

"The fish are glowing in the water?" Dalton asked.

"No, no. Nothing like that. You'll just have to read the story. Trust me on this one."

Dalton paused and took a swig of coffee. "Fine, Eddie. Go for it. Just make it good."

\* \* \*

I heaved my backpack over my shoulder at the doorway. Dalton said I needed a backpack full of gear for every village trip because the volatile Alaska weather can halt air travel for days at a time. If I was going to be stuck in a village overnight, I needed a sleeping bag, a change of clothes, pilot crackers and Spam, toiletries, toilet paper, and a good pair of boots.

The dogs detonated — howling and barking — the moment I walked outside. They hadn't been fed yet. "Easy, guys — breakfast is coming," I assured the pack, knowing Dalton would soon fill their bowls with dog food and a scoop of chicken fat.

I went up the steps at Finn's and let myself in. Knocking was no longer necessary.

Finn sat at his kitchen table with a stupid smirk on his face. On the table rested a vacuum sealer, a cellophane baggie, duct tape, and what I assumed to be an ounce of marijuana. Finn gestured toward the weed like a beautiful game show model presenting a new car.

"I still can't believe you're doing this," he said. "You've got serious balls."

I couldn't totally believe it, either. Especially considering how big a pile of weed stared at me. It looked as big as a head of lettuce. "Will all of that, um, fit?"

"Yeah, it'll fit. It'll shrink down when we smash it and vacuum seal it. Watch."

Finn held the baggie near the edge of the table and dumped the weed off the ledge, into the bag. He placed the bag back onto the table and pounded the weed inside of it with a closed fist.

After that, he inserted the open end of the baggie

into the vacuum sealer and turned it on. (Everyone in Kusko owned a vacuum sealer, a necessity for storing meat.) The machine hummed loudly, sucking out every last molecule of air and sealing the bag tight. The sealed package was narrow and eight inches long, about the size of a large banana.

"Drop your drawers," Finn said.

I unbuckled my overalls. I slid my gray boxers down to my ankles, and Finn slapped my bare ass as hard as he possibly could, just to be a dick. The imprint of his palm and fingers burned into my butt cheek like I was a cow he'd just branded. I almost punched him.

"Easy, Eddie," Finn said between laughs. "I'm just messin' with you. Now, spread 'em."

I held my butt cheeks, and Finn crammed the package inside my crack. Once it was lodged in there well enough, I held everything in place, sidelong, while he cut strands of duct tape and stuck them across my ass.

"Good call on the shave job," Finn said. "This tape is still gonna hurt coming off."

I put my clothes back on while Finn hurried into his bedroom and gestured for me to join him. A full-length mirror hung on the wall near his dresser.

"Profile, please," he requested.

I turned sideways and looked at my reflection. Everything checked out. My overalls were baggy enough that the package was undetectable. I took a few short steps forward and backward, like people do when trying on new pairs of shoes.

"How's it feel?" Finn asked.

"Not great, but I'll live."

I plopped down on his bed to test what sitting felt

like. That wasn't horrible, either.

I stood, looked in the mirror again, and bent over. That posed a problem. If I bent with straight legs, the package broke the plane of my crack enough to reveal a bulge.

Finn looked concerned. "If you have to pick something up, remember to bend your knees."

"I won't forget." I took a few deep breaths and told myself to stay calm. "Who am I meeting again?"

"His name's Casey Cotton — one of my high school buddies. He'll pick you up in Unalakleet. You'll like him."

It was a quarter past six, and we needed to hurry to the airport. The plane was scheduled to leave in forty-five minutes.

\* \* \*

Finn fired up the FJ and we motored away. He loved the truck almost as much as I did, so sometimes I let him drive it.

The ride to the airport was about as long as any trip we could make in Kusko — meaning about five minutes. Finn wasn't playing my wingman. He had to get to work at the airport.

During the drive, every emotion I'd suppressed came bubbling up. I'd previously done an outstanding job of fooling myself into thinking that selling weed wasn't a big deal. I wasn't a drug dealer. I was a good guy who just happened to have a small amount of marijuana, who would just happen to give away the marijuana if someone just happened to give him a few bucks for it. And I barely ever smoked the stuff, which seemed to make selling it more okay.

I thought of how disappointed my dad would be if he knew what I was doing. After all he did to keep the family afloat after my mom died, this was a slap in his face. And what if I got busted? What then? How long would the offense be on my record? A year? Three years? Seven years? Was all of this even worth it? Was I really *this* anxious to get out of Kusko?

I thought of Taylor and the pain and embarrassment I'd feel seeing her around town from now until I left Kusko for good. *Um, yes,* I thought. *This is definitely worth it.*

I dreamed these things with my eyes open, in a trance. Then I remembered that I needed three thousand dollars and had zero, and I heard a voice in the back of my mind. "Own this," it said. I heard it again, and a third time.

"Own this!" Finn said a fourth time, practically shouting.

I snapped to. "What?"

"Own this, dude," Finn repeated, driving with one hand on the steering wheel. "I can see you tweaking in your head over there. Don't. You have to own this. You have to walk inside that airport like you're the shit, like absolutely nothing is up. You have to *own* this."

*Yeah, own this,* I thought.

We pulled up to the front of the airport. "Get your backpack and do this," Finn said. "Don't think. Just do."

I got out, opened the back door of the FJ, and grabbed my backpack. Finn dropped the truck into gear and pulled away toward the employee parking lot. Then he hit the brakes. He backed up the truck and motioned for me to open the passenger door. I did.

"Look at me," Finn said.

I did that, too. Right in his eyes.

"If you get busted, remember something."

"Okay. What?"

He paused for dramatic effect.

"Remember to suck it, nerd."

\* \* \*

As I walked into the airport, my confidence was solid. It drained the moment I got in line to check in for my flight. Three people waited in front of me. A dozen others sat in the dirty blue waiting chairs to my right — Natives young and old, and some construction workers, some of whom were also Native. I was positive they were all on to me. Not only did they know, they knew that I knew they knew. I was sure of it.

I patted my ass to make sure the tape was secure. I did so unconsciously, then caught myself and stopped. As I thought of how patting my ass was the absolute last thing I should be doing, I realized I was doing it again, like a nervous tick. I jammed my hands into my pockets and kept them there.

Drops of sweat beaded at my temples. My right leg shook. One of my eyelids fluttered.

"Next," the ticket lady said.

I stepped up to the counter. The lady was Peggy Paniptchuck, my neighbor from across the street. Her eyes were glued to her computer, which she was almost too short to see over. She asked, without looking at me, where I was going and whether I needed to check any bags. I told her Unalakleet, and one bag to check.

"Are you carrying any explosives, firearms, or illegal drugs?" she continued, still with her head down.

*Own this*, I thought.

"Other than the ounce of weed I've got shoved up my ass, no," I replied.

Peggy's eyes shot up at me. Her mouth was agape, like I'd just announced I had a bomb strapped to my chest. Then her startled expression dissolved into a pleasant smile.

"Good one, Eddie — you had me going for a second!" she said, blushing.

"Got you!" I said.

I had forgotten that Peggy might be working the counter. Had I remembered, it might have chilled me out a little more during the drive to the airport.

Peggy cleared her throat. "Now Eddie, don't hate me for this, but FAA rules mandate that action be taken in the event of an affirmative response to the question I just asked. I'm going to need you to come with me for a moment."

"Seriously?" I said. "But I was only — "

"Sorry, Eddie. Please come with me."

Frantically, I surveyed every area of the airport, jerking and twitching my head around, looking for an out.

"But," I said. "But I'm going to miss my plane."

"Got you!" Peggy said. She laughed, shook her head, and added, "Next time don't mess with me."

I exhaled longer than an old man blowing out his birthday candles. "Dammit, Peggy — you got me just as good! But you know what paybacks are."

"Bring it, Eddie." She was already gesturing for the next person in line. "Now go have fun in Unalakleet. I'll be anxious to read your story, whatever it's about."

I wanted to tell her about the glowing fish, but I figured I'd best get out of there.

"Now boarding for Unalakleet," the flight's pilot shouted near the door leading out to the tarmac.

I got in line. The two people in front of me put their bags on a conveyer belt and walked through a metal detector. The security officer, a Native kid not much older than me, waved them on. No pat-downs.

I was next. I took my first step forward, wondering: *Do I smile at the security officer?*

"Have a nice flight," he said, waving me by.

"Thanks, bro," I replied, using the word "bro" to say, without explicitly saying, that I was a solid dude, and that I thought he was a solid dude, and that solid dudes don't try to bust other solid dudes.

Home free. I strutted toward the glass door leading outside, where a yellow six-seat bush plane warmed up to fly me and a couple others north to Unalakleet, two hundred fifteen miles away.

* * *

Soon we were airborne, and I tried to relax. The fat, middle-aged pilot wore aviator sunglasses and chewed on an unlit cigar. I sat kitty-corner behind him, in front of the other passengers — three old ladies wearing lightweight summer parkas called kuspuks.

The pilot looked over his shoulder and shouted above the sound of the roaring front propeller, "You okay, young man?"

I wasn't okay. Five minutes in, and the flight was scarier than everything I'd just been through at the airport. I hadn't thought the flight would be scary. Dalton said bush planes don't fly much faster than one hundred miles per hour, and they're never much higher off the ground than a mile or so. In theory, even an engine failure seemed survivable. But in reality, every tiny gust of wind felt like the beginning of the end.

I hollered, "Yeah, I'm good!"

"What?" the pilot yelled.

"I said, I'M GOOD!"

"Oh good!" he said. "Don't fret, nothing to be worried about — "

He winced and clutched his chest. My eyes bulged out of my head. Quickly, I peered out the window to see how high off the ground we were. Green tundra and round blue ponds scrolled far, far below us.

I looked back at the pilot. He pointed at me and laughed.

I frowned. "Not funny!" I shouted.

The rest of the flight was a turbulent, find-your-happy-place nightmare. The plane bounced up, down, and sideways in the wind, and I almost barfed when we touched down. The runway was like a bumpy stretch of dirt road.

"Thank you, God," I mumbled as we finally rolled to a stop.

I deplaned and waited for the pilot to retrieve my

backpack from the aircraft's storage compartment. I could see the village from the runway. Mammoth foothills, covered equally by thick brush and green tundra, formed a ring around the town in the far east, several miles away. To the west, the Bering Sea. The Unalakleet River flowed between the foothills and the village, wrapping around the east and south sides of the village and emptying into the sea. Clouds hung overhead.

Several Native families waited next to a red kiosk near the edge of the runway, along with a young guy I assumed to be Casey Cotton, and a middle-aged, red-haired village public safety officer with a crew cut. His uniform was blue, and no gun hung from his belt. Finn had told me VPSOs weren't allowed to carry firearms.

I walked up to greet Casey, practically brushing shoulders with the VPSO. He couldn't have cared less about me.

"What's up?" Casey said with a smile, sitting on a nineteen-eighties Honda Big Red three-wheeler. He was pudgy and much shorter than me. He had the biggest head I'd ever seen, a mop-top of curly blond hair, and a long scraggly beard that must have taken a year to grow. He wore a camo jacket and tan overalls, plus insulated, knee-high boots. It was late May, but still chilly at ten in the morning.

"How long you gonna be here, buddy?" Casey spoke in a high-pitched voice — and so fast I could barely understand him.

"Five hours until my return flight."

"That's plenty of time. Hop on, buddy."

I got on the back of his three-wheeler, and we sped

toward town down a wide, bumpy dirt road. The bumps hurt my butt and made me extra anxious to get rid of the package. I tried to take everything in as we approached Unalakleet, population one thousand. I had never visited a Native village before. It looked like a smaller, scruffier version of Sucktown. Most of the homes looked like glorified ice-fishing houses, with rusty heating fuel tanks outside. Jeans and underwear blew on clotheslines. Strips of king salmon hung on wooden drying racks. People on four-wheelers buzzed in every direction. The steeple of a dilapidated church jutted above the center of the village.

"Is there a store?" I asked as we drove past the town gas pump and onto a narrow ATV trail.

"On the other side of town," Casey said. "It doesn't have much. Whatever food people don't kill for themselves, they ship in from Anchorage."

Soon, shoulder-high shrubs blocked my view of Unalakleet. Casey took us onto a slim dirt trail that snaked around for a mile or two outside the village. Branches spanked at my shins as we sped along. Every time we slowed down to take a turn, clouds of mosquitoes moved in.

Ten minutes later we arrived at a clearing, on the rocky banks of the North River, an offshoot of the Unalakleet River. The foothills towered in front of us. Casey turned off the three-wheeler and handed me an aerosol can of bug dope. I shut my eyes and sprayed my face.

"This is my life," Casey announced with pride, taking in the beautiful scenery. He pointed to my right. "And that, right there, is my home."

Thirty yards down river stood a fish-counting

tower — two stories of scaffolding overlooking a shallow, narrow stretch of river. Alaska wildlife officials contracted people like Casey to count salmon all summer. He sat in the tower for hours at a time, using a clicker to count every salmon that swam by.

"Can't do this job without poking a few one-hitters," Casey said.

"Oh, right," I said, unbuckling my overalls.

I told Casey I needed help with the duct tape. I dropped my overalls and boxers. "Please be gentle."

Three strands of tape covered my ass. I yelped when Casey yanked off the first one. It felt like my skin was being stripped away with it.

After he pulled off the last piece, he plucked out the baggie, walked a few steps forward, and dipped it in the river.

"Wanna test drive that stuff?" I asked him. I assumed the weed was good, but I was trying to sound like a pro.

"No, buddy," he said, shoving the bag into his front coat-pocket. "I don't need to test Finn's weed. His stuff's always the one-hit shit."

Casey handed me a wad of cash, and that was that.

"Okay, buddy. Ready to see something trippy?"

\* \* \*

Back on the three-wheeler, we motored down a trail that was even narrower, heading down river from the counting tower. After a short distance, we pulled into a grassy clearing surrounded by more shoulder-high brush. An ancient-looking Native man stood at a beat-up wooden table in front of a rundown shack made of rusty white metal siding. A tattered wooden skiff, filled with fishing nets, rested on the riverbank fifteen yards away.

Dalton had told me most Native families owned a summer fish camp — a riverfront parcel of land allotted to them by the government for being indigenous Alaskans. The camps I'd seen along the Kuskokwim featured similar shacks for cooking and sleeping.

On the wooden table rested a monstrous king salmon, probably forty pounds. The man cleaned the fish using a strange-looking knife with a circular blade. He cut the meat into long narrow strips.

"I've never seen a knife like that," I whispered to Casey as we dismounted the three-wheeler.

"It's an ulu knife," he replied.

The man used twine to hang a strip of salmon by its tail onto a six-foot-high wooden drying rack. The rack dripped with dozens of bright-red salmon strips.

"What's up, buddy?" Casey asked him.

The man introduced himself as Charles Sampson. He looked quintessentially Native, from his short stature, to his disproportionately large hands, to his bowlegged walk, to his measured, deliberate movements. Being in his presence felt like being back in time. The fact that he wore a weathered-looking caribou leather poncho only added to the sensation.

"The fish are glowing in the dark," Charles told me, his words coming out like drips of water. Charles and Native elders like him spoke incredibly slowly — carefully, it seemed to me.

"That's what I heard," I replied. "Can I see?"

Charles grabbed two strips of salmon from the drying rack and led Casey and me inside his shack. He opened the creaky door to a tiny room with a canvas army cot and a collapsible table with a green portable stove on top.

Then he kicked away the cot to reveal a plastic trapdoor leading underground. Charles opened the trapdoor and descended a short ladder, waving for me to follow.

"You pumped for this, buddy?" Casey asked me, leaning over the pit as I stepped down the ladder. I looked up and nodded.

Soon I stood underground next to Charles, shoulder to shoulder, in a sort of cellar for storing meat. Casey closed the trapdoor above the tiny, dank space.

Pitch blackness. Charles took my right hand and slowly pulled it toward him. He dropped the two fish strips onto my hand.

"The fish are glowing in the dark," he said again.

I lifted the strips toward my eyes. Sure enough, they glowed. Not enough to light up a room or anything, but there was no mistaking the faint, silvery glimmer.

* * *

The next day, I called wildlife officials in Anchorage to talk to a biologist about the glowing fish. The first two biologists I spoke with thought I was crazy. The third did not. He'd heard rumors of glowing fish several years before, researched the topic, and concluded that the phenomenon was the result of a rare phosphorescent bacteria that attaches to the fish in the ocean.

Charles never did say anything more to me other than "The fish are glowing in the dark," but that was all the quote I needed for my piece.

To Dalton's delight, the story did get picked up statewide. It began like this:

## North River Kings Glowing in Dark

By Eddie Ashford
Staff Writer / Delta Patriot

UNALAKLEET, Alaska — When Charles Sampson says the king salmon he's been netting near his fish camp on the North River are glowing, he doesn't mean they're radiating happiness. He means it literally.

"The fish are glowing in the dark," the Native elder said.

CHAPTER 13

# ACCiDENTAL ENEMY

Finn and I scurried up and down the west bank of the Kuskokwim, dip netting for smelt. It was a hot summer night in Suckingham — seventy-plus degrees under a sun that was shining brightly at 10:45.

We fished near Taylor's neighborhood, close to where Joey Bragg had gone wakeboarding. I could see the roof of Taylor's house from the metal culvert I stood on. I kept turning around to look, blindly dipping my net into the water.

Clearly, Finn knew what I was thinking. "Have you talked to her?" he asked.

"No," I said, my eyes glued to her house. "It's a miracle I haven't seen her around town. I hope it stays that way."

I turned my attention back to the river. Next to me, Finn lowered his net into the water and pulled out a dozen smelt. He dumped the little fish into a five-gallon bucket.

Finn had had the idea to take me fishing for

smelt — oversized minnows that arrive by the zillions for several days in late May or early June. He'd explained that people in villages up and down the Kuskokwim would grab a dip net — like a normal hand-held fish net, but with an eight-foot handle — and stand by the river to scoop them up. That's all there was to it. I was just glad to have something to do.

"So, what's the plan for my delivery tomorrow?" I asked Finn, studying the fish flopping in his bucket. We'd netted enough of them that I couldn't see the bottom of the bucket anymore.

"Just like before," Finn said, dropping his net back into the water. "Marijuana up your ass and cross your fingers at security."

Nearly three weeks had passed since my first delivery, and now Finn had arranged for one in his home village of St. Mary's, about a hundred miles north on the Yukon River. But unlike my delivery in Unalakleet, this time I wouldn't be lucky enough to have a customer and news story wrapped into one. I didn't have any story at all and would have to come up with one when I got there. This was a gamble. If I didn't return with a story that was good enough to justify a village trip, Dalton would ask questions.

That scared me, along with something else: the police blotter. If I got busted, my name would appear in the *Patriot* not as a byline, but in that dubious real estate. People never read any of the stories without first flipping to the police blotter to see who'd been busted and for what. It was the best-read part of the paper, according to Dalton. And after a few months in town, I understood why everyone in the YK Delta was deathly afraid of seeing their name printed there. It was all about public shaming.

"Wanna head out?" I asked. "It's getting late."

"Cool," Finn said. "This weekend we'll fry these little guys in beer batter, guts and all."

Finn reached into his bucket, grabbed a smelt by the back of its head, and looked it square in the face. "Suck it, little nerd," he said.

\* \* \*

I didn't feel nearly as nervous at the airport this time around. I stood in line at the ticket counter confidently as Peggy Paniptchuck registered the four people in front of me.

My only discomfort came from the package of weed Finn had lodged up my butt a half hour earlier. After he taped me up, a sharp kink in the package poked at my sphincter. It felt like I was getting stabbed in the bunghole, repeatedly, with a dull knife. But having Finn strip off the duct tape to reset the package would have hurt more, so I dealt with it.

"Are you carrying any explosives, firearms, or illegal drugs?" Peggy Paniptchuck asked me.

"Other than the flask of moonshine I've got shoved down my pants, no," I replied.

"Nice try, Eddie. Enjoy St. Mary's today. Are you going to write about the kids on the four-wheeler?"

Hello, panic. Nice to see you again.

I had no clue what the four-wheeler story was. If I replied no, Peggy would ask what other story I was covering, and I wouldn't have an answer. But if I said yes, she might ask questions about the four-wheeler story as if I knew the details. One lame response, and she could get suspicious. My only choice was to say yes. *Own this*, I thought.

"Yep, the four-wheeler story," I said. "Crazy stuff."

"Really crazy," she said as she went through the motions of checking my ID. "Are you going to interview both of them?"

I set my bullshitting thrusts to supersonic.

"I have one of the people lined up for an interview, but I'm still working on the other one." I glanced at my watch. "Shouldn't be hard to track the other person down in so small a village. Even if I only get that one person to talk, it will still be a good enough story."

She nodded.

"I just can't believe it actually happened," I said without really knowing why. The bullshitting was out of my control now. "I've been thinking about it nonstop. This will probably be one of the most interesting stories I've ever covered."

Peggy handed me the boarding pass, but before I could walk away, she cocked her head and asked, "How did you hear about it?"

"Same way you did." That was the only response I could come up with, and it seemed like a decent one.

"From Tommy Wegscheider?" she said. "How do you two know each other?"

"How do we know each other?" I said, wondering, *Who the hell is Tommy Wegscheider?*

Peggy only nodded and gave me a quizzical look.

"I just meant, you know, through the grapevine," I said.

"Oh, gotcha." She smiled. "Good deal then, Eddie. Can't wait to read the story."

*Yeah,* I thought. *And I can't wait to find out what it's even about.*

* * *

The landing strip at St. Mary's was nowhere near town. I got out of the plane, looked in all directions, but still couldn't see anything. More of the same formidable foothills I'd seen in Unalakleet blocked my view of anything to the north and east. To the south and west flowed the mighty Yukon River. Beyond the river, beautiful green tundra and boggy sloughs stretched to infinity. Hundreds of flying ducks dotted the sweeping expanse of blue sky.

The pilot collected my backpack from the plane's storage compartment and handed it to me. I'd been the flight's only passenger.

"How am I supposed to get to St. Mary's?" I asked.

"Look," he said, pointing to a foothill east of us. A trail of dust rose above the hill, like smoke from the top of a train we couldn't see. "The St. Mary's VPSO is almost here."

A moment later, a little red pickup truck appeared from around a bend, kicking up more dust. The vehicle pulled up just as the pilot climbed back into his plane. I walked up next to the driver's side door. The VPSO rolled down his window. He had black hair and bordered on morbidly obese. Curly chest hair sprouted out the top of his blue uniform shirt, which was missing a button.

"Morning," he said, his gut pressing against the bottom of the steering wheel. "Just you on that flight?"

"Yep," I said. "I'm from the *Patriot*. I'm here about the four-wheeler story."

"Sure," he said.

*Thank God he knows what it is*, I thought. The VPSO looked me up and down, and I tightened my cheeks around my illegal payload.

"You probably need a ride," he said.

"I do," I said, hoisting my backpack into the bed of his truck. "Appreciate the help."

His name was Russ — a white guy in his early twenties. He was so fat he couldn't fasten the seat belt around his bloated stomach. I had never seen a VPSO that out of shape. Most VPSOs were trim because of all the naturally lean foods villagers ate, salmon in particular. But this guy looked like he'd swallowed a beluga.

"Anything newsworthy happening out here, aside from the four-wheeler thing?" I asked him, playing the reporter, as we motored along. "Bust anybody lately?"

"Yeah, I usually cuff a bootlegger every week or two," Russ said, shifting the truck into third gear.

"What about drugs?"

"Not in a while." He glanced at me and added, "But I always know when somebody in town has weed."

*Sure you do, Sherlock*, I thought, scratching my ass, trying to reset the kink. I assured myself that even if he did bust somebody with my stuff, I'd be long gone by then.

St. Mary's was probably a mile from the airport as the crow flies, but two miles on land because the dirt road had to skirt the base of a big foothill. When the village came into view, I couldn't help thinking the place looked like it didn't belong where it was. The cluster of homes and buildings stood on the steep face of a foothill overlooking the confluence of the Yukon and Andreafsky rivers. The way the houses perched on that hillside made me wonder about the wisdom of whoever first chose to live there.

Russ swung through a turn and drove up a hill steeper than seemed safe, and at the top, we hung a right and parked near a small brown house.

"Here we are," he said.

Junk littered the front of the home, including an old dented refrigerator with the door ripped off, two rusty bicycles with deflated tires, and a beat-up four-wheeler.

*Could this be the four-wheeler?* I wondered, getting out of the truck. *What could the story be here?*

"You good then?" Russ asked.

I nodded as I gazed at the rest of the village below us. Five tiers of dirt roads, each lined with houses, rested on the side of the foothill, like steps in a diamond mine.

"If you need a ride back to the airport, I'll be right there," Russ offered, pointing to a shabby yellow house several doors down.

"Thanks, I guess I'll need one," I said. "Oh, one other thing. Do you know where Linetta Wassily lives? My neighbor knows her."

"Way down there, with the red tin roof." Russ pointed to a bright blue house at the very bottom of the foothill, near the Andreafsky shoreline.

\* \* \*

I spent a couple hours inside the little brown house, scrambling to keep up with my note-taking, listening to one of the most impressive stories I'd ever heard. I interviewed two sixteen-year-old Native kids named Sam and Owen. The house belonged to Sam's family.

"We didn't know if we'd make it out alive," Sam said. "We counted six brownies in the area."

His mom sat in a rocking chair, sewing a kuspuk. She never did say a word to me, other than hello when I'd first walked through the door.

The guys and I sat below her, cross-legged on the yellow linoleum floor. Brownish-black globs stained the floor in some places, quite possibly from the dried blood of a caribou that Sam or his dad — whom I never did meet — had gutted on a particularly cold winter day. (No kidding: during winter, one hotel in Kusko put up signs outside its rooms that read: NO GUTTING ANIMALS.)

Owen added, "We saw two males that were both ten-footers. And we saw a sow with two cubs. And we — "

"How close?" I asked, riveted.

"Too close," Sam said. "A young bear that looked way too thin circled around us for an hour, fifty yards away. If you can see a bear's ribcage, watch the fuck out."

Kusko wasn't bear country, but St. Mary's was. In the YK Delta, bears live north of the Yukon River, but rarely south of it.

The story was like this: A week before, without

telling anybody, the two boys drove that old four-wheeler I'd seen out front more than twenty miles north of town, where the kings were running heavy. While crossing what they thought was a shallow slough, the four-wheeler sank all the way up to the handlebars. The guys spent four hours tugging it onto dry land. Although they came prepared with tools for a breakdown, a waterlogged four-wheeler had never made their list of potential problems. Rather than spend two days trudging through the brush on foot, with bears everywhere, never knowing what was around the next corner, they spent forty-eight hours dismantling the four-wheeler and drying the parts over a fire, piece by piece. They reassembled the rig and drove it most of the way back to St. Mary's.

"We heard lots of metal-on-metal," Owen said, "so we knew the thing would take a shit at some point. Luckily, it got us pretty close to home."

Dudes were a year or two younger than me, yet I felt like a boy among men.

I couldn't wait to spring the story on Dalton.

* * *

Interviewing Sam and Owen was so intriguing that I lost all track of time. It was already three o'clock and my return flight would be leaving in under an hour. I had to find Linetta, and fast. I snapped a quick photo of Sam and Owen on the four-wheeler, strapped on my backpack, and made for Linetta's house.

Her home stood far below, past all the tiers of dirt roads. Walking there, I cut through some backyards. One of the homeowners — a Native man who looked older than Charles Sampson — glared at me as though I were trespassing, which I suppose I was.

When I got to Linetta's place, I looked up the foothill toward Russ's house and figured that, given my fat backpack, I'd need about ten minutes to walk there for a ride to catch my flight. I set the alarm on my phone for twenty minutes to remind myself of when I needed to leave.

I knocked on Linetta's door — a rotting wafer board, on a house that looked like a tree fort built with scrap wood by an ambitious group of eight-year-olds. *How's she going to afford this weed?* I thought. *And how the hell does she afford heating oil during winter?*

Linetta opened the door and grinned at me with all three of her teeth. She was skinny and reeked like piss. Her medium-length, oily blond hair looked like it hadn't been washed in weeks.

I couldn't tell her age. Either she was in her forties and partied way too hard, or she was just a dirty old lady in her fifties. She stood barefoot, wearing gray sweatpants and a bright pink T-shirt with sweat stains in the armpits.

"Got my smoke?" she grunted, bypassing introductions.

I glanced around before whispering, "I have it."

"Then come on in."

I looked around again, saw nobody out and about nearby, and stepped inside. The transaction wouldn't take long. It's not like we had a lot to talk about.

Linetta sat down on a musty green couch. A warped

wooden coffee table rested in front of it.

"Let's see," she said.

I dropped my overalls right in front of her. I turned around and shuffled backward, signifying I needed her to strip off the duct tape. Without warning, she slapped my ass like Finn had done, laughing. I snickered too. Life couldn't have gotten much weirder.

Linetta dislodged the package and slit it open with a pocketknife, not bothering to wash it off. She reached on top of the coffee table for a pipe made of antler. She packed a bowl, grabbed her Bic, and sucked three long hits.

"Good shit," she muttered, exhaling a rich cloud of smoke. She handed me a wad of cash.

"How are you and Finn related?" I asked, attempting to forge an actual conversation as I counted the cash. It was all there, and I was that much closer to my goal of three grand.

She didn't answer my question. She took the bag of weed from the table and tucked it into the drawer of her side table. Then she leaned back into the sofa and closed her eyes.

"Run along now," she said.

Before I could move, someone banged on the front door, which Linetta had "locked" by blocking it with a cement block on the floor. The thin board shuddered with each thump from outside.

"I smell weed in there!" a man bellowed. He had the voice of a giant, an angry giant.

I freaked. I was afraid Russ the VPSO had come to bust me. The voice didn't sound like his, though. It sounded as if it belonged to someone I'd like to see even less than the local cop.

"Get out of here, Bronco!" Linetta screamed.

I backed away and watched the door. The man banged on it three more times, and it seemed about to fly off its hinges.

"I said *leave!*" Linetta barked.

The man — Bronco, apparently — kicked open the door. Terrified as I was, I couldn't help but think he didn't look like a Bronco. He was a bald little Native guy in his early twenties, scrawny, and six inches shorter than me. He had a goatee and wore dirty blue jeans. He held a brown paper bag in one hand as he stormed over to Linetta.

"Smoke all you want, but you better have money for this!" he said, pulling a bottle of vodka from the bag.

"I asked for that two days ago," Linetta spat back. "You didn't deliver, so I got weed instead."

Bronco looked me up and down. "From this little dick-suck?"

I told him I didn't want any trouble.

"Well you got trouble," he taunted, taking a step toward me. I backed up. "You think you can come into *my* village and sell weed? You fuckin' crazy?"

I kept backpedaling until I was against the wall.

"Leave, Bronco!" Linetta shouted. "I'll pay for the vodka later!"

For the first time, I felt like a real drug dealer — dirty and disgusting. There I was, feuding with a bootlegger over the money of a sad old junkie, like two vultures fighting over a carcass. This lady should have been using the money she just gave me to buy decent food, or warm clothes, or a nicer sofa to sit on. *Don't look now, but you're adding to the problems of the YK Delta,* I thought, recalling my conversation with Nicolai.

Bronco wouldn't take his eyes off me. "Give me that money!"

My body shook, as did my voice when I said, "This is between you two. I have a plane to catch."

Bronco got between me and the door. "You're not going anywhere until you give me that money, you fuckin' pussy."

"Fuck that," I countered, hoping I'd sound sure and tough.

I'd barely finished the sentence when Bronco unleashed a roundhouse right. I tilted my head back just enough that he whiffed. He'd put everything he had into the punch, hoping to take me out in one shot. As we circled around each other then, I wondered what would go wrong next, how I could get the hell away from him.

Just then, the alarm on my phone went off. It confused Bronco for a split second. Without thinking, I lunged forward and shoved him. He toppled over the coffee table and smacked his head against the corner of the end table, which fell over with him, emptying the contents of the drawer.

Now I was *really* scared.

Blood spurted from a gash on Bronco's head. He rolled onto his side, groaning, trying to get up.

Linetta sat on the couch, dazed, like it was all a hallucination.

"I have to go," I said to Linetta, my voice trembling again. "Sorry!"

I stepped over Bronco to get my backpack, then made for the door.

"Get back here," Bronco said, grabbing at my pant leg.

"Let me go!" I yelled, but he had a good grip. I didn't want to hit him again, but I had no choice. I spun and kicked wildly, catching him square on the nose. My boot sounded like a meat tenderizer smacking a slab of sirloin. He groaned and covered his face with his hands.

"Shit!" I said. I hadn't meant to get him in the face. I looked at Linetta and again said, "Sorry!"

Then I bolted from the house, praying that Bronco couldn't get up and give chase. I darted uphill toward Russ's house as fast as I could, my backpack bouncing like it was filled with bowling balls. I arrived at Russ's house in no time and pounded on his door ferociously. I checked behind me. No Bronco. Russ opened the door right away.

"I lost track of time," I gasped.

"How much time we got?" He wore only a white T-shirt, his uniform pants, and white socks.

"About five minutes."

He didn't even bother with shoes. We just jumped into his truck and tore away.

As we drove the winding dirt road, I rolled down my window and heard an airplane buzzing in the distance. *No way that plane is beating us to the runway,* I thought. *I'll make this.*

I wondered if Russ would find out that Bronco was hurt, and what lies Bronco might spin to explain why his face looked like a gut pile. But I wasn't worried about getting caught for what I'd done to him. I knew that he and Linetta weren't going to say anything. They had their own crimes to hide. Not to mention, Bronco didn't seem like the kind of guy who'd readily admit to getting his ass handed to him by an eighteen-year-old.

Russ slowed the truck as we approached the runway. The plane had just landed. Before I got out, he said, "Hey, just one thing: How'd that four-wheeler story go?"

"Better than I could have hoped," I replied.

## CHAPTER 14

# A GRISLY ENCOUNTER

Heavy gray clouds rolled in from the west as I drove the FJ home to Dalton's place, where I dropped my backpack at the edge of the back dog yard and headed straight for Joanie's house. As I moped toward her, I noticed a blood stain on the front pocket of my overalls. *It's from Bronco,* I thought.

Joanie and I began playing a silly game we'd invented a few weeks before. I hid behind her house, popped up my head, and asked in a stupid voice, "Who eats poop?" When she spotted me, her face burst into a smile.

The dogs took my mind off everything that had gone wrong in St. Mary's as I waited for Finn to come home from work. I could hardly wait to bitch him out for setting me up on such a shady deal. During the flight back to Kusko, I'd been on the verge of hyperventilating the whole way, with the sound of Bronco's skull hitting the table playing over and over in my head, monotonously, like Chinese water torture.

I hid behind Joanie's house again. I crouched down behind her doghouse and sprang up. "Who eats . . . Joanie?" She wasn't there.

Then I felt a nip on my butt. I turned around and, sure enough, there was Joanie. She looked up at me, grinning, as if to say, *Joke's on you this time.*

Finn's cab finally arrived. I ran to his house and got up in his grill before he could give the cabbie a five spot. I was so angry that I started laughing like a lunatic.

"Awesome buyer you gave me!" I roared, all wide-eyed and smiling.

The Albanian cabbie looked at Finn like I was psycho. Finn motioned for him to drive away. "Eaaasy, dude! The hell is wrong with you?"

"What's wrong? *What's wrong?* I'll tell you what's wrong! You gave me a damned junkie to sell to, then some bootlegger broke into her house and took a swing at me!"

Finn stood in his button-down work shirt, silent, processing what I'd told him. *Say something already,* I thought. Every second that passed was more aggravating than the last.

"Two things," Finn finally said. "No, three things. One, you're not selling gumballs and lollipops. You're a marijuana dealer now. Not every buyer is going to be a happy-go-lucky, good-times stoner like Casey. It's just the way it works. So get used to it.

"Two, how was I supposed to know a crazy bootlegger would show up? You're free to be pissed, but you can't be pissed at me for that."

I sighed and shook my head.

"Three," he said, "suck it, nerd."

The kid had some points. I had to concede that.

"Yeah?" I said. "Well, eat it, geek."

I followed Finn toward the front steps of his house. A clap of thunder sounded in the distance, just before I asked, "What's the story with Linetta?"

"She's my ex-aunt, you spaz," Finn said. "I figured that selling to her was safe enough because she used to be family. But the more important question is, do you know who the bootlegger was?"

"Linetta called him Bronco," I said. "I wound up kicking his ass."

Finn's eyes got huge. "You did *what?*"

"He came after me," I said. "It was self-defense."

I explained how I'd pushed Bronco and kicked him in the face and how it'd been kind of an accident — and how it was him or us.

"Bad move, Eddie," Finn said. "Really bad move."

Apparently, Bronco was the wrong guy to mess with. Finn said if you crossed him, you became bear bait. He launched into a story about how, a few years back, Bronco chained a guy by his ankle to a stake and left him to the bears.

"This was five miles up the Andreafsky River in spring, right when the bears woke up from hibernating, all hungry and pissed off," Finn said. "All they ever found of the guy was half his leg connected to the chain. Bronco never got caught, but everyone knows it was him."

Wow. Just, *wow.*

"Whatever you do, stay the hell away from Bronco," Finn continued. "He may be small, but he's got an Alaska-size case of little-dick syndrome. He's an angry, slippery little bastard who knows how to get out of trouble. He knows everybody. He's got connections."

Dalton drove up and cut our conversation short. He parked his blue truck in our driveway, jumped out, and, looking super excited, jogged over with a big cardboard package under his arm.

"Eddie, check this baby out!" he said, handing over the box.

"What is it?" I asked, weighing the box with my hands.

"Just open it."

Finn helped me strip away the packaging. I pulled out a white camera lens the size of a bazooka.

"It's not just any lens, Eddie. It's a two-hundred-millimeter zoom with image stabilization."

I inspected the lens, marveling at its weight.

"Eddie my boy, do you know what this means?"

"What?"

"It means you can capture action shots from much farther away, and in lower light. This lens is good for portraits, too. Your photography is going to improve overnight. Better photos means a better newspaper. A better newspaper means more ads. More ads mean more money."

"Sweet titties!" I said. "More money means I get a raise!"

"Very funny, Eddie." Dalton didn't even smile, though. He just went on admiring the lens.

I felt a raindrop land on my forearm and placed the lens back into the package so it wouldn't get wet.

"And Eddie," Dalton said, "I've got just the assignment for you to give this puppy a test drive."

Before I could ask, he continued, "Quyana Fest in Mountain Village, on the Fourth of July. Photo ops up the wazoo. You can shoot a photo essay and we'll get a two-page spread out of it."

"Giddyup," I said.

"Quyana" was one of the only Yup'ik words I knew. It means "thank you."

Dalton headed inside as a light rain began to sprinkle. Despite the rain, Finn hadn't moved. He stood next to me with a grave look on his face. "Watch your ass in Mountain Village," he said. "It's connected to St. Mary's by a road."

"What?" I asked. "Are you telling me Bronco will be there?"

"It's possible," Finn said. "He could drive there."

Finn said St. Mary's and Mountain Village were among the few villages in the YK Delta connected by road.

I wasn't *too* worried. I'd be at a festival with crowds of people all around. Even if Bronco found me, he probably couldn't do shit there.

* * *

Independence Day came.

"Are you carrying any explosives, firearms, or illegal drugs?" Peggy Paniptchuck asked me at the airport ticket counter.

"Other than the M-80s I've got shoved down my pants, no."

Bada boom, bada bing. I was in Mountain Village.

Beyond my photo assignment, I'd also be making a delivery. Finn hooked me up with one of his former coworkers. He said to look for a small hut in the middle of the festival.

I'd been lucky to catch a flight to Quyana Fest because people from all over the YK Delta were headed to the event. Yute Express and two other airlines had to run extra bush planes to and from Kusko all day and all night. Apparently, Quyana Fest was a big deal.

I landed at four o'clock, deplaned, and looked around. Eighty degrees, no wind, and virtually no clouds. God bless America. Dalton had told me eighty-degree highs didn't happen often in Alaska, except where he used to live, in Fairbanks, where even ninety degrees wasn't out of the question.

More green, hulking foothills everywhere. A proper mountain, capped with snow, stood alone in the far north. To the west, the Yukon River again. The Yukon looked wider and sufficiently mightier than the mighty Mississippi, where I used to fish for smallmouth bass back in Minnesota.

I could see Mountain Village from the runway, which stretched out atop a bluff about a mile from town. No Mountain Village VPSO met the plane at the airport, probably because he had his hands full patrolling the festival. I boarded a yellow shuttle bus parked next to the landing strip. The inside of the bus was buns to nuts; two bush planes had landed right before mine. Half of the thirty people packed inside the bus were children abuzz with giggles, excited for Quyana Fest. The bus dropped us off at the edge of the festival, held along a three-block village street near the banks of the Yukon.

My first assessment: Quyana Fest actually looked

awesome. I stood at the top of a slope that allowed me to see the entire festival at once. Hundreds of people scurried between the games, attractions, and food tables. Salmon smells filled the air. Quyana Fest was like a Native version of my favorite place when I was a kid — the Minnesota State Fair. It had all the same stuff, but with an Eskimo twist. Instead of food booths with deep-fried cheese curds, corn dogs, and bacon-on-a-stick, this place had food tables with moose jerky, smoked sockeye strips, and Eskimo ice cream — a mixture of caribou fat, tundra berries, and sugar.

While the state fair's midway had the human catapult ride, Quyana Fest had the Eskimo blanket toss. I watched as thirty people young and old grabbed hold of what looked like a parachute made of caribou hides stitched together. They launched a teen boy on the blanket high into the air.

I pulled my camera and new lens out of my backpack and photographed the blanket toss. I stood back forty feet to get the whole scene into frame. The lens took some getting used to, but eventually I got "the shot": an exhilarated high school boy, twenty feet in the air, pretending to touch the sun, with a crowd of people cheering beneath him.

A blanket of shade spread over the festival as a renegade cloud temporarily blocked the sun. The loss of light meant I had to adjust the camera's shutter speed. I raised the camera for a test shot, zeroing in on three young Native guys sitting on a knoll beyond the temporary fence behind the blanket toss.

Before I could review the test shot on the camera's digital display, I heard someone call my name. In front of me, through a cluster of festivalgoers, emerged

Bristy and Hope. Both wore tie-dye kuspuks and carried bags of Native jewelry they'd purchased.

"What's up, girls?" I asked, trying to seem happy.

"Hi, Eddie!" they said simultaneously.

"That's quite a camera lens," Hope said.

"I'm shooting a photo essay," I replied, wanting to seem preoccupied.

I felt a tap on my shoulder. I closed my eyes, knowing who stood behind me. "Hi, Taylor," I groaned without turning around.

"Hi," Taylor said cheerfully. She circled around me and joined Bristy and Hope. She wore a blue kuspuk with a floral print. She looked painfully adorable.

I took a deep breath and talked like nothing was wrong.

"So, ladies, how was graduation? Feel good to be done with school?"

"Totally!" Bristy said. "I started crying during the graduation ceremony. I couldn't stop thinking about how I was finally done with school after being there for twelve years . . . or thirteen years, if you count kindergarten. That's, like, more than a decade. I swear, a decade seems like more than a hundred years. When I started kindergarten, I was only — "

Hope interrupted. "Shut up, Bristy. You're *so* annoying."

Taylor chuckled. The sun glared on her from behind, creating a halo effect around her silky blond hair. She looked like an angel — an angel with a slightly wayward eye. As great as she looked, seeing her again was torture.

"Congrats on being named valedictorian," I told

her. Five weeks earlier I had written a news brief about her accomplishment. I didn't have to interview her for the brief, which was a relief at the time, and somehow I hadn't seen her around Sucktown. But here she was in Mountain Village.

"Thanks!" she said, beaming. I didn't like that she beamed. I wanted her to be unhappy to see me, like she regretted not hooking up when she had the chance. I wanted some sign of that regret, not the same supersunny, let's-be-friends Taylor.

I asked, "What are you guys doing now that high school is over?"

"Those two clowns don't know yet," Taylor said. "I'm officially going to be a teacher, like my parents, but I'm taking online classes so I can stay in Kusko."

"Great," I said. "Well, I need to get back to shooting photos. Nice seeing you three. Enjoy the rest of the festival."

"See you later," Hope said as she walked away, tugging Bristy along. Hope turned back to me and added, "I'm taking Bristy to meet a boy she saw. She wants to pull him into the weeds and give him the old Bangkok waffle iron."

Taylor laughed. She glanced at me and told her friends, "I'll catch up with you in a minute."

Great. She wanted to talk.

Taylor moved nearer to me, stepping so close that the tips of our shoes touched. I felt her breath on my chin.

"What, Taylor?"

She peered into my eyes, scowling. I looked at the bridge of her nose, not knowing which eye to lock on to.

"The problem, Eddie, is that I can't let myself like you. You're moving back to Anchorage in less than six months. I'm not going anywhere."

"Then why did you apologize for leading me on?"

"That's what I wanted to explain, but you blew me off," she said. "I wanted to keep hanging out with you. You're a cool guy, Eddie. Us not hanging out would be a waste of something good."

Hearing her say all of that felt bloody good. She had never *not* liked me.

I took a step back. "So, where does that leave us?"

"We keep doing what we were doing before — emailing, texting, hanging out sometimes. We'll see. Think you can handle that?"

"Yeah, I think so."

Before walking away, she smiled and said, "There's only one condition: the next time I see you, don't be wearing those overalls — they look ridiculous."

I stared at Taylor's dreamy backside until the crowd absorbed her.

\* \* \*

The little hut Finn mentioned stood smack-dab in the middle of the festival, next to a table where an old couple sold mukluks made of beaver fur. The structure was made completely of gray sealskin. Above the entrance, a wooden sign read "Shaman Fortune-Teller." I peeled back a flap of sealskin and tiptoed in.

A candle burned on a table, illuminating the face of an elderly Native lady. She wore a headdress made of caribou antlers and long brown feathers.

"Sit. Down," she said in a slow, drawn-out voice.

I plunked down on the folding chair across the table from her. The pulsing candlelight flickered on her wrinkled face and wacky headdress, freaking me out more than it probably should have. Maybe the cellophane up my butt had torn and leaked THC into my system?

"Your. Hand," she said, reaching for me to show her my palm.

I did that, too. Her scaly, deformed fingers twisted in directions as random as tree branches, presumably from the wear and tear of seventy-some years spent sewing clothes, cleaning fish, and picking berries.

She pulled my right hand toward the candle to see it better. She flipped my hand over several times to inspect both sides, slowly dragging her index finger across my skin in small circles, whispering words I didn't understand.

Suddenly, she gasped and looked at me in horror, like my hand had just foretold the apocalypse was nigh.

"What?" I shouted. "What's wrong?"

"You need to cut your fingernails," she said, grinning devilishly.

What was it with old ladies giving me shit all the time? But I might have known something like this was coming, considering what Finn had told me about the lady. Her name was Betty Bennis, and they used to work together at the airport in Kusko. She'd retired and moved back to Mountain Village, her childhood home, and she started this fortune-telling gimmick at Quyana Fest for some extra cash.

"Not funny," I said.

"All right, gussuk — let's see it," she said in a normal voice. Apparently, the Native elder voice was an act too.

I dropped my overalls and stripped off the duct tape myself. While I did that, Betty flicked a lighter and burned a fistful of sage.

"That's aggressive," I told her, knowing she was going to light up on the spot and use the sage to mask the marijuana stink, despite there being a few hundred people just outside the door.

And that's exactly what she did. She slit open the package I gave her, rolled a joint, and sparked it up right then and there. Not only was I was impressed with how fast she rolled it, I was dazzled that she could even roll one in the first place, considering how crippled her hands looked.

"Thank you for bringing this to me. I'm not a dirty old pothead," she said, inhaling a second hit. "I need this for my hands. It helps with the pain and the inflammation."

"You're welcome, but it's not free."

"Of course," she replied. "I have to go to my house for your money. I don't live far."

Once Betty had stepped out, I killed time by looking at all the photos I'd shot. Outside I'd been having a hard time seeing the photos on the camera's digital display, but I could see them perfectly in the darkness of the hut.

I scrolled through shots of cute kids with berry stains on their mouths, venders cleaning salmon at food booths, and the blanket toss. All the photos were money — especially the blanket toss pic with the dude grabbing at the sky. It was front-page material.

I fast-forwarded to my test shot of the three guys sitting on a knoll. I wanted to make sure my camera settings were accurate and that the lens wouldn't blur from camera shake at so long a distance. I looked at the camera's digital display and pressed the zoom button to zero in on the guys' faces.

Then I almost shit myself. The guy in the middle was Bronco. He stared right at the camera, with eyes like he was counting the seconds until he could slit my throat. Either it was a coincidence, or Bronco had perched himself on that knoll on purpose, like a hawk on a telephone poll, surveying a field for prey.

Everything that Finn and I feared could happen in Mountain Village seemed to be happening. Finn had told me that a twenty-mile gravel trail linked the village to St. Mary's and the trip took about forty minutes to travel by truck or four-wheeler. I was guessing Bronco must have driven it to look for me. With how big of an event Quyana Fest was, he probably suspected I'd be there, especially if Linetta had told him about me and my job at the newspaper.

I had to get out of town. Immediately.

\* \* \*

Betty took her sweet time getting my money. But it gave me extra time to size up the situation.

I looked at the photo of Bronco again and figured that the two guys next to him were bigger than him, but not quite as big as me. Still, I had no chance against the three of them.

I considered some options. Maybe I could try hiding out somewhere on the festival grounds, but that seemed hopeless. There weren't many dark corners in the land of the midnight sun. Maybe I could search the crowd for the Mountain Village VPSO and ask for help, but that could mean exposing myself to a lot of questions. Maybe I could ask for help from Betty Bennis, but I didn't want to get her involved, considering I'd already witnessed how scary Bronco could be to old ladies, a la Linetta Wassily.

Just then, Betty peeled back a sealskin flap and walked back in. "Here's your money," she said, handing me the cash. I shoved it in my overalls, down into my jock.

As she sat back down, I peeked my head outside the tent to survey the crowd for Bronco and his goons. Nothing. All I saw were families walking by, drenched in golden sunlight that would be shining strong for hours to come.

Betty settled into her chair. "Everything okay?" she asked.

Apparently I was giving off a scared-shitless vibe, but I pulled my head back inside and said, "Everything's fine."

"Then you won't mind leaving now? I'd like to see some more customers."

Damn. I didn't want to leave the little hut. I wanted to hide in there for as long as I could. But what choice did I have?

The moment I walked out, my prayers were answered. Russ, the fat VPSO from St. Mary's, stood nearby at the salmon-strip stand. Eating.

"Russ!" I hollered.

He turned around. "Long time no see," he said, his voice muffled by what looked like an entire school of dried salmon in his mouth. A glob of Eskimo ice cream smudged the front of his blue VPSO uniform.

"I'm in a jam," I said. "I don't know anybody here who can help."

"I know," he said.

I wasn't expecting that. "You know? What do you mean?"

"The bush planes," he said, wiping his mouth. "I just got back from the runway, and there's a bunch of people waiting for flights. That's what you're talking about, right?"

No idea what to say, I just stared at him.

"Word is that half of them won't make it out tonight," he continued.

Poop stains. If I told him the real reason I was in a jam, he'd start asking questions about why Bronco was after me and he would probably know I was up to something shady.

"Right," I replied. "The planes are full. That's my problem. I gotta get back to the paper. What am I supposed to do?"

"You'll come with me, that's what," Russ said. "Another flight or two will leave St. Mary's tonight. We can make it there in time if we get on the road now."

* * *

The rumbling of the engine of Russ's little red truck sounded like freedom. Even if Bronco knew where I was now, he couldn't touch me. I was with law enforcement. We drove out of Mountain Village, past the airplane runway, and toward the gravel road that would carry us to St. Mary's.

Funny thing, I didn't see anyone waiting for a plane. "I thought you said there were lots of people at the strip," I said.

"Not sure what's up," Russ said. "They probably gave up."

The gravel road was narrow and looked like a big leafy tunnel, with tall tangled brush growing at the edges of the shoulder. Stretches of the road were wider than others, but mainly, there was barely enough room for two vehicles to pass by one another. The radio played old-school country music while Russ dodged potholes and ate moose jerky. He didn't say much, and that was fine with me. I had enough on my mind.

It was obvious then that the whole selling weed thing wasn't such a good idea. It'd been a desperate move, and now my life was becoming even worse than before. Everything sucked. Maybe Nicolai was right — in the end, it really *does* come back.

On the bright side, I told myself, there were only two more deliveries to go until I'd have my three grand and I had almost two whole months to execute them. I could basically cherry-pick those last transactions and take all the time I needed to make sure they were foolproof. If something didn't feel right, I could wait for a safer opportunity. I could play it relatively safe and still be back to Anchorage by fall.

Whatever I did, I'd be steering clear of any village on the western half of the Yukon River, because who knew where Bronco might pop up again. Seeing Bronco again — or the image of him on my camera, anyway — put fear in me.

I wondered what Russ knew about Bronco. He had to know at least something, considering they lived in the same village. I wanted to know more about the little lunatic who might or might not be after me.

"Before I came to St. Mary's last time, my friend in Kusko told me about some dude there who fed a guy to the bears," I said to Russ. "Could that be true?"

"First I've heard of it," he said, biting off another hunk of moose jerky.

*You suck at crime fighting,* I thought, but instead I said, "I heard the guy's name was Buck or Buster or something."

Russ perked up. "You mean Bronco."

"Yeah, Bronco. You know him?"

Russ straightened the rearview mirror, looked into it, and grinned. "Yeah, I know him, and you're about to meet him too."

I looked through the back window and saw Bronco and the two goons speeding up from behind on four-wheelers, kicking up big clouds of dust.

"The fuck?" I said.

Russ didn't say anything more. He kept driving, silent, with a straight face.

I looked back again. Bronco and his buddies were right on our tail, speeding along without helmets.

Bronco looked even smaller than I'd remembered. He wore the same ripped jeans and stained white T-shirt. If the dirty little fool hadn't changed clothes since I last saw him, I wouldn't have been surprised.

The two goons flanked Bronco. They sped along with long, scraggly black ponytails flapping in the wind. Their sunglasses made them look like Native versions of henchmen from an Italian mob. I'd been wrong about them both being smaller than me — one was undeniably bigger.

"What's going on?" I asked Russ.

He still didn't say anything.

"You do realize it's your job to *protect* people from this kind of thing, right?" I said.

That struck a chord.

"I've known Bronco since birth," he replied. "You fuck with him; you fuck with all of us."

"Spare me the brothers from different mothers bullshit," I replied, rolling my eyes.

Bronco sped up on my side of the truck and bounced along near my door, glaring at me and smiling. His face still hadn't finished healing from what I'd done to him. His left eyelid was still purple and yellow.

I flicked him off. He threw his head back and laughed. Then he hit the gas and took the lead.

A minute later, Bronco slowed down and hung a right onto what looked like a hunting trail. Russ followed, with the two goons driving behind his truck. The trail was bumpy enough that nobody could drive faster than a few miles per hour. A foul stench, like a rotting animal, grew stronger and stronger.

"Where are you taking me?" I mumbled.

Sweat sprang from my pores, and my eyes burned — fear made physical. I thought that if these guys only knew me, they wouldn't be doing whatever it was they were about to do. I started pleading as much to Russ.

"Please, seriously, you've got this all wrong," I said. "I never wanted to fight with Bronco. I never wanted to mess with his business. It was a stupid mistake. Total wrong place, wrong time. Whatever you're going to do, don't do it."

Russ kept driving.

"I'm just a kid," I added, hoping the "kid" card might buy me some sympathy. But it didn't. Clearly, they'd be trying me as an adult.

I wanted to open the truck door, bolt into the brush, hack my way to the Yukon River, and swim upstream to anywhere. Before I could finish dreaming of my escape, it was out of the question. We had arrived.

By now, the rotten stench practically singed my nose hairs. The whole area smelled like a bucket of shit and rotten eggs.

"Get out of the truck," Russ commanded, turning off the engine.

Bronco waited ahead of me on his four-wheeler, with the two goons behind. They shut off their vehicles. We stood at the edge of a sandy clearing the size of a hockey rink, surrounded by ten-foot-high brush. In the center of the clearing, a monstrous crater was piled to the sky with garbage — dirty diapers, animal guts, food wrappers, car parts, and other rubbish.

It all made sense. The St. Mary's and Mountain Village dump was the perfect place for a group of no-good assholes to beat my ass in private.

Bronco didn't take his eyes off me while he spoke to Russ. "Dumb shit bought the story about the flights being full?"

"Yep," Russ said, circling the back of the truck. "I found him at the fortune-teller."

"I guess she didn't see us in his future, huh?" Bronco said.

The guys all laughed. I was so focused on Bronco that I didn't notice Russ coming up on me from behind. He got me in a full nelson, throwing his massive arms under my armpits and locking his hands behind my head. I bucked and tried reverse-head-butting him several times, but he was too tall. The back of my head only pounded on his chest. I kicked my legs into the air violently, trying to break free.

"Easy there, little fucker," Russ muttered, like he was a cowboy and I was a squirming calf.

The two goons got straight to work. Standing on both sides of me to avoid being kicked, they pounded the sides of my face with closed fists and sent the occasional boot to my stomach. Each blow felt like a crowbar slammed against my face. I saw flickers of stars every time the bigger goon connected with a punch. When the stars dissipated, the sight of Bronco standing in front of me, cackling, came into focus.

It didn't take long for the goons to knock the strength out of me. When I stopped kicking, Russ let me go. I fell to the ground in a pile, gasping. My stomach ached, my head felt like it'd been run over by a tank, and my jaw felt like I'd been curb stomped.

Bronco knelt down next to me. "That was only a warm-up," he said. "Before we get to the real fun, I'll need that money."

"Please," I said, sliding my hand inside my overalls and pulling a fat wad of twenties from my jock, "just take this and leave me alone. I get the message. I'm sorry. Honest, I am. I never meant — "

Bronco rose and kicked me in the face to shut me up. The tip of his steel-toe boot felt like a hammer to my mouth. I writhed on the ground, spitting out sand, while Bronco counted the cash. "Okay then," he said to the goons. "Carry on."

Russ hoisted me up and reapplied his wrestling hold, and the goons moved in. I didn't know how long this round would last or how much of it I could take. After the first few punches, my face was so numb I couldn't feel the blows connecting anymore. I could only hear them.

Then I heard something else. Everyone heard it. The sound stopped Russ, Bronco, and the goons cold. Russ let me go. I fell down into the sand, rolling over next to the passenger side of the truck. All five of us waited in silence, looking in all directions, listening for . . . whatever that was.

There was the sound again — a whiny, squealing noise. I pinpointed it to where the thick brush met the clearing, twenty yards from the other side of the truck. I was still on the ground and could see, looking underneath the vehicle, the exact area from where the noise was coming.

I saw branches moving low to the ground. I squinted and made out the image of a bear cub peeking his head out. He let out another cry. The cub was the size of Joanie, my favorite dog. Russ, Bronco, and the goons still hadn't seen him and remained fixated on locating the origin of his cries. I inched myself backward, toward the goons' four-wheelers.

Everybody else stood frozen, petrified. We all knew that encountering a brown bear cub in the Alaska wilderness was about the most dangerous situation anybody, anywhere on Earth, could possibly be in. Where there is a cub, a pissed-off mother is close behind.

In the brush forty yards away from us, the forest came alive with the sound of crunching branches and crashing trees, as though a runaway earthmover were plowing through at a hundred miles per hour. In the blink of an eye, the sow burst out of the brush like a football team breaking through a paper banner. She was in full stride, her thick chocolate coat heaving up and down, up and down, with every blazing step.

She went straight for the first thing she could see — Bronco and the goons, only about fifteen feet from me. The three of them quickly huddled together, threw their arms up into the air, and began shouting, "YA BEAR! YA BEAR!"

The sow skidded to a halt right in front of them. She popped her jaws and pounded her front paws on the ground. Her teeth looked bigger than elephant tusks. Her stench was so putrid, it made the village dump smell like lavender potpourri. She must have been eight hundred pounds — an average size for an adult brownie in this region of Alaska, but still big enough to break a man's neck with one swipe of her paw.

I glanced under the truck and watched as the cub began to scamper toward his mom. I did a backward army crawl to the four-wheelers, never taking my eyes off the big bear and the guys. Russ stood against the front of his truck, paralyzed. He could've shot the bear if VPSOs weren't prohibited from carrying firearms. Russ's eyes moved from the bear to me. He must've known I was making a break for it, but there was nothing he could do. Any sudden movement toward me, and the bear would instinctively chase him down.

I crouched behind one of the four-wheelers, using it as a shield to block the sow's view. I inched my head up and saw that the cub had trekked behind his mother and was making his way back into the brush. The sow shuffled a few steps backward, keeping a steady growl. Bronco and the goons kept shouting at her. If the sow hadn't attacked them by now, the chances were slim that she would. She had protected her cub.

I stayed low and hit the electric start, praying that the engine wouldn't spook the bear into charging me. She looked in my direction, then turned her attention back to Bronco and the goons. They kept yelling, "YA BEAR! YA BEAR!"

I lunged onto the four-wheeler, knowing at that point I had two choices: 1) Peel away as fast as I could and hope to outrun the bear if she gave chase, and 2) Wait for the bear to leave and hope that being ready aboard the four-wheeler would give me a big enough head start to outrun the others.

I went with option one, hopping on the rig and slamming on the gas. I whipped a shitty to get myself turned in the opposite direction, buzzed past the truck so I could snatch my backpack from the bed, then hauled ass down the bumpy, uneven road. I pressed my thumb on the throttle so hard, my right thumb felt like it might snap.

After a couple seconds, I swiveled around and saw the bear coming in my direction, but she halted a few steps later. I never looked back again.

In two minutes I'd arrived at the main road. I stopped and turned off the four-wheeler. I couldn't hear any sound of other vehicles following. All I heard was beautiful silence. My only hope then was to bolt back to Mountain Village, ditch the vehicle, and catch the next plane headed to Suckville.

# CHAPTER 15

# DRY-LAND THERAPY

The dog team stomped toward the cloudy horizon on green tundra — extra mushy from the morning dew. The army-green hip boots I wore over my jeans kept my legs warm enough, but my yellow insulated flannel didn't quite cut it on top. *Just wait until winter,* I thought. *Fifty degrees in Alaska will feel like T-shirt weather.*

I liked running the dogs on dry land more than on snow. Dry-land mushing was more relaxing. The dogs couldn't run as fast because the tundra was more abrasive to the bottom of the sled. When I took a header, reclaiming the team was easier.

Just like snow mushing, dry-land mushing had become my therapy. And given what had happened with Bronco and the bear and getting my butt whooped and all that, I needed a fat dose of doggy medicine. Two weeks had passed since the incident and I still hadn't gotten a grip. The beating left me aching and weary, but the outward signs of it hadn't been too bad.

At first my face was swollen and red, but soon the only obvious signs were a cut on my eyebrow, a faint black eye, and a gash on my lip. When anybody asked, I'd told them that I dumped the dogsled or flipped a four-wheeler.

Mostly I just wanted to avoid people. I'd been out mushing almost every day.

This time the dogs and I must have been a mile outside of Suckport. I turned toward town but couldn't see the city limits. I wasn't concerned about going anyplace in particular, so I let Joanie decide. She led the team west. We bounced up and down on the uneven ground, kicking up ptarmigan every couple hundred yards. Without snow, mushing trails no longer existed on the tundra.

As the team strode along, I thought about how otherworldly insane my life had become. In less than a year, I'd gone from normal suburban kid to bush-living, marijuana-dealing, murderer-dodging, broke-ass fool.

The whole caper was a vicious circle. I wanted to leave town more than ever, yet the only way I could get out was to keep doing the very thing that made my life so miserable — selling weed. It was the ultimate catch-twenty-two. I was like an alcoholic, getting drunk to forget about my drinking problem.

To compound matters, since Bronco stole the money I earned during my third delivery, I needed to sell two ounces during my fourth transaction to stay on track financially. If I got busted with two ounces, the cops could nail me for intent to distribute.

I wondered whether Bronco had anything more in store for me. He was still out there. The bear hadn't mauled him and the others. If she had, word would have gotten out and Dalton would have made me write a front-page story about it.

But was the beat-down Bronco and his goons gave me enough to satisfy him? Even if it wasn't, what else could he do to me? Not much, I figured. I was probably safe in Suckonia. I could make my final marijuana deals in villages as far away from St. Mary's and Mountain Village as humanly possible.

Six more weeks. If I stayed the course and played things smart, I could probably be out of town in only *six . . . more . . . weeks*. For as crappy as I felt, that thought made me happy.

* * *

A hundred yards south of us, I noticed a small lake packed with tundra swans. "Haw!" I commanded Joanie and Biff, instructing them to veer left.

Surprisingly, the swans didn't fly away when we approached the lake. They simply paddled themselves, slowly, in the opposite direction. There were dozens of them. I saw the reflection of the clouds in the stillness of the water. The swans looked like they were swimming in the sky.

"Whoa," I said in a hushed voice, to keep from spooking the majestic white birds. I halted the team near the edge of the lake and anchored the sled. I jogged to Joanie and let her off the gangline; she was the only dog I trusted to go free.

Joanie joined me as I slogged my way to the edge of the lake, high-stepping through spongy green tundra.

I leaned over and looked at my reflection in the water. My right cheek was still swollen, and flakes of dried blood surrounded my left eye. *Who are you?* I asked myself, staring at my reflection. I didn't like the person I saw. I was a good person, with a good heart, who was doing bad things. That was my first thought, anyway. Because maybe I wasn't so good after all. I remembered what Nicolai told me in the steam bath. Was I the kind of person who knew what was right but did wrong nonetheless? Or was I getting tricked into thinking that what is wrong is what is right?

I got real with myself. *You're an irresponsible little pussy,* I concluded. *That's all you are. It's all you've ever been.*

I'd always had a major pussy complex. It all started when I was little, watching my dad and Max do guy stuff that I wasn't mentally or physically capable of doing. They fixed cars, landscaped, finished basements — you name it. Growing up in Zimmerman never did my complex any favors, because every guy was a hard-ass. They knocked my dick in the dirt every time a story of mine was printed in the junior high school newspaper. Writing was art, and art was for pussies.

My life sucked right up through most of my sophomore year of high school. My voice still hadn't changed and hair still didn't grow on my balls. The George Foreskin incident I'd explained to Taylor basically sums up most of that year. Late that spring, though, I rounded a corner. My voice lowered an octave. My pubes sprouted. My face grew into my nose. I shot up four inches. My muscles nearly doubled in size during summer vacation.

Around that time I began writing sports stories through an internship at the local newspaper, the *Zimmerman Post*. The guys on the baseball and lacrosse teams liked the stories I wrote about them and dialed back on giving me hell all the time. Gradually it seemed people started thinking, *Hey, maybe Eddie isn't such a pussy after all.*

Soon after Christmas break of my junior year, I started pumping iron in the high school weight room after school. Weight lifting, I discovered, was an athletic endeavor that didn't require me to play a sport and made me look like less of a pussy. Through weight lifting and the guy chatter that goes with it, I honed my cussing skills. The bigger I talked, the less of a pussy I seemed. From then on, I took a keen interest in anything manly that didn't involve playing sports and didn't require any type of mechanical knowledge.

By the time fall of my senior year rolled around, I had been transformed. My single-rep bench-press max topped two hundred forty-five pounds. I cussed like a sailor. Gina Gunderson, the consensus fourth-hottest chick in my grade — some guys ranked her third — let me play with her boobs. After seventeen long years, I had finally arrived at the towering, stately gates of the kingdom of Non-Pussydom.

That's where Alaska came in. When R.J. told me he'd scored a hockey scholarship at the University of Anchorage, my ears pricked up. I had been wanting to go to college someplace rugged and badass like Montana. It quickly dawned on me that Alaska could crap Montana. Alaska would be the most badass place

I could possibly go for college. It's the most fertile ground on the planet for growing balls.

And here I was, dry-land mushing with a kick-ass team of dogs. I snapped out of my daydreaming, glanced at my reflection again, and saw Joanie staring back at me in the water, grinning. Her awesomeness never ceased to amaze.

I led Joanie back to the team, harnessed her, and jumped back on the sled.

"Joanie, home!"

\* \* \*

Dalton sauntered into the office wearing his tan overalls, carrying a thick bundle of newspapers wrapped in a white zip tie. This week's edition had bumped up to twenty pages, up from sixteen pages the week before. With the dividend approaching in two months, the "feeding frenzy" of ad sales had begun.

Dalton dropped the stack of papers on my desk. "Good-looking issue," he said.

"Thanks," I replied.

My front-page photo was money: an older Native husband and wife on the shore of the Kuskokwim, at their fish camp near the village of Kwethluk, showcasing a skiff filled with dozens of sockeyes flipping about. The story: wildlife officials predicted the second run of reds would be coming fast and furious until the end of the week. I had hitched a boat ride to Kwethluk, a twenty-minute jaunt up the Kuskokwim.

Dalton wheeled his chair to my desk. "Ready for our editorial meeting?"

"Sure," I said, right as I pressed send on this message to Taylor:

*Wow, sorry to hear you busted Bristy and Hope smoking weed. Bet you're pissed. I smoked weed once in high school — twice actually, but the first time I didn't feel anything. The second time was a paranoid nightmare. Haven't done it since. I don't know how anybody does. Doing weed is bad news.*

I thought the *doing weed* bit was a nice touch. Putting it that way made me seem ignorant, naive, innocent. Like I thought smoking weed was on par with doing heroine. And I wasn't going to mention the one time I smoked with Finn on the tundra because I still felt guilty about it. In my mind, that time didn't count.

Though it was true I'd only smoked a few times, I knew that in Taylor's eyes, selling the stuff would be an entirely different and deplorable ballgame. I needed to hide my little marijuana operation from Taylor because I thought I still had a chance with her, even though time was running short.

Dalton sat down across from me. "All right, Eddie — what you got?"

"Kind of hard up this week," I said. "I thought I could do a preview of the upcoming run of silvers. Then maybe I could stop by the courthouse and dig into something from the police blotter."

"That's a good start," Dalton said. "Most people don't know this yet, but the principal at Kusko Elementary is about to resign. The district will make it public later this week. Get that story too."

"Done," I said. "But I still need one or two more. Got anything else?"

Dalton didn't respond.

"Dalton?"

"Shh," he said, concentrating.

Dalton was eavesdropping on a conversation in Mikey Colosky's barbershop next door. I'd grown so accustomed to hearing people chatting in there that the conversations sounded like white noise.

I listened closer. There was no mistaking who was getting a haircut — Sheriff Buzz Berger.

I'd interviewed Buzz once over the phone, but we still hadn't met in person, even though I'd seen him at the courthouse. He was a tall, gangly guy who still hadn't shed his long, curly black mullet from his teenage days, and he seemed like a textbook case of a guy becoming a cop to exact his revenge for getting his ass beat in high school. I didn't know where Buzz was from, but he had a southern accent. He couldn't get out a sentence without swearing.

Dalton and I moved over to the wall and leaned in to listen. Dalton cupped his hand to his ear.

"I swear," Buzz said, "we're going to crack down on the fuckers bringing that grass into the villages. Stupid drug-dealing asshole bitch-ass dildo motherfuckers."

*Gulp.*

Dalton dropped his hand and said, "You hear that, Eddie? There's your front-page story. Go talk to Buzz."

I stood there, frozen. *Like, am I to blame for all the marijuana trouble?*

"Is there a problem, Eddie?"

"Sorry, Dalton." I smiled dumbly. "No problem."

I walked through the door separating our office

from the barbershop and saw Mikey, clippers in hand, standing behind Buzz with a "please rescue me" look on his face. Mikey was a heavy guy in his thirties, with scruffy black sideburns down his cheeks and fingers so fat he needed custom-made scissors. He wore a camouflage apron. He never said much — odd for a man in his profession.

In looking at Mikey's bewildered expression, I surmised he'd never even asked Buzz one question. He was just letting Buzz talk, and talk, and talk out his ass some more.

"Sheriff Buzz," I said.

"Hey, boy," he replied.

"I couldn't help but overhear your conversation. Sounds like there have been lots of marijuana busts. Are you willing to go on the record?"

"Bet your sweet little ass I'll talk on the record," Buzz said, grinning at himself proudly in the big dusty mirror.

I walked back to my desk and grabbed a notebook. I glanced at Dalton sitting near my desk. He smiled and gave me a thumbs-up. "Go get 'em," he said.

*Yay!* I thought.

I made my way back into Mikey's shop and sat down on the second barber chair next to him and Buzz. I swiveled the chair so that Buzz and I could see each other in the mirror.

"So, lots of marijuana out there, huh?" I asked.

"Yeah, lots of the shit," Buzz said. "VPSOs have been calling in busts from villages every week since the start of summer. This marijuana bullshit is adding to my paperwork. I got enough going on with all the drunk fuckers everywhere and all the stupid shit they do."

"Which villages?"

"Fuck, let me think here . . . there've been a few busts on the western Yukon, in St. Mary's, Mountain Village, and Pilot Station. Been getting some closer to town too — Oscarville, Kewthluk, Napakiak. Then some others in the far north, in and around Kotlik."

I didn't know what to think. Was I personally responsible for any of this? It's not like I sold bricks of weed that could be broken up and dispersed to lots of customers. Then again, with how precious of a commodity weed was in villages, it was possible that some of the people I'd sold to were divvying up my ounces and selling fat nugs for fifty or a hundred bucks a pop. That easily could have happened with Linetta in St. Mary's and Betty in Mountain Village, then spilled over to nearby Pilot Station. Linetta and Betty were poor enough that they might have been forced to sell some of what I'd given them. And something similar could have happened with Casey in Unalakleet, which would explain the busts in Kotlik and in the far north. It all seemed plausible, anyway. Then again, maybe it was just a coincidence?

But what about the villages closer to Suckwater? I had no explanation for those. Finn had told me I wasn't allowed to sell weed in any villages nearby. I agreed and didn't ask why. I wanted to because transporting weed by boat would be easy. But I didn't have a say in the matter, so I let it go.

Halfway through my interview with Buzz, I wasn't even scared to talk to him anymore. Partly because I realized there was no way for him to know I might have a hand in the village busts, but more because his hard-ass front was so over-the-top it was downright comical.

"Any idea who's smuggling the weed, or how they're getting it to the villages?" I asked.

"Exactly how the fuck you think they're smuggling it — bush planes," Buzz said. "As for the who, I don't know. It's probably a couple dealers; no way one guy could be responsible for it all. And I got half a mind to think there are some crooked VPSOs out there turning a blind eye."

I let Buzz go on until I had all the information I needed. I thanked him and walked back to my desk to transcribe our interview. Considering his filthy mouth, the story would need to be light on quotes.

A few minutes later, as Buzz left the barbershop, I heard him pound on the exit door like a spaz. "Fuckin' thing's stuck!" he hollered in frustration. His door-pounding reminded me of the first time I'd encountered Bronco. I dashed toward the exit, hoping to catch Buzz before he drove off. I caught up to him outside as he slid inside his cruiser, parked next to the FJ.

"You forget to ask me something?" Buzz asked, clearly annoyed.

"You know anything about a guy named Bronco?"

Buzz's face got mean. "Little asshole bootlegger from St. Mary's who feeds guys to bears? Nah, never heard of him."

"What can you tell me about him?"

"I can tell you that the next time he gets busted for

something, that little fucker's going down, and going down hard. Why do you ask? You got something on him?"

"Oh, I don't. I just . . . I've heard people talk about him. I thought maybe he's responsible for some of the problems out there in the villages."

"Well I wouldn't be too shittin' surprised," Buzz said, buckling up. "Now if you'll excuse me, I've got some motherfuckin' crime fighting to goddamn take care of."

\* \* \*

Later that day, I worked off supper by picking up shit in the dog yards. Three days' worth of turds had piled up because I'd forgotten to clean it the day before. I wore jeans, a long-sleeved sweatshirt, and a bug net over my head. The mosquitoes were vicious, attacking the top of my ass crack every time I bent over to scoop a poop.

Five minutes after I started on the side dog yard, Taylor pulled up in her parents' rusty silver Chevy truck. Waving through the window, she parked next to the FJ and hopped out. "Hey, Eddie!" she said, circling around the front of the vehicle. She wore jeans and a sweatshirt, too, with her hair pulled back in a ponytail. Even in plain clothes she looked to me like a movie star.

"What are you up to?" I asked.

"Just driving around," she replied. "Thought I'd stop by and say hi."

She was about to sit on the flat roof of Lenny's

doghouse, but I stopped her. "I just cleaned shit from there," I said. She thanked me for the heads-up, waving mosquitoes away from her face.

"Sucks about Bristy and Hope," I said. "Are you guys fighting, then?"

"No, but they keep avoiding the topic."

I picked up the two wooden pallets near Kuba's house, one by one, and set them aside to clean the shit underneath. Taylor grabbed the black plastic bag on the ground and opened it up for me while I shoveled shit into it. I loved that dog poop didn't bother her.

"Speaking of weed," Taylor said, "what happened the second time you smoked it? What got you so paranoid?"

I dropped the first wooden pallet back into place and said, "The sound of my buddy's air conditioner fan outside — it just freaked me out. I thought it was cops in helicopters circling the house."

Taylor laughed. "And?"

"And I hid in his closet and ate an entire tin of cashews. The next day, my poop came out like pea gravel. It felt like I'd torn something."

Taylor doubled over in laughter, swatting at more mosquitoes. I laughed along with her as I repositioned the second pallet.

"K then," Taylor said. "I gotta run. These mosquitoes are too much."

"I don't blame you," I said. "Text me this week. Let's set something up. Maybe I can take you dry-land mushing."

"Deal," she said.

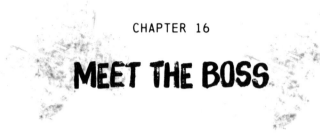

# CHAPTER 16

# MEET THE BOSS

Crumbs littered Finn's kitchen table like sand in a sandbox. I wiped them away and sat down. I used his digital scale to weigh two ounces of weed, taking from a mound of the stuff he had been drawing from, indiscriminately, for his own personal use.

Finn stretched sideways on his black couch, comatose, his blank face aiming toward the image on TV or the lava lamp next to it. He wore blue basketball shorts and no shirt. White drool stains dotted the cushion by his head. I gathered he'd been playing Madden football — and getting crushed by the computer — when he dozed off. The glowing screen showed Finn's Seahawks (he always chose the Seahawks) were down 35-0 to the Steelers.

Finn had been off work the past two days, smoking away his downtime. He'd started each day with a wake-and-bake, then kept the bowls packed at all hours. I'd never seen him on such a bender. His clothes were scattered all over the floor, and the sink overflowed with dirty dishes. On his stove rested two pots filled with crusty, dried-up macaroni and cheese he'd forgotten to eat. *Wow, Finn really sucks at the munchies,* I thought.

I finished weighing the green and licked the stickiness off my fingers. The following morning would be my next delivery, in the village of Russian Mission. The stakes were high with this delivery. Get busted with two ounces, and I could see jail time. Succeed, and I'd have just one more delivery to go.

"Finn."

He didn't respond.

"Finn!"

Still nothing.

"Finn!"

"Wha?" he groaned, staring ahead blankly.

I stood up from the table, stomped over, and got in his face. "Get your shit together! I need your help!"

"K," he said without passion, rubbing his eyes.

I grabbed Finn's hand and pulled him to his feet, like a lineman helping up a sacked quarterback. He could walk, but barely. He stumbled to the kitchen table and sat to my left. He began marveling at the fingers on his right hand, wiggling them around. "Electronic signals," he said.

"Yeah, electronic signals," I said, placating him. "The electronic signals from your brain to your hand. It's like the electricity is, like, coursing through your veins and shit."

"Yeah, dude. *Wow.*"

He kept gawking at his fingers in wonderment.

I rubbed my feet back and forth vigorously on the shaggy red rug underneath the table. Slowly, I raised my left index finger and touched his cheek. The shock popped like a fork stuck in a wall outlet. Finn jumped in his chair and nearly hit the ceiling. "DUDE!"

"How's *that* for some electricity?" I said. "Now pull your head out of your ass, dummy. We have work to do."

I fired up the vacuum sealer and sealed two packages of weed that I'd pounded flat as pancakes. For this delivery, I'd need to strap flat packages to each butt cheek. I was positive two ounces wouldn't fit in my crack — one barely did.

"Here," I said, handing Finn the packages. I stood up, pulled down my overalls and skivvies, and bent over. Once Finn saw my bare butt, he tried slapping it like he did before my very first delivery. He missed and toppled onto the floor, laughing. I laughed with him and, reaching for the duct tape on the table, said, "See this tape, Finn? Think you can stick it over my ass?"

Finn slapped his own face a few times, trying to suck it up. "Yes I can, Eddie. Yes. I. Can."

Finn held a package to my right cheek. Just as he began placing a strand of tape, the front door opened. I froze. I couldn't see who was there because my back was to the door. Finn couldn't see either because he was facing the same direction as me, on his knees, working on my butt. I sensed he was freaking too. Freaking not only because he had more marijuana in his house than normal, but because from behind us, it must have looked like he was doing something awfully naughty to me.

Hope's gruff voice filled the room. "What's this, Finn? Are you giving Eddie the old Jamaican salt lick?"

Wild laughter from Bristy. "You are the funniest bitch EV-AR!"

Finn and I still hadn't turned around. He asked from behind me, "What's a Jamaican salt lick?"

"Long story, Finn."

We turned around and saw Bristy falling apart on the floor in hysterics. Hope stood tall next to her, smirking, proud of her remark.

"First off," Finn began, "you two are stoned, so this looks weirder than it actually is."

"We are not stoned," Hope insisted.

"Yes you are," Finn countered. "Gay people have gaydar. I have stone-ar."

"Fine," Hope conceded. "We're baked. That's not the issue. The bigger issue is, what were you doing to Eddie?"

Suddenly, the implications of the situation hit me. Bristy and Hope were about to discover I sold weed. I liked their friend, Taylor. Taylor couldn't know I sold weed. This was not good.

I inserted myself into the controversy.

"No, Hope," I began, "the bigger issue is that you and Bristy are here to buy weed knowing your best friend doesn't approve of you smoking weed because she doesn't need, as you once put it, 'any extra bullshit.'"

Hope said it was none of my business, but I said it was, because I cared about Taylor.

She replied, "You care about Taylor so much that you let Finn give you rim jobs?"

We all laughed. As comical as Hope's comment was, I understood her tactics. She was forcing our hand to explain what we were doing. She knew that most guys who get accused of engaging in rim jobs with other guys tend to want to set the record straight quickly.

Finn knew the explanation wasn't his to give, so I dove right in. "Come on in," I told Bristy and Hope. "Do I ever have a story for you."

The girls sat down on opposite ends of the couch. Finn sat between them and started weighing out their eighth.

It took me ten minutes to lay everything out. The whole time, Bristy and Hope stared at me, flabbergasted, like they were finding out Santa Claus flies his sled drunk.

"But you're a reporter," Hope said. "You selling weed doesn't make any sense."

*None of my life in Sucktown makes sense,* I thought.

"It's not like I'm proud of this," I said. "It's not like I'm some burnout selling weed to make money just for the sake of making money."

When I said that, I pointed at Finn conspicuously.

"Suck it, nerd," he said.

"In all seriousness," I continued, "the reality is that I hate Kusko. If things were to work out with Taylor, I might stay. But those odds are slim. So, desperate times, desperate measures."

I asked the girls if they were on bad terms with Taylor because of the weed thing.

"She's not happy," Hope said. "We wouldn't be in this situation if Bristy wasn't such a dumbass."

Bristy looked ashamed. She pulled her cell phone from her front pocket, pressed the screen a few times, and tossed the phone to me. "Check it out," she said.

I read the text thread.

Bristy: "OMG Hope! I'm so stoned! I just peed down my leg cuz I forgot how to work the doorknob in my room! I can't get to the bathroom! I'm trapped! I'm peeing again now! HELP!"

Taylor: "This is Taylor."

Bristy: "OMG Hope! I just sent Taylor a text meant for you. I said I was stoned! What do I do now? I'm too baked to think!"

Taylor: "Still Taylor. We'll all need to talk."

"For the record," Bristy said, "the peeing in my pants thing didn't actually happen. I just thought it would be something hilarious to send to Hope."

I wanted to lecture Bristy and Hope about what real friendship is, but I didn't have much of a leg to stand on. Although I hadn't lied to Taylor as bad as Bristy and Hope had, I wasn't being forthright with her. I was a weed-selling hypocrite.

I got so buried in those thoughts I didn't realize an uncomfortable silence had overtaken the room. Bristy, Hope, and Finn looked around, dazed, like stoned buffoons. Bristy finally said, "So, Eddie, we can keep a secret if you can."

"Deal," I replied. "You don't know anything about me selling, and I don't know about you smoking."

The girls handed Finn some cash and started to leave. Just before they closed the door behind them,

Hope peeked back inside and said, "Okay, boys. Carry on. Finn's got that look in his eye, like he's ready to give Eddie the old Memphis blow horn."

Those lines weren't as funny anymore. I pulled my overalls and skivvies back down so Finn could finish the job. After he taped up both packages, I put my clothes back on and looked in the mirror in his bedroom. The packages were discreet enough under my baggie overalls. It would work.

I headed for home with the stuff taped to my ass cheeks, and I left it in place when I crashed for the night. While it wasn't exactly comfortable, I could live with it. Nothing was jammed into my crack like on previous trips, and it had been an ordeal getting Finn to help tape the bags for our supposed test. I didn't want to push my luck before an early flight the next morning.

\* \* \*

Finn was running well behind schedule when I knocked on his door the next morning. The disheveled idiot hadn't showered. He looked and smelled like a big hairy poop. I spent ten minutes in his entryway waiting for him.

"Hustle!" I said, watching him scramble to throw on his gray button-down work shirt and jeans. His shift at the airport started at seven-thirty. My flight to Russian Mission departed at 7:45. By now it was 7:21.

We walked outside into the soggy morning air. Finn hopped to the passenger side of the FJ on one leg, trying to get his other shoe on. He stepped in a puddle and splashed mud on the bottoms of his legs.

We arrived at the airport parking lot at 7:29. Finn opened his door before I came to a complete stop. "Trust me, there won't be any drama during this deal," he said. "The guy you'll be selling to — everyone calls him Bossman — is totally cool."

"Good," I said as Finn trotted off to start work. "See you tonight."

"Suck it, nerd!" he said over his shoulder.

I grabbed my backpack from the back of the FJ and speed walked behind him. I arrived at the ticket counter in ninety seconds flat. While in line, I searched my thoughts and determined I felt less concerned about the legal consequences of getting busted than I did the ramifications of what Taylor might think of me should I get pinched. If I got caught selling weed, I could kiss my chances with her goodbye.

Before I knew it, Peggy Paniptchuck was staring me in the face. "Are you carrying any explosives, firearms, or illegal drugs?" she asked with a smirk.

"Other than the one — count 'em, two! — ounces of weed strapped to my ass, no," I replied.

"Three would have been funnier," Peggy said. "Have fun in Russian Mission."

* * *

The bush plane circled above Russian Mission, seventy miles north of Suckfield. Russian Mission was nestled right next to the Yukon, with a lake a couple hundred yards across wrapping around the south side of town. Miles beyond the lake and the Yukon, green mountains covered with pine trees surrounded the village like the stands of a giant outdoor football stadium. The mountains were proper mountains, not the hulking foothills I'd seen in other villages.

Two other passengers flew with me in the six-passenger plane. One, a Native elder who I doubted spoke a lick of English. The other, a young Asian guy wearing khaki pants and a red short-sleeved oxford. I guessed he was a teacher. The shirt was a tell.

Finn had told me to track down the guy called Bossman, who was leading a construction crew in the village. As the plane descended, I watched out the window as a steamroller was off-loaded from a river barge. Bossman and his guys probably hadn't started their work yet. *Won't take long to find them in town,* I thought.

Although I'd promised myself that I'd make my final two deals in villages far away from Bronco's haunts on the western Yukon River, Russian Mission was a bit of a gray area. The place was on the Yukon, but more than one hundred air miles east of St. Mary's, with five or six villages in between. I would have preferred to make this transaction on the eastern Kuskokwim River, in a Bumfuck, Egypt, village like Red Devil or Sleetmute.

Skittish as I felt about Russian Mission, I trusted Finn that the deal would be a painless transaction. He said my customer owned an Anchorage-based asphalt company and would be in Russian Mission with his six-man crew for a week paving the village's new airplane runway. Finn knew one of the crew members, and said they all smoked weed, but that Bossman didn't have the balls to fly any in for them.

I felt safe selling to an entire construction crew. In the unlikely event that Bronco came after me again,

I'd be safe hanging with Bossman and his guys for the afternoon — strength in numbers.

The runway story was an easy sell to Dalton. *Patriot* readers in villages across the YK Delta would want to know how a dinky town like Russian Mission scored funding for such a runway. Almost every other village runway in the region was a dirt strip. During the nearly seven months I'd lived in Kusko, I'd written two stories about bush planes winding up ass-over-teakettle while landing on dirt runways.

* * *

The plane touched down on the dirt runway, bouncing up and down so hard I almost kneed myself in the chin, and soon I stood next to the plane with my backpack on my shoulders. The sun was shining, the air brisk and clean. I gazed at the Yukon River and saw half a dozen boats on the water, their occupants netting silvers.

The runway was practically connected to the city's main drag. The Russian Mission VPSO waited at the edge of a short dirt road leading to town. He had brown hair and was in his late twenties, and his muscular chest practically popped the buttons off the front of his navy blue uniform.

The elder and the teacher walked just ahead of me, toward the VPSO. The VPSO stopped the elder and started talking to him jovially in Yup'ik. I'd never met a young white man fluent in Yup'ik. The VPSO and elder chuckled together as the teacher and I passed by. The officer didn't even look at me when I ambled past. Yet again, I was home free. At home I had twelve hundred bucks in cash under my mattress. After this two-ounce deal, I'd have twice that.

"You there," the VPSO said.

The teacher and I both turned around. The teacher pointed at himself with a confused look on his face.

"Not you," the VPSO said. "I'm talking to you there, newspaper boy."

Me? What did he want with me? And how did he know I worked at the *Patriot*?

My face went redder than a spawned-out sockeye salmon. My ears felt like they were on fire.

"Yes, sir," I said, trying to project confidence by making my response sound more like a statement than a question.

"Come with me," the VPSO ordered.

"What is it? I'm here for a story, and I need to get right to work."

"Come with me," he said sternly. "Now."

The elder and teacher stood there, staring at me like I was some kind of criminal. I dropped my head and followed the sound of the VPSO's footsteps on the gravel.

* * *

The VPSO's office building stood at the edge of the village. It looked like a smaller version of a typical bush home — another glorified ice fishing house on stilts, made of wafer board weathered gray. Only two other buildings stood closer to the runway — city hall, and a shipping and receiving warehouse.

"What's your name?" I asked as we approached the office.

"Jed." His massive, V-shaped back looked like that of a professional bodybuilder.

"Jed what?"

No answer. He opened the office door and led me inside. The place stunk like mildew and rotting wood. I scanned the room. A third of the space was a holding cell sectioned off by black iron bars. The bars seemed pointless. A motivated prisoner with strong legs could probably kick down one of the walls of the flimsy building and go free.

Inside the cell was a filthy twin-size mattress — that explained the mildew smell — and a plastic two-liter Coke bottle half-filled with drinking water.

Jed motioned for me to sit down near his desk on an overturned five-gallon bucket. His desk was made of scrap wood. On it rested a police radio, an old yellow computer, and paperwork. He sat down on a paint-chipped, taupe-colored folding chair.

"Sorry, Jed, but that was a long flight and I haven't shat since yesterday," I said, a desperation move. "Mind if I hit the can before we talk?"

He thought for a second. "Go ahead."

He let me walk halfway to the door before saying, "But before you go, I'll need that marijuana."

Busted. *This cannot be happening*, I thought. *How could he know? What's he going to do to me?*

"What are you talking about?" I asked.

"I'm talking about the weed you're trying to smuggle into my village. Where is it?"

"It's nowhere, because I don't have any."

"Bullshit," he replied. "Where is it?"

"I'll tell you again — nowhere, because I've got nothing."

Defeat loomed. If I was going down, I would go down swinging.

"I've had enough of this, Jed," I said. "Remember, I'm a newspaper reporter. I think I see a 'VPSO harassment' story with your name written all over it."

He wasn't deterred. He grabbed my backpack off the floor and rifled through it, dumping out a pile of Spam, pilot crackers, socks, underwear, toiletries, winter boots, and other supplies. Nada.

"Are we done?" I asked.

"Not even close," Jed said. "Stand up straight and hold your arms out."

I shut my eyes. *The beginning of the end,* I thought.

He patted my arms, sides, chest, and back. I heard him kneel down, after which he passed over the insides and fronts of my legs. He began patting the backs of my legs, starting at my ankles and moving up to my knees and thighs. In the split-second before he reached my ass, a call came in on his radio. He stopped patting to listen to the chatter.

"Ten twenty-nine near Holy Cross. Suspicious boater on Innoko River."

Jed shook his head. "That doesn't concern me," he muttered.

He continued patting, taking a swipe over my crotch. Then I heard him stand up.

I opened my eyes. Jed sighed. He kicked the bucket I'd been sitting on, and it went sailing across the room.

Dude forgot to check my ass. The police call sidetracked him.

I felt epic relief. The tension in my body dissolved faster than snowflakes on a stove top.

To sell my innocence even more, I started unbuckling my overalls. "Ready for a body cavity search?" I asked smugly.

"Fuck you," Jed said, fuming.

The momentum had swung. For all he knew, I really *was* clean.

I finally had a moment to think. *Bronco is responsible for this. But how?*

The only explanation I could muster stemmed from what Finn had originally told me about Bronco — he knows everybody and has connections. Clearly, Bronco's tentacles extended to more villages than I'd given him credit for. Russ wasn't the only VPSO Bronco had under his spell — Jed was under the same twisted trance.

But how did Bronco know I'd be in Russian Mission? Did somebody at Kusko Airport tip him off? Or did Bronco put out an APB to all the crooked VPSOs he knew? If so, how many crooked VPSOs were there, and in which villages?

I wanted answers.

"About that newspaper story," I began, instructing him to please sit down. I remained standing. "I like the headline 'VPSO Searches, then Seizes Harassment Charge.'"

"Fuck you," Jed repeated. "What is it that you want?"

I told him I wanted to know if Bronco was behind this, and Jed said he didn't know anybody by that name.

"Well then," I said, "you can expect to be famous across the YK Delta in the very near future."

"Write the story — I don't care," Jed shot back. "I know everybody out here and I have a stellar reputation. I'm a gussuk who knows how to speak Yup'ik. You're a cidiot from Anchorage. It'll be your word against mine. Nobody will believe you."

He had a point. But I wasn't going to concede, especially considering I had no designs on writing the story in the first place. I had nothing to lose.

"Don't care. I'm writing the story anyway," I said. "Last chance now — did Bronco put you up to this?"

Jed revealed a faint smile. "I don't know anybody named Bronco."

Bullshit. The asshole knew.

I shoved my stuff into my backpack and left.

\* \* \*

I tracked Bossman and his crew to the only restaurant in town — if you could even call it a restaurant. The greasy spoon was located inside the living room of a larger village home. The joint's name, The Muddy Rudder, was spray-painted black on a hunk of wafer board propped up against the house, near the front doorstep.

I opened the creaky screen door and walked in. Four four-person tables filled the room. Along the far wall, a short old Native woman wearing a blue kuspuk washed dishes in the sink, next to a black gas range.

The construction crew ate scrambled eggs and bacon at two of the tables, which they'd pulled together. My contact sat at the corner of the table with his back to me, wearing dirty jeans and a sleeveless softball

T-shirt with BOSSMAN printed above the number 29.

"Anyone got a match?" the crew member next to him asked, an unlit cigarette in his mouth.

"Yeah, I got a match — my dick to your arm," Bossman said.

Everyone laughed, including me. Bossman heard me chuckle behind him and turned around.

"You must be Eddie," he said.

I nodded and made some lame small talk before ducking into the bathroom to strip away the weed packages from my ass. After that, Bossman and I did our business underneath the breakfast table.

I spent the rest of the morning and the early afternoon with Bossman and his crew, shooting photos of them doing prep work on the runway and interviewing them about the logistics involved with hauling in heavy equipment and tons of asphalt to a remote Alaskan village. Starting the next day, nobody in town would be able to get into or out of Russian Mission via airplane for a week. If an emergency came up, folks would have to call in a chopper from Suckington or catch an airplane by boating to the village of Marshall, one hundred river miles west.

I never did find the person I needed to talk to about the funding for the runway and the politics involved — the Russian Mission mayor, Vern Cheney, who skipped town to net silvers at his fish camp. I'd have to call him after I got back to Suck Francisco.

At two o'clock I heard what sounded like a giant lawn mower in the sky. I jogged over to Bossman. "That's my ride home," I told him, pointing to a bush plane circling above.

He shut off his jackhammer, flipped up his protective goggles, and shook my hand. "Thanks for the hookup," he said.

Just after takeoff, I peered back down at Bossman and his crew working on the edges of the runway. I could hardly believe a businessman and seemingly decent guy would want to buy pot for his crew. *Alaska is a different world*, I thought.

## CHAPTER 17

# SEEiNG MoRE OF TAYLOR

After eating my fifty-third moose stew supper in seven months, I rifled through the two metal file cabinets that were my clothes dressers, trying to decide which shirt to wear. I narrowed it down to either a green button-down chamois shirt or a plaid red flannel. I owned only one nice pair of pants — pleated khakis — so wearing those went without saying.

I carried both shirts to the bathroom to look at my reflection in the mirror. Dalton sat on the couch digesting and watching TV. "Big date tonight?" he asked, a fat after-dinner chewsky wedged in his craw.

"Something like that," I said from inside the bathroom, fastening the buttons on the red flannel. I looked better in that shirt than the green one. Case closed.

I sat down on the boot bench in the entryway, laced up my casual leather shoes, and opened the front door. "Later, Dalton."

I fired up the FJ and backed out of the driveway. Dust whipped everywhere, like a dirty blizzard blowing through town. Across the street, Peggy Paniptchuck was power washing away the layer of brown soot and dust that coated the west side of her house. That was a summertime routine out here, like mowing the grass back home. On the way to Taylor's house I dodged neighborhood kids on bikes. The kids didn't care about the wind and the dust, just like Peggy didn't care. They were used to it.

\* \* \*

"Come in!" I heard Taylor's dad shout from inside. I felt nervous to meet Taylor's parents. My chances with her were already slim enough. If her folks disliked me, there was no chance I'd have a shot at her before I left Suckdale. I let myself in and stood in the empty foyer, wondering where Taylor was and what I should say or shouldn't say to her mom and dad.

"Shoes off, please," I heard her dad say. His deep voice was more gravelly than the dirt roads I'd just driven.

I took off my shoes and walked down the short hallway to the living room. There sat her dad on the couch, using a yellow oilcloth to polish the blued steel of an antique side-by-side shotgun with a walnut stock. He wore blue denim overalls and a red flannel shirt similar to mine. His head was shaved bald, and a sturdy black beard grew from his bronze cheeks and chin. He wasn't smiling.

"Where's Taylor?" I asked. I was spooked,

considering the guy was holding a gun and I liked to look at his daughter's boobs. "Nice to meet you, I mean. Is Taylor home?"

"This isn't what it looks like," he said. "I'm not polishing my shotgun to make a statement."

"Whew," I said, exhaling loudly.

Then he did smile, before dropping the oilcloth onto his lap and shaking my hand. His shake was vise-like and transferred a slippery sheen of gun oil from his hand to mine. I wiped it on the back of my pants. He said I should call him Bruce.

"Taylor took off with Bristy and Hope," he said. "I don't know what's so important, but she said they'd be back soon. You might as well have a seat."

The room went quiet.

"Nice shotgun," I said.

"It was my grandpa's, then my dad's, and now it's mine. When I'm gone, it'll be Taylor's."

Awkward silence again. I cleared my throat and made a lame comment about how nice it was that the gun had stayed in the family — a comment that launched Bruce into a long backstory filled with tangents and dead-ends, from which I learned more about Taylor's family than I cared to know — maybe more than Taylor cared to know. Bruce told me his grandpa, Barney, traded a stack of wolf pelts for the gun in the forties. Barney had lived and died in the tiny village on Anvik, where Bruce's dad grew up before coming to Kusko, where he met an Italian girl named Isabella who became his wife and Bruce's mother. And on and on he went.

By the end of it I knew Bruce had lived in Kusko his

whole life and he'd met his wife, a Swedish immigrant named Cindy, in a biology class at the University of Anchorage's extension campus in town. I did a lot of nodding and tried to stay focused on him while I mostly just wanted Taylor to show up and rescue me.

"Here comes the prettiest girl on Earth now," Bruce said as the sound of footsteps came from the hallway.

I stood up and turned around to greet Taylor, but in walked someone who looked like an older, paler version of her. I wouldn't have said Cindy was the prettiest woman in the world (or even in her own house), but she had things together. Dressed in black jeans and a white blouse, Cindy smiled and said hello. She had Taylor's pouty lips and butt-chin, and she looked fit as an Olympian.

"So, Eddie," she said. "Are you enjoying summertime in Kusko?"

"I guess so, but I could do without the wind and the mosquitoes," I said. "I'm just glad there aren't any wood ticks."

I wanted to groan at my own stupid comment, but it only sent Taylor's folks into another stream of shit I could not have cared less about. Cindy hadn't seen a wood tick since she lived in Sweden. Bruce couldn't recall having seen one at all. They had ticks in Alaska, but they were very rare. They attached to imported livestock, but the state . . . oh my God! It took every once of effort I could muster to keep nodding, to keep looking interested, to keep from falling asleep.

But when they started asking about me and my story, I wished we could've stuck with the ticks.

"I've been reading your stories in the *Patriot*,"

Bruce said. "Nice work. You seem like a smart kid."

"Dalton keeps me running," I said. "I hope I'm doing okay."

"How much longer will you be in Kusko?" Cindy asked.

Her question caught me off guard. Had Taylor not told Cindy and Bruce I was supposed to leave at the end of the year? If so, was it because she didn't care enough about me to tell them? Or did they know and they were only testing me? What did and didn't they already know about me?

"I'm supposed to leave in late December," I said, leaving my answer somewhat open-ended.

"That's a long ways off," Bruce said. "If you stay that long, you'll set a new record."

"Record for what?"

"In the past few years, no reporter has lasted more than a few months," Bruce said. "They can't hack Kusko."

"Oh, *that* record," I said, cranking up the B.S. machine. "Yeah, I know about that. I took my job fully aware that my boss hadn't been able to find a reporter for quite a while. I like a good challenge. I'm not a quitter."

Cindy cleared her throat. "But, didn't you quit in college?"

*Wood ticks,* I thought. *How can I get them back on wood ticks?* But maybe, in a roundabout way, their giving me the third degree signified I had a chance with Taylor. Why else would they want to know the dirt on me? Maybe Taylor had told them she liked me. I shut down the B.S. machine and tried the opposite approach.

"That's not quite right, Cindy. I didn't quit college," I said. "I flunked out, actually."

Bruce and Cindy exchanged frowns, then stared at me poker-faced.

"I took this job to make up for my mistake," I said, hoping I wouldn't have to divulge the reason (beer) behind my academic missteps. "My goal is to get back into college and ace every class."

"That's commendable," Cindy said without a smile, or a nod, or any visible indication of understanding. "Everybody makes mistakes."

"Cindy and I are teachers," Bruce said. "In this household, we take education seriously."

*Sweet, merciful fuck*, I thought. *Where is Taylor?*

She had no apology when she finally did show up. She only shouted "Hey, guys!" from the entryway and headed upstairs. When her dad called her into the living room, she looked at me, scrunched her brow, and said, "Didn't you get my text?"

"Crap," I said, standing up and pulling my phone from my pocket. I'd been so nervous before I came over and so overwhelmed with talk since I arrived that I hadn't thought to check.

Her message read: "Emergency meeting with Bristy and Hope. Come at 8 instead of 7. We can hang out after."

"Shoot," I said. "What happened to Bristy and Hope?"

"They're outside firing up the steam bath," Taylor replied. "I wanted to fit in a steam with them before you came over."

"Go join them, Eddie," Cindy said. "Have you ever had a steam?"

"Yes, one time. I liked it."

But wait now. A steam? With Taylor? And Bristy and Hope? With them naked? With me naked? Was this a joke? A mom suggesting that a strapping young lad strip down with her gorgeous daughter inside a tiny, hot, steamy, dark room?

"Excellent," Bruce said. "Enjoy your second one."

\* \* \*

As I stood outside the small building in the Sifsofs' backyard, the purple bath towel I'd draped over my shoulder flapped in the cool, dusty wind. The steam bath was about the same size as Nicolai's but with a larger vestibule. It was also much newer, with fresh, varnished logs fused together by caulk instead of mud. Taylor had told me to give her a two-minute head start to get situated with Bristy and Hope.

I ducked into the vestibule and saw the girls' clothes lying on the floor. Their towels hung on wall hooks. There wasn't another hook for my towel, so I dropped it on the ground near the steam bath door, next to a small stack of wood and a long fire stoker.

I knocked on the door and said, "Ready for me?"

"Come in," I heard Bristy say from inside.

I stripped off my clothes and dumped them on top of my towel, then opened the door. A rectangular patch of light glared into the pitch darkness and exposed the girls' feet. Total darkness enveloped their bodies from the ankles up.

I saw two sets of feet to my left and one set to my right. Straight in front of me, the light illuminated the bottom of a stove. I guessed I was supposed to sit in the vacant spot to my right, closest to the door.

"Shut the door, Eddie," Hope said, her voice coming from my right. Those were her feet nearest the stove and next to the empty spot. "Hurry."

I closed the door and got situated, and in that moment, the atmosphere went from hot to suffocating. My pores gushed sweat. My hair felt like I'd dunked my entire head underwater.

"You're good right there," Hope continued. "You're welcome for giving you the spot closest to the exit. If your vagina gets too hot, jump outside to cool off."

Taylor and Bristy giggled.

Hope sounded just like my brother back home, which didn't amuse me.

"Dear Lord!" I said, coughing.

Laughter from all around me.

"Give it a second," Taylor said. "You'll get used to it."

I pinpointed Taylor's voice. She was sitting directly across from me. It struck me: The girl of my dreams was sitting five feet in front of my face, naked. No bra. No panties. No nothing. Not even a bracelet around her wrist. *Naked.*

Insta-bone. I was grateful for the dark, which was still nearly complete, even as my eyes had time to adjust. I leaned forward and tried to think of anything except Taylor. I couldn't.

She spoke up. "Sorry about my parents. They try to come off as laid back, but they can be intense."

"Good people," I said, knowing it sounded stupid but not caring.

"What'd you talk about?" Taylor asked.

"You know, this and that," I said. "But at the end, I told them I flunked out of college. They might think I'm stupid."

Taylor went quiet for a moment before saying, "You're not stupid, Eddie. You were just really thirsty for a few months. But you're good now."

I loved, loved, *loved* that she said that. But I wondered whether she said it to be nice or because she was into me.

Hope poured water on the rocks. The water sizzled into a scorching cloud of steam that rolled across the ceiling a few inches above my head. Gradually, the heat descended across my head, shoulders, and chest.

"Taylor's mad at us for getting high," Bristy said.

In that moment, my chubby deflated. Bristy and Hope knew too much about me, and if they were coming clean with Taylor, would their confessions include Finn and me? They knew I dealt the stuff, that I only had one more delivery to go to earn the final six hundred I needed. One whisper of that, and I'd be dead to Taylor.

"Oh?" I said. I didn't know what to say next, so I played stupid.

"Well," I continued, "I'm sure you guys will patch things up."

"Oh, we'll see," Taylor said. "Tonight was one of many conversations we've had and will continue to have. Meanwhile, we're doing our best to set the issue aside and not allow it to do any more damage."

"Well, that's mature," I said, hoping the topic would end.

We sat in the dark and quiet, and I stared at Taylor's feet. She wiggled her toes, and I wondered if she knew what I was up to.

"Have you ever smoked weed?" Bristy asked.

*Very funny,* I thought. I went with my pat story, which used to be true.

"Yeah," I said. "Twice in high school. The first time, nothing happened. The second time, I got real paranoid. Haven't done it since."

"Have you ever *sold* weed?" Hope asked.

Why were they screwing with me? They must have been pissed that they were in trouble with Taylor but I wasn't. Did they know I smoked with Finn on the tundra? How far were they going to go with this?

I sighed in frustration. "If I don't *smoke* weed, why the hell would I *sell* it?"

Saying that out loud made the marijuana deals I'd been making seem all the more ridiculous.

"I don't know," Bristy said. "You're always flying out to the villages. You could stick it in your ass and make a fortune."

Hope laughed. Taylor didn't.

"Quit bugging him," Taylor said. "You two are not funny."

"Stoke up that fire, Hope," I suggested. "Those rocks aren't kicking out much steam anymore."

She had just poured more water on the rocks, but the steam didn't seem nearly as powerful. My eyes were finally adjusting, and as the steam faded I could see Taylor's form across from me, just her shape in the darkness.

"Open the door and grab a couple more logs," Hope said. "There should be a fire stoker too."

I got on my knees and felt for the door. "Okay, ladies. Unless you want to see all of me, shut your eyes for a second."

Light blinded me as a wash of cool air doused the hot coals in my lungs. I felt around for the logs and fire stoker. I found both and pulled them into the sweltering humidity of the steam bath.

"Here," I said to Hope in the dark, touching the stoker to her leg. I heard Hope shuffling things around before she opened the stove door and threw the first log in, then the second. She used the stoker to stir the hot coals. The first log caught fire right away. The second one was being stubborn.

"Come on!" Hope said, agitated, poking the coals.

The second log burst into flames, lighting the space like a camera flash. In that split-second burst of light, I saw all of Taylor. Everything. Every last inch of skin. From head to toe. I might've gasped. Just before the light faded to blackness, my eyes met Taylor's. Her face went from surprise to a slight smile.

In the dark again, everybody acted as if the flash of light never happened.

Everybody except Bristy.

"Eddie has a boner," she said.

CHAPTER 18

# STING

Dalton left the office early to go bowling, ducking out just after five o'clock. He competed in a league at Kusko Lanes, which was the closest thing to a bar in town. Although Kusko's laws forbade alcohol to be served in public places, the cops pretended not to notice that all the bowlers scored in the hundreds during their first games and tossed gutter balls at closing time. Every team showed up with a cooler filled with liquor and mixers and solid-colored plastic mugs. As long as the cops couldn't see the drinks, the drinks didn't exist. Even Sheriff Buzz Berger was in the league. He liked to pound whiskey Cokes from a coffee thermos, Dalton said.

Mikey Colosky hung up his camo apron for the night right after Dalton left, leaving me alone in the Quonset hut. I sat at my desk, putting the finishing touches on a story about the Kusko School District's budget problems. Droves of parents had attended a board meeting the night before to ream out the school board for upping the price of school lunches by fifty cents. I never realized how much shit school board members ate until I started writing stories about the decisions they made. I didn't feel altogether sorry for them, though. Half the time the parents were right.

I finished writing and shut down my computer. I sat in silence for several minutes, listening to the wind blowing outside and the electric hum of florescent ceiling lights, thinking about the phone call I was about to make.

I stared at the phone. Its buttons were coated with the same dirty gray residue as the keys on my computer's keyboard. I rubbed my thumb over the phone buttons and created enough friction to lift the residue away in little clumps that looked like eraser shavings.

*You're stalling*, I thought.

I picked up the phone and dialed. Three rings later, Linetta Wassily answered.

I said, "This is Eddie, the guy who sold you the weed."

Her TV blared in the background. Apparently, I'd interrupted her busy day of doing jack squat.

"Yeah?" she snarled.

"You want some more?"

She paused a moment. "Yeah, okay. But I don't have the money right now. Pay you back?"

I, too, paused to think for a moment. "No problem," I said. "I'll drop the stuff off Monday. I'll fly to St. Mary's again when the dividend checks get cut next month."

"Fine," she said. "See you Monday."

I hung up and made another call, this time to Betty Bennis in Mountain Village.

After that, I drove to Kusko Lanes to talk to Sheriff Buzz Berger. I found him seated at a scoring table, ten lanes down from Dalton, who never saw me through the crowd of other bowlers. Buzz wore a black button-down bowling shirt that read STRIKE FORCE on the back. I pitched him a plan that would help both of us.

\* \* \*

Just before the flight to Mountain Village took off, I sent my dad a text saying that I loved him. I had forgotten to tell him so during a short phone conversation we'd had on Father's Day. I was too nervous to remember, stumbling over my words, trying not to get caught in all my lies. I wanted him to know now, just in case something went wrong.

I landed in the village just after ten in the morning. Its VPSO waited near a kiosk by the runway. He was a short, middle-aged Native guy who appeared to have dusted off his navy blue, state-issued VPSO parka for the first time since spring. It was late enough in summer that morning temperatures hovered in the forties. The titanic foothills surrounding the runway were covered in low-lying brush that was beginning to show hints of fall color.

I walked straight to the VPSO after I got off the plane.

"Ivan Hurley," he said, with a crippling handshake. "You're the newspaper kid, right?"

"I am, sir. I was here for Quyana Fest last month but didn't see you. It's nice to meet you."

"What brings you here?"

"I couldn't get a flight to St. Mary's today, so I came here," I said as the pilot handed me my backpack. "Do you know where Betty Bennis lives? I'm going to borrow her four-wheeler and cruise over to St. Mary's for my story."

Ivan gave me a ride to town in his truck, dropped me off at Betty's place, and went on his way.

The four-wheeler parked in Betty's front yard looked like it was worth more money than her dilapidated home. She opened the door with a smile and handed me the keys to the vehicle. I took off the leather boot on my right foot and pulled out a nug of weed. To keep the nug from smelling like athlete's foot, I'd covered it with a cellophane wrapper from a pack of cigarettes.

"Thanks for agreeing to this, Betty," I offered, extending my hand for a shake, with the nug in my palm. She shook back and collected the weed. Her crippled fingers felt like brittle twigs.

"Just make sure the tank is full when you drop my four-wheeler back here," she said. "When will that be?"

"I'll be back before my return flight leaves at three o'clock."

\* \* \*

During my drive to St. Mary's, I passed the trail to the city dump. I could smell the garbage all the way from the road. The putrid aroma took me back to the incredible events that had transpired there, reminding me of how deeply I hated Bronco. If anything, the stench gave me even more motivation to do what I was about to do.

I hit the gas and kept driving, ducking overgrown branches that extended to the center of the bumpy road. Twenty minutes later, I arrived at the edge of a sandy cliff overlooking the St. Mary's runway. I parked the four-wheeler behind some bushes, stayed seated, and waited for the next plane to arrive.

Soon, I heard the buzz of a bush plane flying in from the south. Just after it landed, two pickup trucks drove down the long road from St. Mary's and parked near the plane. Russ got out of one of the trucks. The fat-ass was impossible to miss, even from several hundred yards away.

I turned on the four-wheeler and drove down the winding dirt road to the runway. I crept along a straightaway next to the runway and kept my eyes fixed on Russ, like a fighter plane on missile lock. He was helping unload boxes from the plane. At the exact moment he turned his head to look in my direction, I snapped my eyes to the road, pretending I didn't notice he'd spotted me. I kept putzing, casually, like a Sunday drive.

*Good*, I thought. *Russ saw me.*

\* \* \*

At Linetta's house, near the banks of the Andreafsky River, three black bags of stinky trash sagged in a pile outside the front door. Walking ten extra steps to reach the garbage bin at the end of her walkway was too much work for her.

I knocked, and Linetta answered in all her pitiful glory. She stunk like she hadn't showered in days. Her oily blond hair was a matted mess. She wore flip-flops, a neon yellow shirt, and black sweatpants stained with crusty white stuff.

"Come in," she said.

I took off my backpack and sunk into Linetta's couch. A rainbow-colored ashtray rested on top of the wooden coffee table in front of me. Next to the ashtray was an antique photo album with a faded leather cover. "Mind if I look at this?" I asked, attempting to buy time.

"Go ahead," Linetta said from the kitchen, waiting for a pot of water to boil. She was making tundra tea — a YK Delta favorite made from tundra shrubs that look like evergreen leaves.

I opened the album and beheld pages upon pages of photographs taken all over the YK Delta at fish camps, Quyana Fests of yesteryear, family gatherings, drinking parties, berry picking excursions, moose and caribou hunts — all kinds of nostalgic Alaskan scenes. Linetta was about the only white person in all the photos. Judging by how young she looked, the photos must have been shot in the nineties. She was surprisingly beautiful in her youth.

I noticed familiar faces in the photos. It seemed that Peggy Paniptchuck and Linetta were friends, because both of them appeared in several berry-picking photos. I saw Betty Bennis, too. She was in almost every fish camp photo, cleaning salmon.

"Are you related to Betty Bennis?" I asked Linetta. "She's in most of these fish camp photos."

"No," she replied, stirring the pot of water. "But I saw her a lot. Their fish camp was next to ours."

I didn't understand how Linetta could be white and have a fish camp. Only Native families had fish camps. I asked her as much.

"My ex-husband is Native," she said.

*Duh*, I thought. *Linetta is Finn's aunt. She was married to one of Finn's uncles.*

Halfway through the photo album, a pint-sized Finn started appearing in lots of the pictures of fish camps and family gatherings. In several photos he wore a kid-sized poncho made of seal skin, over-smiling for the camera as only a toddler can. He wore a similar poncho as a tween. If I'd have flipped the pages fast enough, it would have looked like Finn growing up in time-lapse photography.

Seeing him as a kid was interesting. He never talked much about his youth or his family.

"Is the house Finn grew up in nearby?" I asked, perusing more pages.

Linetta didn't say anything. She shuffled to the couch and sat next to me. She opened the coffee table drawer and pulled out a moose antler pipe and the cellophane baggie of weed I'd sold her earlier in the summer. She used her index finger to scrape out what little shake was left in the bag and sprinkled it into the pipe. Then she snatched a lighter from her pocket and sparked the thing up.

She exhaled the biggest hit I'd ever seen. The smoke poured out as if she had a bonfire in her lungs.

"You're in it," she said.

"What?" I asked, astonished. "Finn grew up in *this* house?"

I surveyed the shithole interior. The rotting linoleum floorboards slanted downhill like a funhouse. All the windows were cracked, with mosquito-filled spiderwebs between the panes of glass. Duct tape plugged chinks in the walls. Back in Minnesota, the place would have been condemned.

I wanted to ask Linetta a million questions. But the questions would have to wait.

*THUMP!* I flinched at the thundering coming from the front door. *THUMP!*

"Not again!" Linetta cried.

She stayed seated while I got up to answer. I knew this was coming. But I was way more scared than I thought I'd be. I walked to the door as calmly as possible, grasped the doorknob, and took a deep breath. I knew who was on the other side.

I opened up, and looked into the eyes of Bronco. The two goons stood on either sides of him.

Bronco's face was curled into a snarl.

"Listen, Bronco," I said. "Before you — "

The bigger goon popped me in the kisser, and I hit the floor tasting blood before I realized what was happening. Linetta screamed as Bronco and the goons stormed inside and shut the door behind them. I floundered on the floor. My lower lip throbbed like it'd been stung by a swarm of wasps. I wiped my mouth and blood stained the back of my hand.

"You're not getting away this time, you little gussuk fuck," Bronco sneered, circling above me. "You actually thought you'd sell weed in my village again? Like I wouldn't know you came in from Mountain Village?"

Bronco kicked me in the gut, knowing I was powerless to retaliate with the two goons backing him. The three of them kept circling me, waiting for me to answer.

"Yes and no," I groaned.

"What do you mean, yes and no?" Bronco asked, kicking me in the gut when he said "no" to drive home his question, knocking the wind out of me. His leather boot felt like it'd driven through my stomach and out my backside.

"I mean," I said, coughing and gasping, "that I meant to sell weed here, but I also meant to tell you about it."

I held up my hands, rose to my knees, and asked for a chance to talk. The snarl on his face didn't change, but he held back and waited for me to get my breath and go on. I laid out my story: I was going to sell to Linetta and give him a cut, and I came from Mountain Village on a four-wheeler because I knew Russ would be all over me if I got off the plane in St. Mary's.

He just snarled and stared at me. I'd reached a pivotal moment. If Bronco didn't buy what I was saying, he and the goons could wind up thrashing me beyond repair. Worse yet, I could become bear bait. The silvers had quit running, effectively ending the year's salmon run. If some of the younger bears hadn't gotten their fill, they'd be looking to fatten up however else they could before winter.

"Or," Bronco scoffed, "we could pound your ass now, take your money again, and call it a deal."

"Just think a second," I said. "I could earn you a lot of side cash with no work and no risk for you."

I rose all the way to my feet. "I'm telling you, Bronco — there's room for us to coexist."

Bronco stroked the goatee on his chin. He must have been contemplating what was more important to him — money, or punishing me for the many ways I'd humiliated him.

The goons sat down on the couch, on each side of Linetta. She looked dumbfounded, like I was charming a poisonous snake.

"What's the cut?" Bronco asked.

"Thirty percent."

Bronco motioned for the goons to stand up and prepare for Round Two.

"Okay, okay — forty percent," I conceded.

The goons sat back down, and it seemed like Bronco was actually buying it. And why not? For all he knew, I was a career dealer with no plans to leave Suckwood. He'd seen firsthand the weed I was selling and had no reason to believe I wasn't legit.

He asked, "How do I know you won't make deals under the table and keep my cut?"

"Because the moment you find out otherwise, I know it's my ass," I responded, stroking his ego. "I don't want to mess with you, Bronco. I know what you're capable of."

Bronco smirked and asked, "How will you get me my money?"

"We can keep hashing out details, but this probably isn't the best place," I told him, pointing at Linetta.

"Good point," he said.

I picked up my backpack as Bronco and the goons walked out the door. Linetta asked from the couch, "But where's my weed?"

"I'll come back later," I said.

Outside, the brisk late-morning air gave me a shiver as I trailed Bronco and his cronies on a dirt road next to the Andreafsky River. They headed toward three shitty little houses — shacks, really — clustered at the end of the gravel street. I assumed one of the houses was Bronco's. After we'd walked a while, I glanced back at Linetta's house. Sheriff Buzz peeked his head around from the back of her house and gave me a quick thumbs-up.

* * *

Inside Bronco's house, the last of the three shacks, he gestured for me to sit down on a new-looking red recliner. He and the goons pulled up chairs at the kitchen table, like they needed to confer before they'd bring me into the conversation.

The place consisted of a single open room with synthetic wooden walls, like an RV from the eighties, only the bathroom didn't even have walls. A shower and a toilet stood in one corner, surrounded by a pink polka-dot curtain. Although I was sure the pink curtain came with the house, I very much wanted to call Bronco a fruity-ass for it. But small as it was, the place looked surprisingly livable. The kitchen appliances in one corner and living room set in another might've been new, too. Bronco clearly had some money coming in.

"Let's have a drink," the smaller goon said in a

high-pitched voice that matched his stature. Finally, I'd gotten to hear one of the goons speak. I'd wondered if they were mutes.

Bronco got up from the table, walked to the center of the room, and peeled back a musk ox rug in the middle of the living room floor. He lifted away some floorboards and pulled out a jug of home brew from a pit brimming with dozens of other containers of the stuff — one-gallon milk jugs, two-liter pop bottles, and other disposable cartons. All were filled with a red-orange liquid, which was a fermented mixture of juice, sugar, and yeast that had a lot of fans in the YK Delta. I also spotted a few one-liter glass bottles of proper vodka.

Bronco walked back into the kitchen, swiped four glasses from his cupboard, and started pouring.

I'd never been so nervous. I checked the kitchen and side windows, circumspect, looking for any sign of Sheriff Buzz. *He'd better be out there*, I thought.

I cleared my throat. "If we're going to do this deal, I need to know that all your VPSOs are on the level."

"What do you mean?" Bronco asked.

I told him to call Russ over — I wanted to hear it from Russ's own mouth that he wouldn't bust me again. If I heard it from him, I wouldn't worry about selling in St. Mary's, or Russian Mission, or wherever else Bronco was hooked up.

"You're lucky you got past Jed in Russian Mission," Bronco said while dialing Russ.

*I knew it*, I thought.

Bronco, the goons, and I stared at the floor, counting the seconds until Russ showed up, sipping our drinks. The home brew tasted like a warm mixture of orange soda, cherry juice, and regurgitated vodka.

A few minutes later, big fat Russ labored into the house and pointed at me.

"It's been an hour since I told you he was in town," he said. "Why hasn't his ass been kicked?"

"Shit's cool," Bronco assured him. "Sit your ass down and listen."

Bronco filled him in and waited for Russ to weigh in on the plan.

"Okay," Russ said, his ass oozing off the sides of the kitchen chair. "I won't bust this fool again. But I better get a cut."

Bronco grabbed one of the kitchen chairs and set it down three feet across from me. I sat up straight. "Now, Eddie," he said, sitting down, stroking his scruffy little goatee. "About those details."

I crossed my fingers, praying that all the pieces of my plan were in place. With Russ and Bronco and the goons in the same room with all that alcohol, everything hinged on these next moments. I was scared shitless.

"First," Bronco began, "how will you get me my money?"

I didn't have an answer. I didn't have any weed on me to sell to Linetta, either. I'd never had any in the first place, other than the little bit I'd given Betty. Seconds from now, Bronco would discover I was full of crap.

*Here goes nothing,* I thought.

"Now!" I screamed at the top of my lungs.

Bronco and the others looked at one another.

"NOW!" I screamed even louder, jolting up off the

recliner and dashing toward the door. "NOW, BUZZ! NOW!"

Sheriff Buzz burst through the door with a chrome-plated tactical shotgun at his hip. He shouted his two favorite words in the English language: "Freeze, motherfuckers!"

Buzz swung his shotgun to and fro, stomping his feet up and down like a psyched-up linebacker anticipating the snap. He had a barbaric smile and crazy eyes. He stalked toward the men, continuing an entrance so outrageously overdramatic he must have practiced it in front of a mirror. Awesome.

"Eat the floor, shitheads!" Buzz ordered with his finger on the trigger, hoping somebody would make just one false move. All four guys fell to the ground. Buzz took a few steps backward to where I was standing by the door. "Hold this," he said, handing me his shotgun. "If one of them sons a fucks moves, shoot off his penis."

I could tell Buzz meant to say something more badass than penis, but I let it go. I didn't want to spoil his moment.

Bronco lay in the center of the room. Buzz hustled to him and cuffed his hands behind his back.

"Hey, Bronco," I said, looking down on him, with the shotgun pointed at Russ and the goons in the kitchen. "You know what this is about, right?"

Bronco looked up at me from the ground and gave me the stink eye.

"This is about those pink curtains of yours. They're so pussy, it's illegal."

Buzz belly laughed. It was his kind of joke.

He had laughed just as hard at the bowling alley three days earlier when I'd pitched him my plan for the bust. I'd asked him a simple question: if I could get Bronco, his goons, and Russ in the same room with all of Bronco's alcohol, could we pull off a sting? I hadn't needed to ask twice. He was so housed off whiskey Cokes he practically wanted to fly to St. Mary's right then and there. He didn't ask how I could make the situation happen because, quite frankly, he didn't want to know. All he cared about was taking down Bronco by whatever means possible.

That's all I cared about too. Because Bronco had to go. If Taylor changed her mind about me and I stayed in Kusko at least a little longer to be with her, I couldn't have Bronco hanging around. He'd come after me again. And considering the smile Taylor had given me in her steam bath, I was sure her mind was changing.

Buzz had just finished cuffing Russ when I noticed the time. I had a long drive back to Mountain Village and a plane to catch. "Buzz, you got this under control?"

"Bet your sweet titties," he said, his perma-grin still going strong. "Nice work, sport."

# CHAPTER 19

# THE STIFF ARM

After the flight from Mountain Village to Suckford, I walked off the plane feeling ten feet tall. I was more exhilarated than if I'd bungee jumped off a cliff with a boobie in one hand, and in the other hand a rifle with which I was shooting a trophy bull moose. I felt unstoppable. Empowered. Euphoric.

I couldn't believe that I'd actually pulled it off. I, Eddie Ashford, had taken down a notorious bootlegger in bush Alaska. *Me*. Nothing could ever be more badass than that. I wanted a statue made of myself, with my face like I was all *Hell yeah!*

I sauntered through the airport lobby and saw Peggy Paniptchuck typing at her desk. "Peggy!" I said, happier than a ray of sunshine. "You're beautiful!"

"Thanks?" she replied.

I kept walking, out the door and to the parking lot, thinking outstanding thoughts. Half of me wanted to write a big fat news story about every detail of the bust because it was just that awesome.

*Easy there, Big Eddie,* I thought. *Hold your horses now.* Writing such a story would be counterproductive. The story would be so sweet that every Alaska media outlet would want to cover their own version of it, and in doing so, would want to interview me. They'd ask lots of questions I wouldn't want to answer. Namely, *How was it you knew Bronco?*

Thankfully, Sheriff Buzz said he would keep my role in the bust on the down-low. So, for now, I'd need to keep my dink in my pants. I could blather about the bust *after* I'd left the YK Delta.

Speaking of, I needed to figure out, immediately, whether my departure would come two weeks from now or much further down the road. I only needed six hundred to pay my (and my truck's) way out, but I also had a girl to kiss. Considering all the positive momentum I had going, I had to strike while the iron was hot.

After strutting through the airport parking lot, I peeled away in the FJ. It was just after four o'clock. Taylor told me she'd be volunteering at the elementary school every afternoon this week, helping teachers decorate their classrooms before the new school year started.

I arrived at the school and backed into a parking space in front of the main entrance. I sat in my truck and stared at the glass doors nervously. Teacher after teacher filed out.

*Screw it,* I thought. I pulled out my phone and sent R.J. a text: "Just helped bust one of the biggest bootleggers in the YK Delta. Am the shit."

He texted back ("Seriously? What's the story?") just as Taylor floated through the school doors. She wore black short-shorts and a tight white tank top. Her long, muscular legs belonged in a magazine. I put my phone away as she approached, got out of the FJ, scrambled to the rear of the vehicle, and opened the tailgate to retrieve my backpack. I unzipped the top of the backpack and rummaged through it, just to look busy. To my left, I heard the click of Taylor's shoes on the pavement.

"Eddie?" she said.

I looked in all directions, acting befuddled. "What? Who said that?"

"Right here!"

I looked left and our eyes met. I threw my hands up in surprise, as if running into her were some crazy coincidence. "Taylor! Good to see you!"

"You too!" She gave me a smile.

"How was your day?" I asked.

"Really good. I had a —" She narrowed her eyes and peered at my mouth. "Wait, what happened to you?"

I'd almost forgotten that my lower lip had been split open. It had stopped bleeding during my flight but still felt raw. "Oh, that," I said, touching it gently. "Joanie got excited and accidentally head-butted me."

"There's blood on your shirt," Taylor said, her smile gone now. "When did this happen?"

"It's nothing," I said.

I could practically feel the awkward silence descend. I had to talk, so I told her I was there for the paper, that I wanted to get some teacher reactions to the school-lunch controversy.

"Actually, I was hoping I'd bump into you," I added. For as fearless as I felt about wanting to kiss her, there was no easy way of doing it. We were in a parking lot, in broad daylight, with teachers walking past, and my efforts toward a little conversational foreplay petered out. But I was having a powerful day, and I wanted to act while I had the momentum. *Stop being a pussy and get on with it,* I thought. "Actually, I mainly wanted to see you. Actually, that's the only reason I came."

"Yeah?" Taylor said, her grin returning. "Why is that?"

"Because I wanted to give you something."

"Give me what?"

"This." I took two little steps toward her, cupped her hand, closed my eyes, and went in for the kill.

I never got there. She let go of my hand and pulled away.

I backed up a step, with my eyes still closed. When I opened them, Taylor looked at me like I'd puked on her shoes.

"Oops," I said with a dumb smirk, feeling like a world champion dipshit but trying to make light. "Can I try again after my lip heals?"

"I don't think so," she said, her expression as blank and empty as the tundra.

Gut punch. She might as well have gotten a running start from across the parking lot, drove a sledgehammer into my stomach, and stomped on my entrails when they seeped out. If only Taylor knew what was going on behind the scenes. I wanted to tell her I was about to leave Suckland for good, that this was her last chance, that she'd probably never see me again. But I couldn't do that. If I did, I'd have to explain everything I'd gotten into.

"Sorry, Taylor. I know I jumped the gun. But after the look you gave me in the steam bath — "

She glared at me with both eyes locked in perfect alignment.

"You're leaving and I'm staying," she said. "What part of that don't you understand?"

She walked three parking spaces away to her parents' silver truck, hopped in, and sped off.

\* \* \*

Soon I got to my place, parked the FJ, and took a moment to calm myself. I sulked my way next door to Finn's place and entered without knocking. He was crouched in the center of his living room, taking a shit on a honey bucket — a five-gallon pail with a toilet seat on top and a disposable plastic liner inside.

"'Sup, dude?" he said with a smile, seemingly finding it funny that I'd walked in on him dropping a deuce.

Seeing him pooping really *was* funny, but I was in no mood. "Out of water?"

"Until tomorrow," Finn said with a wipe of his ass. "No money for an emergency water delivery."

There were so many things I wanted to talk to Finn about — the sting operation on Bronco, my knowing about the shitty house he grew up in and how hard he'd had it, and my getting Heismaned by Taylor. But I was too glum to talk about it. I shifted gears.

"I'm going to need another ounce."

"Your final delivery!" Finn said, pulling up his pants. "But what about Taylor?"

"Don't ask," I said.

Finn explained how it was a good thing I was asking for weed now, because he might not be selling the stuff much longer. That surprised me. But it was a good kind of surprise.

"I was late for work the other day," he said. "I'd stayed up all night. I can't be late again."

"You're going to stop smoking *and* stop selling?"

"I'm thinking about it. I'm living on my own now. I can't fuck around."

I asked what he would do to earn the extra money he needed to get by. He said maybe work nights at Kusko Dry Goods, or weekend janitor shifts at the hospital.

"But I can still put this last order in for you," Finn said, pulling the plastic liner from the honey bucket and tying it off. "No problem there."

"Thanks, Finn," I said, heading toward the door. "And good for you."

Finn still wouldn't tell me who his supplier was, or why I couldn't sell in villages near Suckmont. I'd given up on asking a long time ago because the conversations always went nowhere. I didn't even care about the identity of his supplier. I just didn't like that he couldn't trust me with the information.

\* \* \*

Dalton knocked on my bedroom door. "Are you awake, Eddie? Time to get going."

I'd been up for a while, lying in bed in a T-shirt and plaid pajama pants. Quickly, I grabbed a spray bottle from underneath my pillow and squirted water onto my face. I put the bottle back and rubbed my eyes to make them look puffy.

"I can't," I moaned, feigning misery. "I have tuberculosis or something."

Dalton trampled in and saw me underneath my covers, looking like a sweaty mess. "Whatever, Eddie. You don't even know what tuberculosis is," he said, calling bullshit. "But you're right, you don't look so good. Stay home and get some rest. I'll head to the office and hold down the fort."

Fifteen minutes after he left, I sat down on the living room couch and placed my phone on the coffee table, along with a piece of scratch paper with some phone numbers I'd scribbled.

My first call was to R.J., but he didn't answer. I left him a message: "I'm coming back, sucka! Expect me in a week or two. Got some crazy stories to tell you besides the bootlegger thing. Call me."

I knew that living with R.J. again at Chateau Eagle River wouldn't be an issue. He'd be pumped to have me back. But I wondered how I'd handle living in a party house again. Could I resist the temptation?

Next I called my admissions counselor at the University of Anchorage, Mr. Westbrook. He didn't answer, either. I left a message saying I'd be moving back to Anchorage a few months early. "I'm wondering what other types of local jobs or activities would help me toward getting in position to reenroll in college this winter. Please call me."

If Mr. Westbrook didn't have any ideas or leads, moving back to Minnesota wouldn't be out of the question. I was borderline clinically depressed, suffering from a nasty case of the fuck-its.

I saved the worst call for last — Yute Cargo. The customer service lady said they could fly my truck out four days from now, on Friday. "Pencil me in," I said.

I sunk into the couch and sighed. Scheduling my truck for delivery to Anchorage was supposed to feel terrific. It was supposed to be the triumphant culmination of all the hard work I'd put into getting myself out of Suckshire.

But it didn't feel terrific. It felt demoralizing. All because of a girl named Taylor Sifsof. Until I'd met her, I never imagined that anything could make me want to stay in Suckramento.

"Thank you, Mr. Ashford," the lady said. "But I'll need a two-thousand-dollar nonrefundable deposit by day's end."

"Done," I said, feeling extra grownup to have that much money. "I'll drop it off this afternoon."

Although I only had twenty-four hundred, and was still short of paying Yute Cargo the entire balance of three thousand, I wasn't worried about counting my chickens. With Bronco out of the picture, earning the final six hundred was a non-issue.

I'd become an old pro at selling weed. I could unload that final ounce in my sleep, blindfolded, with one hand tied behind my back.

## CHAPTER 20

# CHANGING COURSE

Casey Cotton needed more weed, and in forty-five minutes, I'd be on a plane to Unalakleet to give him some. I'd gotten to Finn's house early in the morning, and we were almost finished with the packing ritual. Having torn off a third strip of duct tape, Finn knelt behind me in his living room and ceremoniously placed the last strand he'd ever strap over my butt cheeks.

"How's it feel?" Finn asked.

I sipped from a mug of instant coffee he'd mixed me. "The tape is pulling. I didn't have time to shave."

"That's not what I meant," Finn said, smoothing the tape.

I knew what he meant. In a few days, according to my plan, I'd be leaving Sucksburg for good. I'd net six hundred with this delivery, and I'd be free to pay my way back to civilization.

"I'm jacked to get out of here," I said before taking

a long sip. "The only bad part is you. I'll miss you, brother. I really will."

"What do you want, a farewell reach-around?" Finn said.

"Get the hell out of here!" I said with a laugh, swatting his hand away.

I'd spent all my extra money on a flight scheduled to leave Saturday. Having become preoccupied with leaving Suck Center — even more intensely once it seemed at hand — I hadn't bothered to tie up loose ends with Finn, Dalton, or Taylor during the past few days.

Not that I had much to smooth over with Finn. Although I'd told him about the Bronco sting — he was aghast it had happened — I didn't mention that I'd discovered the truth about his childhood home and the circumstances he'd grown up with. Between the condition of Linetta's place and Finn's never talking about his family, there was no sense in making him dredge up bad memories. Some things are best left unsaid.

As for Dalton, he had no clue I was leaving. I didn't even have a story to cover in Unalakleet, where'd I'd be delivering to Casey. Even if I did have a story, by the time it was due on Tuesday morning, I'd be gone. So whatever. Whenever I started thinking about how angry Dalton would be when he found out I'd left him high and dry, and how guilty I'd feel about screwing him over, I stopped thinking.

And Taylor. I hadn't heard from her since she denied me five days earlier. Nary a text or email. Again, whatever. I couldn't wait to get far, far away from her. It was embarrassing to be in the same town, to know that Bristy and Hope had heard all about my failed move, to know that I could run into any of them anytime.

I pulled up my overalls. "It's my birthday, you know," I told Finn. "I'm nineteen."

He stood up and high-fived me. "That's awesome! Why didn't you tell me sooner? We could've had a little party."

"Thanks," I said, buckling the straps on my overalls. "But it doesn't feel awesome. A year ago, practically to the date, I was driving the FJ to Alaska, ready to take on the world. Instead, the world kicked my ass. I pissed away the last twelve months, and somehow nineteen sounds a lot different from eighteen."

Finn opened the fridge and pulled out two Mountain Dews for the drive to the airport. "Did you learn anything in the past year?" he asked.

"Tons of shit," I said. "Mostly bad."

"Mostly bad, my ass. You didn't piss it away. Since January you've lived in a part of the world few people get to see, doing a job few guys your age get to do. Put that in your pipe and smoke it."

I smiled. "Thanks, Finn."

"Happy birthday, Eddie."

It was time to leave. I stepped into the kitchen to retrieve my backpack resting against the stove. My phone starting ringing as I walked toward the door, and I debated whether to answer. My flight would be taking off in a half hour.

I pulled the phone from my front pocket. I didn't recognize the number. *This better be quick,* I thought.

"This is Eddie."

"Good morning, Mr. Ashford. This is Gordon Westbrook, your admissions counselor."

I dropped my backpack onto the floor, surprised, and sat at the kitchen table, listening to Mr. Westbrook talk. Finn sat down on the couch. "Yeah?" I said to the counselor. "What's the good news?"

He said he'd checked out my work in the *Delta Patriot* on the paper's website, and that he spoke with the UA admissions board about it. All were convinced that I was ready to be a college student again. I dropped the phone to my chest and mouthed "Shit yeah!" to Finn.

I put the phone back to my ear. "Can I enroll for this fall?"

"Yes. But first you'll need to — "

Just then, my phone hiccuped. Someone else was calling me, and when I checked, I saw "Dad" on the screen. Perfectly terrible parental timing. As always.

*Why's he calling me now?* I thought. *He should be working at the car wash.*

"Mr. Westbrook, I'm going to have to call you back. My dad's on the other line. I'm afraid I have to take the call."

I hadn't spoken with my dad since Father's Day, and that talk had only lasted a few minutes. I had ended the conversation quickly because every word I'd told him was a lie about how well school was going, that I'd be taking a few summer classes to get even further ahead. The longer we would have chatted, the better the odds of me tripping up.

"Happy birthday, son," my dad said. His voice was slightly high-pitched like mine but had lowered with age.

"Thanks," I said. "Are you at work?"

"No. Max and I took the day off to go walleye fishing on Mille Lacs Lake. We just docked the boat in Garrison to eat an early lunch. We figured we'd call now. There's no cell coverage on the water."

My dad said they'd been fishing since six a.m. and that he was going on just a few hours of sleep. He'd poured drinks at the Zimmerman VFW until one a.m.

"Enough about us," my dad said. "How's nineteen feel so far?"

"Pretty good," I said. "I'm on my way to Kusko Dry Goods to buy cigarettes. I'm a smoker now."

"Sure you are," my dad said, chuckling. "What's Kusko Dry Goods?"

Crap. My head wasn't clear enough to formulate proper lies. I still hadn't woken up completely.

"It's this store by me," I said.

"Kusko? Where does that name come from?"

"I don't know, Pops."

He didn't respond. "Hello?" I asked. "Are you still there?"

"I'm here, son."

I waited again. Still nothing. I watched fifteen seconds tick on the clock above Finn's kitchen sink. And in that moment it dawned on me what his silence meant.

"You know," I said.

"Yes, son," my dad replied calmly. "I know you're in Kusko."

I glanced at Finn sitting on the couch. He pointed at his watch. "Hurry, dude," he whispered from across the room. "We gotta go."

I asked my dad, "Did you know when we talked in June?"

"I did," he said flatly.

"Then why didn't you say anything?"

My dad paused. "I wanted to let you figure it out on your own."

"Figure what out?"

"Life," he said.

Total shocker. My dad wasn't known for playing games. He was an old-school, straight-shooting man's man. He explained that he'd known since April, when Max stumbled onto one of my stories online. My dad had then made a bogus call to the University of Anchorage, saying it was a family emergency. Then he learned they had no record of an Eddie Ashford registered for spring classes.

I sat there speechless, duct tape straining against the stubble on my ass, facing the reality that I had no clue about what other information my dad had gathered. Had the college people told him I'd been kicked out for a year? If so, how would I explain my early departure from Suck City?

Finn waved his arms frantically from the couch. "You're going to miss your flight," he said.

"Where's the FJ?" my dad asked.

"With me," I said. "My boss paid to fly it here."

"Is he paying to fly it out?"

"Yes, after my year is up."

Another mistake. I should have said "yes" without

adding more. But I was too rattled, and still too tired, to forecast the implications of my words.

Then, after another one of his silent pauses, my dad said, "I'm proud of you."

"What?"

"I said I'm proud of you, Eddie. You've taken responsibility for your mistake. In the process, you've gained valuable experience."

I let his words sink in. "You're not mad I flunked out of college?"

"Of course I'm mad. And I'm even madder that you lied about it. Incidentally, you're a bad liar. You mentioned Kusko Dry Goods during our Father's Day conversation too."

In the background, Max shouted, "Dumbass!"

"Sorry about that, Dad. Really, I am. The truth is that I've been in over my head ever since I moved to Alaska. It's brutal being so far from home on my own."

"I know it is, but you're figuring it out. Through your mistakes, you're learning to do the right thing. Your mother would be proud."

I patted the package of weed lodged in my butt crack. *No, she wouldn't,* I thought.

"Thanks," I said. "I really do need to get going."

"Let's talk again soon."

"Love you, Pops. Have fun fishing." I stood up from the kitchen table and shoved my phone back into my front pocket. Finn bolted from the couch to the kitchen and grabbed my backpack.

"I'll put this in your truck," he said, hoisting the backpack onto his shoulder. "If we don't leave this second, you won't make it. You can feel guilty about your daddy talk later."

Finn scurried out the door. I still hadn't taken a step. I stood frozen, reflecting on the conversation I'd just had.

*You're figuring it out,* my dad had told me. *You're learning to do the right thing.*

I envisioned my mom looking down on me from above. I wanted her to be proud of me. Between selling weed and smoking weed and ditching out on Dalton and pounding beers every day in college and failing my classes and lying to people to cover up my misdeeds and being pissed off all the time over a situation I created, I was sure the Alaskan version of me would not make her proud.

At that moment, everything I wanted, and everything I'd worked for, was laid out before me on a platter — college, my friends in Anchorage, mountains, fast food at two a.m., movie theaters, car washes, department stores, freedom from Sucktown. All of it was there. All I had to do was sell one more ounce of weed.

I walked outside and stopped myself near the hood of the FJ. Finn had already started the vehicle. He sat in the passenger seat of the truck as it idled. I opened the driver's side door, got in, and sat down on the black vinyl seat. I grabbed hold of the key in the ignition and took a giant breath. I twisted the key, forty-five degrees counterclockwise.

"You're shitting me," Finn said.

# CHAPTER 21

# STILL IN SUCKTOWN

When I was nine years old and new homes were being built in my neighborhood, my friends and I would sneak into the attics of the half-built houses and jump around on the pink fluffy stuff. Later, around the time I'd go home for lunch, a slow burn would heat up in my hands, arms, and legs. By nightfall, the microscopic shards of fiberglass in my pores would ignite into an itchy inferno. The pain would blaze until I ate my corn flakes the next morning. Then, the next day, I'd do it all over again.

I'd forgotten all about the itch and burn until I helped Nicolai Vawter insulate homes in Napakiak, a three-hundred-person village ten miles southwest of Kusko. My forearms already started to tingle as we worked. I'd left them exposed between my utility gloves and the rolled-up sleeves of my sweatshirt. I knew from experience that once I fell asleep that night, I'd scratch those areas of skin until they were raw.

"Son of a — " I said, cutting myself off when I glanced at Nicolai, the pastor, standing right next to me.

"When you get back to Kusko, mix baking soda with water and spread the paste onto where it itches," he said. "Keep it there for a half hour. After that it'll feel better."

Napakiak was linked to Kusko not only via the river, but by an old trail that postal workers from the early- to mid-1900s traveled, via dogsled, to deliver the mail. During winter, the trail shaved several miles off the journey to and from Kusko for mushers and snow-machiners who'd otherwise have to travel the frozen Kuskokwim. Saving those few miles was a godsend for people who needed to get to Kusko in sub-zero temperatures for emergency supplies, medical attention, or a greasy burger at Delta Delicious.

The trail was the same one that connected to the mushing trail that started in Dalton's backyard.

Nicolai and I wore dirty work jeans and disposable white dust masks. We fit the insulation ahead of two other church volunteers — a Native father named Willie, and his son, Willie Jr. — who covered the walls with Sheetrock behind us. They ran a construction outfit in Kusko. Our goal was to insulate three homes that Saturday.

Nicolai, the Willies, and other church volunteers had spent the past two months erecting the three homes, working on the weekends. Each house was the same: an efficiency space with room for two bunk beds, plus a small kitchen area. None of the homes had enough room for a couch; the families would need to watch TV from their beds or from their kitchen tables. No plumbing work was needed — the families would use drums of water for drinking, cooking, and cleaning pots. Behind the houses, Nicolai and company had built a steam bath for the families to share. For toilets, they'd use honey buckets or the great outdoors.

I had arrived with Nicolai and the Willies aboard two wooden skiffs powered by forty-horse outboards. Each skiff was stacked high with construction materials. It was late October, and winter was coming up fast. More than two months had passed since the day I bailed on my last delivery, the one that would've put me over the top. After talking to my dad and finding out he knew the truth about my situation, I'd been keeping my commitments in Kusko.

Nicolai told me this week would be the last that anybody could travel the Kuskokwim by boat. In five or six weeks, the river would become a frozen interstate for trucks and snow machines. Ice had already begun to form along areas of the shoreline.

"Two houses down, one to go," Nicolai said, stapling the final strip of insulation inside the second home. He'd funded the construction of the homes with a share of the summer's church offerings. Nicolai put on his jacket. "Let's take five before we start on the third."

I put on my red hunting coat and followed him outside. As Nicolai headed toward the river to get more insulation from one of the skiffs, I circled around the back of the house to take a squirt. It was dong-shriveling cold outside, windy, and getting dark.

I unzipped my jeans and did my business, pointing my stream downwind into some weeds. Napakiak must have been the blandest, most boring village I'd visited in the YK Delta. It was nothing more than a wide dirt road lined with ramshackle homes on stilts. Spruce trees, abutting a universe of tundra, surrounded the homes and road.

I was whizzing away when I heard commotion to my left. Two houses down, a short, thirty-something white guy wearing tan coveralls tried to light a cigarette. He swayed like a tall tree in high wind.

"You've got it backward!" I shouted.

"What?" he asked, looking in my general direction, adjusting his red stocking cap.

"Flip your smoke around — you're lighting the filter."

"Oh shit," he muttered.

He lit his smoke just as I finished peeing. He started talking again before I could zip up and walk away.

"Hey, kid," he grumbled, stumbling in my direction. "You holding?"

"Sorry, brother. I got nothing," I said, watching him come closer.

"Then you fuckin' suck, dude," he said, coming up to me and exhaling a puff of smoke.

The insult didn't faze me. Like many village guys, he was a hard-ass. If I didn't return fire, I'd lose his respect. If I lost his respect, he'd start messing with me. I'd been in the YK Delta long enough to know how these guys operated.

"Whatever, cockrocket," I said, choosing an extra-strong insult and taking a step toward him to signify I wasn't afraid. "I was about to ask you the same thing."

He blurted a drunken chuckle. He took off the leather glove on his right hand and extended his arm. "I'm Cal."

"Eddie," I said, taking off my utility glove to shake back. "What do you need, Cal?"

"I need a lot of weed is what I need," he said. "Been dry here for a while. Napakiak is the last stop on our supplier's run. Sometimes he sells out before he gets here."

"Want me to throw a line out when I get back to Kusko? I know people."

I was just saying that. I didn't want anything to do with this guy. Not to mention, I was done selling weed. Forever. I was trying to straighten out my act, to live so I didn't have anything to hide, and I'd been helping out Nicolai to try to even the scales in my mind after all the bad shit I'd done in Alaska.

"Nah," Cal replied, stumbling a bit. "You don't need to ask around. That'd be a mistake."

\* \* \*

I walked up the wooden steps to the third house and swung the door open. I found Nicolai inside, unraveling a roll of pink insulation. I stepped aside as the two Willies carried in Sheetrock.

"Let's get back to work, Eddie," Nicolai said, handing me a stapler. "I want to get back to Kusko at a decent hour."

As I took the stapler and checked to see if I needed to reload, I found myself still thinking about my encounter with Cal. Being in the presence of His

Holiness, Nicolai, always kindled my conscience. I thought about when I'd sold weed all those times, about how by selling weed I'd enabled people like Cal. I imagined his story probably went something like this: His parents didn't know how to parent, so he sucked in school. By sucking in school, he didn't learn the basics, and without the basics, he couldn't land a decent job. Without a good job, he was poor. In being poor, he was pissed that he couldn't make a good life for himself. In being pissed, he needed something to take his mind off how shitty his life was. To take his mind off things, he smoked weed and got hammered. By smoking weed and getting hammered all the time, his life got shittier.

"You okay?" Nicolai asked me.

I was so spellbound by what I believed to be Cal's tragic life that I still hadn't moved while Nicolai had gotten back to action. "Yeah, I'm okay," I said, eyeing the stapler in my hand.

"You want to talk about something?" he asked.

We got back to work, and as I did, I told Nicolai about meeting Cal outside and everything I assumed to be true about the guy.

"That's a fair assessment," Nicolai finally said from atop his ladder as he rolled a strip of insulation down the wall. "But don't go thinking it's just poor people who smoke marijuana and drink too much alcohol."

Here we go. Nicolai was going to tell me not to be so closed-minded, because there were still plenty of functional drunks and junkies out there, like suburban car salesman dads who swilled vodka in the garage after their families went to bed, and lonely housewives who started drinking red wine earlier and earlier in the day the more depressed they became. My dad, the bartender, had already filled me in.

But Nicolai said, "I'm living proof that addiction doesn't discriminate."

I continued stapling, pretending I wasn't nearly as interested as I actually was to hear the dirt on him. He started telling me how he grew up in a good family, that he married a good woman. He supported her by working construction in villages along the Yukon River.

"Then life happened — we had a kid, I lost my job," Nicolai said. "One night, I took a drink to take the edge off."

The two Willies walked outside to grab more Sheetrock from the skiffs.

After they shut the door, Nicolai continued. "It snowballed from there. I got fired from construction job after construction job. My wife stuck with me for the sake of our son."

Nicolai explained how he got so bad that he once traded his snow machine for three cases of beer and two ounces of weed. I stopped looking at him and stared at the floor. The conversation was getting too intense. I turned around to fit more insulation.

"That's crazy," I said, sounding insincere.

When I looked up, Nicolai had his arms folded, like he was scolding me. Dust coated his face except where his mask had covered his nose and mouth.

"You need to take this seriously," he said. "It creeps up on you, Eddie. It's a thief that steals little bits of your life. You don't know it's happening when it's happening. Then, one day, everything you had is gone."

"Why are you getting worked up, Nicolai?" I asked. "Just because you couldn't handle yourself doesn't mean I can't. I don't even party anymore. I learned my lesson in college."

"I'm not a fool," he replied. "You're at a dangerous age right now. You think you know everything, but in reality, you're always one impulse away from doing something monumentally stupid."

"Thanks for the talk," I said.

Nicolai shook his head and sighed, frustrated that I was brushing off a subject so personal to him. I felt bad that I'd offended him. I figured that a happy follow-up question would patch things up. "How did you go from where you were to becoming a pastor?"

Willie Jr. opened the door, clad in camo coveralls. A muscular guy not much older than me, he had short hair and bushy black sideburns.

"Pick up the pace, gentlemen," he said. "It's getting cold out there. We need to get back to town."

* * *

Nicolai, the Willies, and I landed the skiffs at the Kusko boat launch. It was dark outside and hard to see much of anything. The instant my and Nicolai's skiff touched the sandy shoreline, I jumped off the front and darted toward the FJ, which was parked near a Dumpster. I ran at record speed, like I was trying to escape gunfire on the beaches of Normandy.

"Eddie!" Nicolai hollered after I was halfway to

the truck. "Aren't you going to help us unload?"

"Can't talk, gotta poop!" I yelled back from under the yellow light of a lamppost, kicking up rooster tails of sand behind me. "Sorry!"

I didn't really have to poop, though. I just wanted to see Taylor, and less than five minutes later, I pulled up to her house and flipped off my headlights. It was just before seven o'clock.

I knocked on Taylor's door, and she opened it. I fell backward, pretending like I'd been knocked over by a hurricane. "Holy smokes, Taylor — your hotness just blew me away!"

"You're a dork," she said. She wore black yoga pants and a gray sweatshirt. Her hair was pulled back into a ponytail. "Get inside, you. It's cold out here."

Lately I often gave Taylor shit about being hot. Joking about it helped me live with the idea that we would never be more than just friends. My failed kiss attempt in the school parking lot seemed likely to end our relationship, but it didn't. Instead, I'd tackled the awkwardness head-on. I'd reached out to her, apologized, and made light of it. Taylor was cool with that.

I took off my red hunting jacket and walked down the hallway to the living room. I laid my jacket on the couch and sat on it to avoid dirtying the furniture with my work pants. Taylor sat on the opposite end of the couch and clutched a red velvet pillow to her chest. She said her parents had gone to visit some friends.

"How are your classes going?" I asked. "Do you think college is tough?"

"It's harder than high school, but so far I'm doing

well," she said with a shrug. "How'd the volunteer work go?"

"Great," I said. "We insulated three homes."

"Feels good, doesn't it?"

"What?" I asked. "The work?"

"No," she said. "I mean helping people without expecting anything in return."

It did and it didn't. After I decided to stay in Kusko, I resolved to make the most of my downtime by doing positive things. My dad's speech about taking responsibility had inspired me. I wanted to make him proud and give my mom a reason to smile, wherever she was. And I wanted to prove I could handle the situation I'd created by making some good out of it. So far, I'd painted a few rooms inside Nicolai's church, and twice bagged up groceries for families at the Kusko food shelf.

But even after all of that, Kusko still kind of sucked. Doing the "right thing" was hard work. In my off time, I'd have preferred reading, napping, mushing, or beating Finn's ass in Madden football. I still couldn't wait to move back to Anchorage, but I'd decided to stick it out for my full year. Until it was over, I was just going through the motions, regretting the day I handed Yute Cargo most of my marijuana earnings for that stupid two-thousand dollar nonrefundable deposit.

"Yeah, I guess it feels good," I said. "Last week, when I handed a bag of groceries to a poor old man, he gave me a hug."

"That's what it's all about," Taylor said, getting up. She walked to the kitchen. "Want to bake cookies?"

"What kind?" I said, rising to my feet. I was starving.

Taylor opened the fridge and pulled out a tube of sugar-cookie dough. She stripped away the wrapping and used a spoon to press down on the tube, popping it open. She opened a drawer beneath the range, grabbed a cookie sheet, and set the oven for three hundred fifty degrees.

"What are you up to tomorrow?" she asked, rolling a wad of dough between her palms.

"I might see what Finn's doing."

Taylor never asked about Finn selling weed, but she knew he did. After she and I patched things up in early September, I came clean about my friendship with him. I told her I hadn't wanted her to know I was friends with Finn because I didn't want her to think I smoked weed.

"What's Finn like, anyway?"

"He's a funny kid," I said. "One of the coolest dudes I've ever met, actually. I saw where he grew up when I was in St. Mary's for a story. Didn't look so great. He doesn't complain about anything, though."

"I don't know what to think of him," Taylor said. "But, still, it's cool that you're friends with Finn. He probably needs a good influence."

*Am I a good influence?* I wondered.

"And I think you have to love people no matter who they are or what they do," she said.

"Really?" I replied. "But, like, didn't you disown Bristy and Hope after you first caught them smoking weed?"

Taylor's face went from a pleasant grin to a slight

sneer. "What?"

"A year or two ago, when you first busted them. Hope said you stopped talking to her and Bristy for a while."

"And?" Taylor asked.

"And, is that unconditional love?"

"First off, that was a long time ago," Taylor began, dropping a wad of dough to illustrate her displeasure. "I'm more mature now — mature enough to know that in busting Bristy and Hope this latest time, I'm not going to flat-out disown them because of it."

"Didn't it piss you off that Bristy and Hope had been lying to you?" I asked.

"Of course," Taylor said. "But now that the truth is out there, we've been able to talk about it. I told them it was sad that they're basically choosing drugs over our friendship. They said they're just having fun and I'm being a bitch about nothing. They stated their case, and I stated mine. In the end, I'm just trying to be the bigger person."

I broke eye contact with Taylor and started rolling the last glob of cookie dough. I hadn't meant for the conversation to blow up. I'd just been trying to keep it real.

"Look, Eddie," Taylor said in a softer tone, closing the oven door. "I've spent most of my life with Bristy and Hope. I'm willing to ride out this storm, even if I have to keep them at arm's length for a while. I don't want to lose their friendship forever."

I folded my arms and smiled. "Well then, you're a better person I am."

"It's not that hard," Taylor said sarcastically.

I flicked her off and asked, "Is this our first fight?"

"Yes, my friend," Taylor said with a grin. "And you lost."

# CHAPTER 22

# INDEBTED

Ten months into my tour in Kusko, and Dalton still hadn't bought a new computer for me to use. I flipped on the boxy relic, knowing I'd have to kill five minutes while it booted up.

I took off my red coat and slung it over my office chair. The snow on the arms and shoulders of the coat had begun to melt into droplets of water. It was seven a.m. now, and a storm hadn't stopped dumping since yesterday afternoon. The weather forecast called for whiteout conditions until at least sunrise, which was at around ten in the morning.

I had the office to myself because Dalton was home in bed with a stomach bug. He said he'd felt fine going to bed, then woke up at two a.m. with it coming out both ends. As I poured water into the coffee percolator on the fax machine table near my desk, I noticed a manila envelope in the mail tray next to my computer. Dalton must have dropped it there after I left the office the night before.

This qualified as an exciting development. I never got mail. I sat back down at my desk, grabbed the envelope, and studied it. The return address said University of Anchorage. I ripped it open and pulled out two sheets of paper that were stapled together. The top sheet was a letter, printed on University of Anchorage letterhead.

My eyes bugged out when I started reading. My student loans didn't cover my first semester, and after a bunch of policy mumbo jumbo, there was this: "Students are ineligible to enroll in additional classes until the tuition fees associated with the failed semester have been paid in full. Successfully completed semesters will not be billed until after graduation."

The letter ended with a bullshit apology from a student loans administrator named Ernie Dickmeyer, who wrote that the college didn't notify me earlier because they couldn't find me until "Mr. Westbrook alerted us to your whereabouts in Kusko."

I flipped the letter over to the second page — a bill for almost four thousand dollars.

\* \* \*

Lunchtime loomed, and I still hadn't finished my story. I was too overwhelmed to think straight. *Four thousand dollars*, I kept thinking. *Four thousand dollars.*

With every extra minute that passed, I'd be working that much later. My two stories had to be finished that day because I'd be taking the following day off work to spend Thanksgiving with Taylor and her folks. Instead of turkey and cranberry sauce, Taylor's dad was supposed to cook a white-fronted goose, while she and her mom prepared a jam-like spread made of tundra berries they'd picked earlier in the fall. I'd been excited for my first Thanksgiving in the YK Delta — and with Taylor, to boot — but that all went away. *Four thousand dollars,* I thought again and again.

For another hour I did my best to pound out the first story, but it was hard. As I read my notes from the last city council meeting, I thought of my new debt anywhere the notes included a number. One chicken-scratch line read: "Three hundred arrests in 2010," but what I read was, "Four thousand arrests in 4000."

Eventually, at almost two p.m., I finished the story. It opened like this:

## Drug, Alcohol Busts Increase 50 Percent

By Eddie Ashford
Staff Writer / Delta Patriot

KUSKO, Alaska — Local police say they've arrested 50 percent more people for drugs and alcohol in 2010.

Sheriff Buzz Berger, speaking at the Kusko City Council's Nov. 25 meeting, reported that the number of suspects cuffed for bootlegging or drug possession has eclipsed 300 arrests in 2010, up from about 200 arrests during the same 11-month period in 2009.

"I'm sick of this (redacted)," Berger said to Kusko mayor Marty McCambly, before unleashing an elaborate tirade of profanity that led several audience members with children to cover their kids' ears. "I have a (redacted) message for all the (redacted) drug dealers and bootleggers out there: you can (redacted) run, but you can't (redacted) hide."

My next story was a sports wrap-up about three high school basketball games — one girls' game, two boys' games — that had been played the night before in village schools in Chevak, Shageluk, and Aniak. After every game, coaches would email the *Patriot* the box scores and a few quotes from themselves and any key players. Sometimes they'd even send photos, which I liked because photos filled pages and required me to write less.

But I couldn't bring myself to start working on that sports story. Stress had been building all day, and I was too frustrated to concentrate anymore. *I'll come in early tomorrow and work on Thanksgiving after all,* I thought.

I burst outside the office, into the four-p.m.-twilight cold, all pissed off. Next to the FJ, I slipped on some ice hidden under a foot of snow and fell onto my back. I would have knocked my head on the ground had the snow not cushioned my fall. I got up and brushed snow off my jeans and coat, even more pissed off.

I got inside the FJ. It was so frigid outside that the truck's engine wouldn't turn over. It only whimpered. I pounded the steering wheel. "START, DAMMIT!"

With a groan, the engine finally started. I backed out and peeled away to Finn's house, in desperate need of somebody — anybody — willing to hear me vent.

I rolled into my driveway, next to Dalton's blue truck. I looked to my right and saw lights on inside Finn's house. I stomped over to his place and opened the front door. "You here, Finn?"

He hollered to come in. I knelt in the entryway to take my shoes off.

"Four fucking grand," I said, untying the laces of my leather boots.

"What?" Finn said from the kitchen. I heard water running.

"I just found out I can't reenroll in college until I pay four thousand dollars," I said, hanging my coat on a wall hook near the door. "I was literally one week away from choosing my classes before the next semester starts in January. Now this."

"Dude, that's a disaster," Finn said sincerely as I sat down on the couch.

Finn stood in front of the kitchen sink, scouring burn stains off the bottom of an iron cooking pot. He wore baggy blue jeans and a red T-shirt that read "Alaska Grown." The text overlapped a cartoonish bushel of green marijuana leaves.

Before I could bitch more, I paused to admire the cleanliness of Finn's house. It was almost too clean. Fresh vacuum tracks streaked across the living room carpet. Every inch of the gray linoleum kitchen floor sparkled, and the shaggy red rug underneath the kitchen table looked almost as good as new. The place smelled like an operating room.

I glanced down at the old black couch upon which I'd situated myself. Somehow, Finn had cleaned all the drool stains and dried pizza sauce off of it.

"What'd you do, rent an upholstery cleaner?" I asked.

"Nah, bro," Finn said, ferociously scrubbing a thick burn mark. "I cleaned the couch with some spray stuff and a brush. Looks good, huh?"

"Yeah, looks good," I said.

He kept working at the sink, so I shifted back to my situation. "Dalton said he can fly me and my truck out around Christmas, but once I get back to Anchorage, I don't know what I'm supposed — "

I stopped talking when I noticed a popcorn bowl full of weed resting in the middle of Finn's kitchen table. I got up from the couch to take a closer look. The bowl practically overflowed with weed, like soda pop poured too fast.

"Geez, Finn," I said. "How much is in there?"

"Just under six ounces."

I didn't understand — Finn had stopped selling weed about two months ago. Not to mention, why did he need so much? Back when I used to sell, he rarely held more than an ounce. Sure, there were times when he possessed two ounces — one for me, one for him. But he never held my ounce for more than a day or two before I took it off his hands.

"Why so much?" I asked.

Finn stopped scrubbing and stepped next to me at the kitchen table. He picked up the popcorn bowl and tossed the buds up and down like they were actual popcorn. "Because I lost my job."

"Shit. When?"

"A few days ago," he said, setting the bowl back down. "I showed up late again. A power surge goofed up my alarm. Total bullshit. I haven't touched weed, or anything, in almost a month."

Finn said he had no choice but to sell full time until he found another job. I understood his dilemma. I'd be freaked, too, about so much uncertainty hanging over my head. In Kusko, they weren't exactly handing out jobs on street corners.

"Is that why you're cleaning house? Because you don't have anything better to do?"

"Yep," Finn said, sitting down at the table. "Makes me feel slightly better about myself, like at least I'm not a *total* fucking loser."

"Call me crazy," I said, "but maybe you wouldn't feel like such a loser if you, I don't know, put on a different shirt?"

I didn't mean to kick Finn while he was down. It was just a lame joke, but he took it personally.

"Whatever, Eddie. If I wanted your opinion, I'd have asked for it."

"Don't get pissed, Finn. I'm just messing with you."

He pulled the bowl of weed closer to himself, grabbed a nug the size of a strawberry, and studied it. "I don't know what to do," he said.

I thought for a moment, then replied, "Maybe you should come to Anchorage with me."

I blurted it out without thinking, but once I'd said it, I saw that it made sense. There were plenty of jobs in Anchorage, or he could join me in college. He could sleep on the couch at Chateau Eagle River as long as he needed while he figured things out.

"I don't know," Finn said.

"You should, dude. Get out of here for a while. Do something different. You can always come back."

I took the bowl of weed between us and shoved it aside. I slid my hand across the table to grab him by the wrist. I wanted him to know I was serious.

He chuckled. "Sorry, bro. This isn't a good time for me to stroke you off."

"I'm not kidding."

"Okay?" Finn said, stretching his arm across the table. "You're freaking me out, Eddie."

I clutched Finn's arm. "I know you grew up in that rundown house Linetta lives in. Between that house, and the fact that you never talk about your family, I'm pretty sure you grew up with some shitty stuff."

Finn stared down at the table, and I squeezed his wrist tightly. He looked up.

"Come to Anchorage," I said. "Start something new. Why not?"

"Maybe," he said, looking away. "We'll see."

CHAPTER 23

# CRIME OF OPPORTUNITY

I woke up just before six a.m. on Christmas Eve
and couldn't get back to sleep. I sprawled across the
bed and stared at the ceiling, listening to Dalton snore
through the wall. But Dalton's log sawing wasn't what
had woken me. During the past two weeks, I'd been
wide awake anytime I opened my eyes after five a.m.,
regardless of whether Dalton snored. I was too excited
to sleep.

Because the countdown had officially begun. I'd
be out of Kusko, for good, in five more days. Dalton
had purchased my airplane ticket and scheduled my
truck to be shipped. My old bed was waiting for me at
Chateau Eagle River. Soon I could start picking away
at my big college bill working a job in Anchorage, or
back in Minnesota — I still didn't know.

All I really knew was that I'd survived. In Kusko.
For one year. Halle-friggin'-lujah.

Every morning in December, I'd been lying awake

and imagining everything I'd do after I landed in Anchorage. First, I'd eat everything on the menu at the first decent restaurant I saw. Then I'd pop inside the nearest ice cream shop for a quadruple-scoop waffle cone. Then I'd go back to the Chateau and take the longest and hottest shower of my life, splashing and frolicking like an overjoyed sea otter, never worrying about running out of water. Then I'd gear up for the welcome-home throw-down R.J. was sure to organize. One night of partying wouldn't hurt.

When I got out of bed to brew a pot of coffee, I walked to the kitchen with a spring in my step. I checked my phone while the coffee brewed. Taylor had texted me the night before, after I'd fallen asleep.

Taylor: "Hey! X-mas Eve festivities start at 5. What time are you coming over?"

I tapped out a reply saying that I'd have to work late and wouldn't get there until six. I finished with: "See you then. You're hot."

I would miss Taylor, and not because of her big bombs, long legs, and snare-drum behind. She'd become a pretty good friend. Granted, I'd still want to cast haymakers at the first ball washer to land her as a girlfriend after I left Kusko. But such is life.

Dalton opened his bedroom door and staggered to the bathroom to take a leak, wearing a T-shirt and boxer briefs. He sniffed the air and caught a whiff of the coffee. "You brew some for me?"

"Got you covered," I said.

I poured myself a cup, sat on the couch, and flipped on the morning TV news. Dalton eventually made his way into the kitchen, explaining he'd be gone all day to help his buddy build four new doghouses.

We had finished the week's edition of the *Patriot* a day early because Dalton wanted to free up his Christmas Eve and Christmas Day, but I still needed to write two stories to help Dalton get ahead for the following week, when I'd be back in Anchorage. I'd planned one about how villagers in Upper Kalskag were without water because the town's well had jammed with ice.

"I'll look for another story in the police blotter," I told Dalton.

"Get to the courthouse early — they close at noon today," he replied. "Thanks for playing hard until the whistle blows. I'll already be busy enough after you leave next week. I still haven't come close to finding your replacement."

"Have you interviewed anybody?"

Dalton sighed and explained that in the past two months, he'd received only three applications. Two of the people accepted other jobs, and the other person never got back to him.

I felt bad for Dalton. I wondered how much longer until he threw up his hands and sold the *Patriot*. After seven years, the paper still only treaded water.

Dalton opened the fridge, pulled out a one-liter carton of cream, and poured some in his coffee. "Are you sure you don't want to stay in Kusko?" he asked.

*Effing positive,* I thought.

"Pretty sure," I said. "I'm ready to get back to civilization."

"But what about that big college bill you can't pay? You could stay here another six months, work it off, and reenroll this summer. I'll give you a raise."

"Thanks, but no can do."

Dalton walked back into his room to get dressed. A few minutes later, he flipped on the outside floodlights and went out to feed the dogs before he left. The sun wouldn't be rising until ten thirty.

For another half hour, I drank coffee and watched TV in my pajamas. I spent most of the time thinking about Finn. He was still on the fence about moving with me to Anchorage. His biggest barrier was the lease on his crappy house, which wouldn't expire for another couple months. In the five weeks since he'd been fired, he still hadn't found a job. A *legal* job, anyway.

I turned off the TV, got up, got dressed, and poured coffee into a thermos to take with me to Finn's house. I thought it would be cool to stop by and brainstorm ideas about how he could get to Anchorage after his lease expired. I bundled up for the short walk. It was seven forty-five a.m., and stars shined in the sky. The temperature couldn't have been above zero.

I didn't want to knock on Finn's door before eight, so I decided to pass the time with Joanie. I walked to her house on a snow trail through the side dog yard. The dogs peeked their heads out of their houses, but they didn't bark — Dalton had fed them. The water he'd poured in their dishes had already frozen.

Joanie's house was near the shed in back. She peeked her head out of her house and smiled. I squatted beside the opening to her house. She shot out like a rocket and ran in circles, kicking up a mixture of snow and dog shit. Then she settled and sat down in front of me.

"Good girl!" I said, scratching the fluffy white fur on her neck.

Then I shuffled behind her doghouse for a game of Who Eats Poop? She got into position at the front of her house. I crouched down, waited a second, and sprung up like a jack-in-the-box. "Who eats poop?" I asked. Joanie barked with delight, explaining in dog language, "I do! *I* eat poop!"

I kneeled down and motioned for Joanie to come. She placed her front paws on my lap and licked my face. "I'll miss you girl," I said, grabbing her by the ears and kissing her cheek.

I left Joanie and made my way to Finn's house. I rapped on his front door. No answer. I waited a moment and then twisted the doorknob. The door was unlocked.

"Finn?" I said through the crack before pushing the door open and going into the entryway. "Anybody home?"

I checked out the living room, kitchen, bedroom, and bathroom. The house, in all its silence and immaculate cleanliness, was empty. So I decided to wait for ten or fifteen minutes and finish my coffee. *Who knows, Finn might show up*, I thought. I took a seat at the kitchen table, where Finn's popcorn bowl sat in the middle, now covered with tin foil. I snatched the bowl and peeled back the foil. Inside, the bowl still brimmed with weed. I figured Finn must have secured a fresh new batch to sell after Kusko Dry Goods denied him a job a few days ago. Finn had said the guy who interviewed him knew his former boss at the airport. He said being blacklisted was a common occurrence in Kusko — if you got fired anywhere, everybody knew why.

I glared at the bowl of weed. *He's got five or six ounces in there,* I thought. *That stuff must be worth . . .*

My conscience became a battlefield.

Part of me said to take the stuff and sell it. Now. If I found a village buyer, I could dump the weed for as much as forty-five hundred, if I was right about the amount he had — and I was pretty sure I was right. I figured I could pay Finn his costs and then split the earnings with him. He could use his cut to get ahead on rent and move with me to Anchorage. I could use my cut to help me get back into classes at the university. I'd still be short of paying the entire four-thousand-dollar bill I owed, but I was almost positive my dad could scrape together the rest, assuming I swore to pay him back. *And Finn might even be happy I sold his weed,* I told myself. He'd have his profits in a matter of hours, not weeks.

The other part of me sounded like an overcrowded room of overbearing parents. I heard my dad say I should leave the weed alone and take responsibility for my actions. I heard Nicolai say not to get fooled into thinking that what is wrong is what is right, that I was one bad decision away from doing something monumentally stupid. I heard my mom say that despite my good intentions, taking Finn's weed would still be stealing.

I muted the lame side of me. *The biggest problem of my life could be solved in just a few hours, with minimal effort,* I thought. *Sure, Finn always said I couldn't sell in villages near Kusko. But whatever. It's one deal.*

I decided to make a phone call and leave the situation to chance. If I didn't like the answers I got,

I'd scrap my idea.

I stood up from the kitchen table, pulled out my cell phone, and dialed information. The operator connected me to a gentleman in Napakiak named Cal Smeaton.

Cal answered after four rings. "Who?" he asked groggily. I must have woken him up.

I told him I was Eddie, the guy he met in October. "I was peeing. You were lighting a cigarette backward."

"Oh, right. Why the fuck are you calling?"

"You said you can always use a whole lot of weed. Is that still true?"

"Shit yeah, it's true."

"I have some, but I'd need to make the delivery soon. I mean, like right now, as soon as humanly possible."

We went back and forth about how much I had and how much I wanted for it. He tried haggling, but finally said he'd probably take it at my price but that he'd need to find a friend to go in on it with him.

"Call me back," I said. "And please be quick."

Then I was all action. I dashed out the front door and ran home to put on my mushing gear. If Cal called back with good news, I wanted a head start. Finn could be home at any minute. I started prepping the dog team as though it were game on. I planted the sled near the shed, at the foot of the snow trail that led to Napakiak, and anchored the ice hook. I harnessed Biff and Joanie and connected them to the gangline.

Twenty minutes passed. Just as I began harnessing Boris, my phone rang. I held Boris between my knees and put the phone to my ear. "That you, Cal?"

"Come on down," he said.

"I'm harnessing my dogs now," I said. "It's eight forty-five. I should be in Napakiak just after ten."

"Ten?" Cal said. "In that case, wait another fifteen minutes before you leave."

"Fifteen minutes? Why?"

I looked back toward my house and Finn's, praying that he or Dalton wouldn't return. I doubted Dalton would be back anytime soon. But Finn was a different story.

"Just wait another fifteen fucking minutes. Let me get ready," Cal said angrily. "You got that?"

He hung up. Waiting awhile was fine, but I'd need to do it out on the tundra, once Kusko city limits were out of view. I resumed harnessing the nine remaining dogs and finished in less than ten minutes. Next, I had to commandeer the weed. I'd saved that for last in case Finn came home while I was wrangling the team.

I clumped over to Finn's place in my bulky winter wear. I opened the front door. "Finn?" I said.

No answer. I took off my boots in the entryway, not wanting to track snow into the house. I rummaged through the wooden chest in the living room, looking for Finn's electronic scale. I found it, placed it on the kitchen table, and started weighing. He had just barely five ounces.

I scoured the kitchen for some one-gallon plastic baggies and found a few under the kitchen sink. I dumped the weed into three of the baggies and shoved them down my jacket.

I stopped just as I was about to walk out the door and wondered whether I should leave a note explaining the situation. Without a note, Finn would freak the moment he realized his weed was gone.

*Nah,* I thought. *I'll let him sweat. When he realizes how much money I made him, he'll forgive me in a hurry.*

I hustled back to the dog yard and crammed the weed into a cinch pack hanging from the handlebars of the sled. I stomped the foot brake into the ground and locked it into place. I walked ten feet behind the sled, dislodged the ice hook, and threw it into the sled before hopping back on and unlocking the foot brake.

"Hike!" I commanded the dogs.

# CHAPTER 24

# THE TUNDRA RUN

The dogs approached the fork in the snow trail, four miles from my house. I commanded Biff and Joanie to veer left onto the trail to Napakiak rather than take the roundabout and head back home. "Haw!" I shouted.

Joanie looked back to me, confused. She'd expected me to yell "Gee!" to steer her and Biff to the right, onto the roundabout. "Haw, Joanie! Haw!"

She and Biff merged the team onto the trail to Napakiak, leading southwest.

We cruised along as the trail unrolled into an endless straightaway. No clouds blocked the rising sun behind us. The dogs barreled toward the pink horizon atop a desolate, treeless landscape that looked like a vast white sheet. The windless day was so quiet, the only sounds I heard were the patter of the dogs' paws on the narrow snow trail and the whooshing runners of the sled. Once again, I'd bundled myself in my favorite red hunting coat, black snow pants, and my heaviest boots.

I saw something ahead in the distance. To my right and far off the trail stood a guy wearing a furry parka, the kind made from animal pelts. He stood knee-deep in snow and clutched a rifle at his side.

I wasn't alarmed. I'd seen random guys with guns in the middle of nowhere plenty of times before. He must have been out for an early hunt.

I checked my watch. *A little after ten a.m.*, I thought. *If I finish this deal fast enough, I can make it to the courthouse before noon.*

I turned my attention back to the trail. I squinted to get a better look at the guy up ahead. He appeared to be raising his rifle. But I didn't see any game anywhere. It looked like he was aiming in my direction. Then I heard the bang of a gunshot.

*Wait, did that dumbass just fire in my direction?* I thought.

I glanced down at myself and at the dogs speeding along. We were all in one piece.

*Holy balls,* I thought. *Close call.*

"Hey!" I hollered, waiving my right arm in the air. "Are you blind? Watch where you're shooting!"

One thing was certain: the guy wasn't hunting small game. The rifle shot sounded way too big for rabbit or ptarmigan. It was the unmistakable crack of a .223, which sounds heftier than a .22, but lacks the bigger boom of calibers .243 and larger.

I didn't understand why he'd be carrying a .223. That round would disintegrate a little animal. And everyone knew the caribou were long gone — the Mulchatna herd was last spotted near the Kilbuck Mountains, in the far east. I'd written a story about it. Maybe he was hunting fox?

Whatever he hunted, he was one hell of a careless shot. He had my full attention. I couldn't take my eyes off him.

I squinted again. It looked like he was shouldering his rifle a second time. I couldn't tell where he was aiming. To be safe, I ducked down and peeked my head above the handlebars.

I heard that crack again, and the earth exploded five feet in front of the team, splashing snow onto the faces of Joanie and Biff.

*My God, he really is shooting at me.*

I snapped to my feet. "Stop shooting!" I shrieked, ten times louder than before. "Stop!"

Adrenaline gushed through my system. My heart pounded in my ears. I was hyper alert, like I'd just chugged a gallon of Red Bull through a beer bong.

*Why is this happening?* I wondered, terrified, scanning the tundra in all directions, looking for someone who could help. *Because of the weed? Is the shooter Cal? Or is the shooter just some wayward lunatic? Or is this about something I'm too rattled to even think of?*

I couldn't hide anywhere. The tundra was so flat, I could practically see the back of my head in the distance.

I couldn't turn us around either. The snow was way too deep off of the trail. The dogs would spend an eternity trudging through that white garbage. I'd need to get off the sled and guide them on foot. We'd be fish in a barrel.

I could only keep going, and pray the shots wouldn't scare my lead dogs. If Joanie and Biff stopped running, the team stopped running. If the team stopped, my life stopped.

By now the shooter stood one hundred fifty yards to my right at two o'clock. He'd have his easiest shots in less than twenty seconds, when he'd be perpendicular to us, cutting his shooting distance to less than one hundred yards. That'd be a layup, no matter if he aimed with a scope or iron sights.

*If the dogs can speed up and get through this stretch of trail, I might just make it,* I thought. *The dickhead with the gun already missed me twice.*

"Hike!" I commanded the dogs. "Hike!"

I felt petrified, pissed off, confused, and frustrated all at the same time. "Fuck, fuck, fuck!" I said to myself out loud.

*Stupid weed,* I thought. *That's what this is about. But why would this guy want to kill me over a few measly ounces?*

The three sacks of pot were tucked inside the cinch pack hanging from the handlebars. I unzipped the cinch pack, pulled out one of the sacks, and held it high in the air. "See this?" I screamed. "You can *have* the weed! Just stop shooting!"

I was certain he could hear me. Sound travels forever on the tundra.

And immediately I deduced that the shooter certainly could hear me. Even at that distance, I could hear him chambering another round.

*BANG!*

Lunchbox, the wheel dog on my right, stumbled and his snout hit the snow. Poor Lunchbox blurted out a squeal and collapsed.

"Fuck you!" I yelled at the shooter. "You killed my dog! You killed Lunchbox!"

No time to grieve. My own life was at stake. I shoved the sack of weed back into the cinch pack and gripped the handlebars tight.

Lunchbox became dead weight, dragging and bouncing behind the team. The ten dogs in front of him continued running because he ran last in line and they didn't see him. But his running mate, Diesel, began to slow. He repeatedly jerked his head to the left, agitated by the extra weight Lunchbox's lifeless body had added to the right side of his collar. "Shake it off, Diesel! Hike!"

I figured the next bullet would hit me. The three shots had gradually gotten closer, which meant the shooter had been using trial and error to determine how far he needed to lead me. Now that he'd killed the dog closest to me, he needed only to aim a few more clicks to his left and I'd be toast.

I crouched down to make myself a smaller target. The shooter stood at three o'clock now, so if he wanted to take me out, this was his big chance. I was practically gift-wrapped.

*BANG!*

He missed again.

Or did he? I was intact, but I heard a yelp. I rose to my feet to assess the damage. My right swing dog, Boris — second in line behind the lead dogs — limped, favoring his back right leg. Drops of blood spilled onto the snow behind him like a trail of bread crumbs.

Despite his injury, Boris managed to scamper on three legs, fast enough to keep up. This didn't surprise me. He was the toughest dog in the pack.

We were still in this. We were down a dog, and our pace had slowed, but we were in it.

Now I hated the guy as much as I feared him. The fuck stick killed one of my dogs and injured another. He would kill more of them if he didn't get me first.

*He has no right to do this*, I thought. *I wish I had a gun to even the fight.*

I eyeballed the shooter. He stood slightly behind us, at four o'clock. With every step the dogs took, we were that much farther away from him. Another seventy-five yards and we'd be home free.

*BANG!*

He missed. By the time he chambered his next round and got another shot off, we might be in the clear.

I took off my right mitten and twisted my body toward the shooter. "Try this on!" I howled, waving my middle finger at him.

He leveled his gun. I ducked again.

*BANG!*

Another miss.

I rose and turned toward the trail, filled with hope. The dogs ran strong. They were tired and panted heavily, like distance runners sprinting the final leg of a mile-long race. But they weren't letting up. I was proud of them.

I faced the shooter one last time. He had yet to connect with a shot from so far away, or at such a crazy shooting angle.

"You can't hit dick!" I yelled with unrestricted fury, certain we were safe.

*BANG!*

Joanie let out a yelp and leaped straight up into the air, like a scared cat. She went limp before she could hit the ground. She landed sideways, and her body slid to a halt.

Every dog in back of Joanie smashed into one another from behind, like a multicar pileup. I heard clanking collars and the crunch of bone-on-bone collisions.

Then I flew headfirst off the sled and landed in the middle of a furry heap of chaos. The dogs were all around me, tangled in the gangline, snapping, growling, whimpering, choking. I covered my face to avoid being bitten.

I swam my way out of the pandemonium. I tripped and fell onto my belly at the front edge of the pile, near Joanie. I crawled up next to her.

She was alive, but barely. Every time she took a breath, a puff of steam spurted out the exit wound near her left shoulder.

Joanie and I lay on our sides, half buried in snow, with our heads next to each other. I looked into her eyes and stroked the puffy white fur on top of her head. At that moment I didn't care about the shooter. I was too concerned about Joanie's life to worry about my own.

Because Joanie wasn't a dog. She was a person. Back home in the dog yard, she'd get so excited to see me that she'd shake her butt with enough force to hip-check a hockey player through Plexiglas. And that smile of hers.

"I'm so sorry, girl," I whispered. "I love you so much, Joanie. You're a good girl. You're such a good girl."

She smiled at me, but life drained from her eyes. Another wisp of steam rose from the hole in her body, then nothing more.

I was defeated. After what had just happened, and what was probably about to happen, I didn't care anymore. If the guy wanted to kill me, so be it. I could do nothing to stop him.

I rolled over in the snow, three feet from the dogs, and found the shooter. He was lumbering in my direction, high-stepping through deep snow, less than a hundred yards away. He wasn't in any hurry. He knew it was impossible for me to run or hide.

The tangled dogs saw the shooter too. They stopped moving and grew silent. They sensed a mortal enemy approaching.

I stumbled to my feet and locked my eyes onto the shooter as he plodded toward me. The rising sun painted the left side of his body pink. He wore a gray sealskin parka, with a bushy hood covering his head and a furry scarf wrapped around his face. He swung his left arm to keep his balance through the snow, gripping his rifle at his right side.

The anticipation was excruciating. I couldn't take it anymore.

"Get on with it, you shit fuck!" I roared in a strange, guttural, hysterical voice I'd never heard myself conjure before. "WHAT ARE YOU WAITING FOR?"

He dropped to one knee and pointed his rifle at me.

Piss cascaded down my legs. My entire body rattled. I shut my eyes, waiting for the shot.

It didn't come.

I opened my eyes. The shooter had resumed trampling toward me through the snow.

*Why didn't he take me out?* I wondered. *He must want to say something to me before he shoots me point-blank, execution style.*

I figured I had thirty seconds to live. I thought about my dad, Max, and Taylor. When they learned I'd been murdered, they'd be just as devastated as they would be baffled. They'd wonder, just as I did, *Why did Eddie have to die?*

I hoped the shooter would tell me what I did to deserve this. That would give me *some* bit of peace, and a clue about the reasons for my demise that my family and Taylor might come to know.

If not, what if the guy never got caught and the case went cold? My family and Taylor would never have answers. They might assume I'd been living a secret life. Their memory of me would be stained.

Even though I kind of had been living a double life in Kusko, I didn't deserve this. The bad things I'd done warranted nothing more than a couple days in the clink, a fine, maybe some community service, and a stern talking to. If I'd known that selling herb would lead to this, I wouldn't have done it. I would have listened a lot closer to Nicolai Vawter when he said that in the end, it all comes back.

The shooter trudged through the snow about forty yards away, taking longer to arrive than I'd originally forecast. Joanie lay motionless a few steps from me, with blood still trickling out of the hole in her lung. The ground beneath her looked like a cherry sno-cone. Biff licked the top of her head, concerned that his best friend wouldn't wake up.

Biff stopped licking and fixed his eyes on the shooter, releasing a low, steady growl. Diesel and Lenny grumbled at the shooter too. The rest of the dogs stared at me, whimpering and whining. It was as though they were looking to me for guidance, waiting for me to take action.

I again glanced at the bodies of Joanie and Lunchbox. Boris sat near Joanie, licking the gunshot wound in his back right leg. I stared at Joanie next to him, my lower lip quivering, wishing I could take back the last hour of my life.

I looked back toward the shooter. He was ten yards away, his rifle still pointed at me, bobbing up and down with each step he took.

*I'm really, actually, surely about to die,* I thought. *This is happening.*

I became desperate. I turned toward the trail in the direction of Kusko, jumping between Lenny and Kuba to make a break for it. But that's as far as I got. I tripped on the gangline connecting the dogs and fell onto my face. When I rolled back over, I was staring down the barrel of a gun, two feet from my eyes. I threw my hands up. "Please don't kill me."

The shooter pointed the gun upward, indicating I should stand up. I did as instructed, while he took three steps backward.

The dogs went silent again, as if they knew they'd die next if they raised too much of a stink.

The shooter stood five feet in front of me. The furry scarf covered most of his face, but I could see his dark blue eyes. They were icier than the sub-zero temperatures and meaner than a wolverine's.

"Turn around," he said bluntly.

This guy wasn't Cal, and he wasn't Native. I could tell that much. A small part of me wondered if he might even be Bronco, but that wasn't possible. I'd never know who he was or why this was happening.

"On your knees," he ordered.

So it was going to be execution style after all.

I dropped to my knees, facing the dogs. They stared at me, motionless, whimpering softly.

"I'm sorry for the bad things I did," I said, attempting to rattle off everything I wanted the world to know before I died. "I'm sorry to you, God. I'm thankful for the nice friends I had. I'm happy for the good things I did. I love my mom. I love my dad. I love — "

The light went dark.

CHAPTER 25

# HEADACHES

For the first few seconds, I couldn't tell if I was alive, dead, conscious, or unconscious. I stopped wondering once I felt pain inside my head. I heard something humming, but I couldn't open my eyes because my eyelashes were frozen together. My left cheek, my chest, and the fronts of my legs felt numb from pressing against the frigid ground. Frozen piss glued my legs and snow pants together. I couldn't feel my fingers or toes.

I pried my eyes open with the backs of my mittens. The sunshine was gone. Snow fell, and I could see only a hundred yards in any direction. I didn't know if that was because of the snowflakes, or because my brain had partially shorted out. I felt as though I were inside a freshly jostled snow globe.

I tried rising to my knees. I collapsed back onto the ground; my icy limbs wouldn't function properly.

My head pounded like house music. I brushed

my right mitten across the back of my cranium. Even through the mitten, I felt a sizeable lump. Touching the lump produced indescribable agony.

I rolled onto my back gingerly. My front side began to warm immediately, feeling like it was being pricked by a thousand needles. I stared up at the gray sky for a while to allow my strength to return. Snowflakes fell on my face, but I couldn't feel them land. The humming grew louder.

Finally, I summoned the strength to rise to my feet. I looked around in every direction, on spaghetti legs. Nothing but flat white tundra, snowfall, and clouds. I could see a full two hundred yards now. But there still wasn't much to see.

My memory of the shooter came rushing back. Until now, my encounter with him hadn't crossed my mind because there were no dogs around — live ones, anyway — to have reminded me of it.

The team was gone, and enough snow had fallen that I couldn't see their tracks. I wanted to know which direction they went on the trail — back to Kusko, or onward to Napakiak.

I replayed the awful episode with the shooter to retrace its events. I bumbled near the trail, looking for any disruption in the snow that might give me a clue to Joanie's and Lunchbox's whereabouts. I kicked around in the snow, and my boot found them. They were buried next to each other under a pile of snow six feet off the trail. The shooter must have cut them from the gangline and tossed them together.

My heart began to throb worse than my head. Seeing the dead dogs sickened me. It was wholly nauseating to think that Joanie and Lunchbox were murdered and tossed aside as if they never mattered. They were good dogs, and I believed they would have been willing to die for me. They deserved better. And I was to blame.

I heard the humming again. The sound wasn't a symptom of getting cracked in the skull with the butt of a rifle. It was man-made.

I looked in the direction of Kusko but didn't see anything. I turned southwest, toward Napakiak, and made out the twinkle of a headlight flickering through the snowfall. I bent over and scooped snow onto Joanie and Lunchbox to cover their bodies before I wobbled back onto the trail toward the snow machine. The driver spotted me and began to slow down. He drove a black Polaris and wore a black snowsuit and yellow full-face helmet, its shield tinted black.

The driver motioned for me to get on the back of his ride, never even stopping completely. He must have known it was an emergency, that there was no time for introductions.

"Kusko!" I shouted above the high-pitched crackling sound of the two-stroke engine.

As we sped away, I looked back at where I last saw Joanie. The tip of her tail poked above the snow.

*Joanie, home!* I thought.

* * *

As Kusko approached in the distance, I pointed over the driver's shoulder, to the right, the southwest side of town. He veered off the trail onto the thick snow, gliding across the tundra like a water-skier on a glassy lake. The sun hung low in the sky, casting golden light onto the flat white landscape. I guessed it was around three o'clock. I'd been out cold for a while. I pointed right again as Dalton's and Finn's houses came into view. A minute later, the driver dropped me off where the tundra met Finn's backyard.

I hoisted myself off the sled, took off my mitten, and shook the driver's hand. "Thank you," I said, trying to catch any hint of his face through the dark helmet shield. He only nodded, then punched the throttle.

I wasn't surprised that the driver never said a word to me. So many fucked up things happened in the YK Delta. Like everyone else, he'd already seen it all.

As quick as the driver sped off, my mind raced way faster. I had a million things to think about, all with one thing in common: I was screwed. Soon, Finn would know I'd lost his weed. Dalton would find out that Joanie and Lunchbox were dead and the rest of his team was — where? I had no idea. Together, the dead dogs and Finn's weed were worth thousands of dollars.

Then again, financials were the least of my worries. The bigger issue: I'd officially become a shady scumbag. A certifiable asshole. A selfish, dodgy bastard. I could kiss goodbye my relationships with Finn, Dalton, and Taylor.

I took a deep breath to collect myself. I glanced at Finn's house and could see the silhouette of him through the big window in his living room. He appeared to be pacing back and forth.

\* \* \*

I arrived at Finn's front doorstep. I heard him yelling inside. I looked to my left and saw that Dalton's pickup wasn't in our driveway. *He doesn't know about the dogs yet,* I thought.

When I knocked on Finn's door, he opened it while screaming obscenities into his cell phone and motioned for me to come in, never taking his voice off the gas. "Don't give me that shit. You fucking know something!" he roared into the phone.

I took my boots and jacket off and wobbled toward Finn's couch. As I walked past his bathroom, I glanced at my reflection in the mirror and saw terrible things. My face was beet-red, ice crystals hung off my eyebrows, and globs of frozen snot stuck to my cheeks. I looked like I'd just walked across Siberia and back.

I flopped down on the couch. Finn, wearing a heavy brown sweater and blue jeans, paced around the kitchen table, fuming. The person on the line wouldn't stop fighting him. "Fuckin' suck it, nerd!" Finn shouted, throwing a saltshaker across the room. "Next time I call, you better have answers! Got that?"

Finally, he hung up in a huff. He couldn't find anything else to throw, so he chucked his phone. It bounced off the couch cushion next to me and smacked my thigh. I tossed the phone back to him.

"Sorry," Finn said. He sat down, propped his elbows up on the kitchen table, then put his head in his hands and sighed. "Eddie, whatever this is about, I can't handle it right now."

*Here goes nothing,* I thought.

"I know you can't, Finn," I said, mustering courage. Finn dropped his hands from his face and looked at me. "Why do you look like a frozen shit-cicle?"

"Listen closely," I began, calmly and deadly serious, like an army officer about to tell a wife that her husband was killed in action. "I'm in a lot of trouble. And you're all I've got. I need you to be cool."

His curious look morphed to rage. "You stole my weed," he said, swallowing loudly.

"Yes," I replied.

"And you sold it in a village near Kusko."

"Tried to. Yes."

"I specifically told you never to sell around here."

"Yes."

"But yet you did. And you did it with *my* weed."

"Yes. And the weed was stolen from me."

Silence. Except the ticking sound of the clock above the kitchen sink.

Finn palpitated in his chair, anxiously, like a rodeo bull itching to break out of a bucking chute.

He couldn't contain himself any longer. "You motherfucker!" he screamed, kicking away his chair and charging toward me.

He picked me up and slammed me against the wall. Before impact, I tilted my head down to protect the lump. Whatever pounding he was about to inflict, I deserved. Finn grabbed a fistful of the front of my shirt and cocked his right arm, ready to punch me in the face.

Time seemed to pause. I got lost in Finn's snarled expression. In his crazy eyes I saw the ripple effects of the bad decisions I'd made. I pictured Dalton. He'd probably have to sell some valuables to buy new dogs. He'd spend hundreds of hours — time he didn't have — on training them. I pictured my dad. He'd wonder where he went wrong raising me. He'd blame himself for working so much after my mom died. I pictured my mom. Somewhere, she was ashamed. I saw Finn before me. I pictured him selling more drugs to make up for what I'd done. He'd get caught, go to jail, and lose everything. He'd get out of jail, not find work, and repeat the same process. I saw myself. I didn't know who I was anymore. I did right, and I did wrong. I didn't know how to always do right. I had no identity. I was all over the map.

Finn held his fist there, cocked and ready, but seemed locked in his own spiraling thoughts over whether he should drive that fist into my face.

"I'm sorry, Finn," I said, my voice docile and earnest. "Please don't hit me. I need you right now. I need your help."

He unloaded his punch, but it landed on the wall next to my head. He retracted his fist and punched the wall three more times in quick succession.

\* \* \*

We didn't know where to begin. Under different circumstances, I'd have left his house so we could both decompress. But I didn't have that option. I had nowhere to go. Finn retreated to the kitchen table, and I went back to the couch.

I blurted the first thing that came to mind. "This is the worst thing I've ever done. I'm going to make it right."

"You're damn right you're going to make it right."

Silence again until Finn finally spoke up. "So, then, what happened?"

I told him everything: I'd wanted to sell the weed and split the earnings with him. A guy shot at the dogs and me. I thought I was going to die. Joanie and Lunchbox were dead. The other dogs were missing. Finn had an I-told-you-so look on his face during my entire story.

When I finished, he said, "Now you know why I said not to sell in villages near Kusko. That territory is spoken for, and if you mess with it, you get trouble."

"I know you said that, but I didn't know it'd be a matter of life and death."

"We sell weed, dumb shit," he replied. "People in this line of work don't fuck around. You should have known that."

He gave me the whole story then, even poured himself a bowl of generic frosted flakes as he talked. My friend with the gun had been his dealer — the guy he bought from and, in a one-degree-removed way, the guy who'd been supplying my deliveries to the distant villages. Finn said the guy was the exclusive seller in all six nearby villages, from Napakiak on up to Akiak — all of which didn't absolutely require air travel from Kusko. The guy didn't mind supplying Finn because the Kusko market was too big for him alone. He didn't care if I sold in far-off villages because he never traveled to them. But the villages near Kusko, those were his babies.

"Why would he shoot at me when he'd already

made his money off the same weed I was holding?" I asked.

"He didn't know you'd lifted my weed," Finn said. "For all he knew, you were a new dealer moving in on his turf."

But, I wondered, how could he have known the exact moment I'd be traveling to Napakiak? Less than two hours had passed between the time I called the buyer and the time I left Kusko with the dogs.

Finn shoveled up another mouthful of cereal. "Remember when that VPSO in Russian Mission almost busted you?"

"Yeah."

"Just like Bronco had connections, this guy does too. I'm sure your guy told my guy what was going on. In return, my guy gave your guy a free sack of smoke for his loyalty. To sell weed out here, you need strong networks in place."

I paced the room, attempting to warm myself. The house couldn't have been warmer than fifty degrees. "But why would he kill the dogs?"

"To send a message. He wanted to give you a good scare to make sure you never tried selling in one of his villages again. I know how he rolls. Last winter, he shot out a guy's four-wheeler tires when the dude tried selling in Kwethluk."

I told Finn it seemed more like the guy wanted me dead, because I easily could have frozen to death. I'd been knocked out, in the sub-zero cold, for who knows how long. Another hour or two and maybe I'd have died.

"Wrong," Finn said. "He wasn't going to let you freeze. In fact, I'd bet money the guy who gave you a ride here was him. Black snow-machine? Yellow helmet?"

After Finn finished his last spoonful of cereal and drank the milk from the bowl, I asked if he might have an idea where the dogs were.

"You're on your own with that one," Finn said, wiping milk from his chin. "But I'm sure you'll find out soon enough."

Thinking of Dalton, I went to the window by Finn's front door and looked outside. His truck was parked in the driveway next to mine. Either he knew the dogs were missing, or he figured I'd taken them for a run.

"Dammit, Finn," I said. "Dalton has no idea I ever sold weed. I can't believe I have to go have this conversation with him."

"I know," Finn said from inside the kitchen. "Total Pearl Harbor job."

"I need to call Taylor," I said, staring outside. "Where's my phone?"

Finn picked it up from the floor, where apparently it had landed during our scuffle.

"She's in your recents, huh?" Finn said. "It's ringing. Come and get it."

I took the phone from Finn and sat back down on the couch. When I looked back at him, red and blue lights flashed in through the window across his face.

"Oh shit," I said.

"Oh shit, is right," he replied, rushing over to peer out the window. "You didn't get the weed from me, Eddie. Don't go dragging me into this."

I had the phone to my ear, but still couldn't hear it ringing. I was too hypnotized by the flashing lights. I thought I'd be able to hash everything out with Dalton, just him and me, but now cops were involved.

"Hello," I heard Taylor say.

I was too stunned to talk.

"Hello?" Taylor asked. "Eddie, is that you? Did you butt-dial — "

I hung up and said to Finn, "Whatever happens, I might need you to call Taylor again later."

\* \* \*

When I stepped outside, a wash of frigid air scraped at my face. The snowfall had lightened. It was starting to get dark. Dalton stood in his driveway bathed in flashing lights, talking to Sheriff Buzz at the front of a beat-up squad car.

As I approached I realized Buzz was giving Dalton the third degree.

"But they're *your* motherfuckin' mutts, Dalton," I heard him say above the idling of his police cruiser, his mullet curls swaying in the breeze. "There was more marijuana in the sled than a goddamned Cheech and Chong movie. Can you blame me for questioning you?"

"I'm telling you, Buzz, I had nothing to do with this," Dalton said.

"Maybe so," Buzz said. "We'll still need to get to the bottom of this shit down at the station."

Up close, Dalton looked mortified. Half of him must have been floored by being questioned for something he hadn't done, the other half stunned by the fact that his dogs had been taken.

"What's going on here?" I asked as Buzz stared down Dalton.

"Eddie!" Dalton said. "I thought you'd taken the dogs out mushing. Then Buzz showed up. He said the VPSO in Napakiak found ten of my dogs abandoned near the village, with a bunch of marijuana in the cinch pack. Two of my dogs are missing. I can't believe this is happening."

I had two choices — fess up or play stupid. If I played stupid, nothing would happen to me in the short term. It might be days before the crime came back to me, giving me enough time to leave Kusko. If I confessed, I'd take it in the ass. It occurred to me that if I was going to play dumb, I should have been acting surprised.

"What? How could two dogs be missing?" I blurted. "Who would take the dogs?"

"We don't know, Eddie," Dalton replied somberly. "This is crazy."

Nicolai Vawter pulled into his driveway and shut off the headlights of his red pickup. He got out and rushed over, wearing a black woolen coat over his Sunday best. Soon he'd be leading his Christmas Eve service. "Everything okay?" he asked.

Dalton asked Nicolai, "Did you see anybody take my dogs?"

Nicolai said no, he'd been gone all day.

"I'll ask the questions, Dalton," Buzz chimed in. "No more bullshitting. Let's get on with this."

Buzz turned Dalton around and pushed him toward the back of the squad car. I got out of the way as Buzz opened the car door, shoved Dalton in, and slammed the door shut. All I had to do was shut up and let Buzz drive away. Buzz dropped the car into reverse, and the tires of his police cruiser squeaked through the snow.

I watched the police car backing up, then looked at Nicolai. I looked back at the police car, then at Nicolai again. Every time I looked at Nicolai, I felt more ashamed.

The angel on my shoulder couldn't be muzzled any longer. I ran toward the sheriff's car and waved my hands in the air.

"Stop!" I shouted, blinded by headlights.

Buzz hit the brakes, rolled down his window, and hung his head out. "You got something to say, sport?"

As I walked toward Buzz, I remembered when my dad told me how he wondered all through his twenties whether or not he was a man, as if there were some specific incident that needed to happen in order for that status to become official. In the wisdom of his thirties, he came to realize that he gradually became a man sometime in his late twenties, when he began making a concerted effort to do the right thing and take responsibility for his actions. My life was playing out differently than my father's. I had to become a man right this second, at nineteen.

"Dalton didn't do it, Buzz. I did." I spoke to him through the open window. I didn't lean over. I didn't want to see Dalton's face. "That was my weed. I got his dogs killed. I'm responsible."

# CHAPTER 26

# SILENT NIGHT

I had always envisioned jail cells as being cold and dank. But this one, inside the Kusko Sheriff's Department, was blazing hot. Underneath my cot, a heating vent kicked out warm air nonstop. My throat felt itchy and dry, like I was being gagged with cotton balls. Only an inch of water occupied the plastic milk jug at my side. I needed to ration it for the long night ahead.

I stripped down to my boxer briefs, lay on my bare back, and stared up at the fifteen-foot-high ceiling. The cot, slippery from my sweat, was a torn-up mat suspended two feet off the ground by an iron frame.

The concrete blocks of the ten-by-ten cell were painted mint green. In the corner opposite my cot rested a stainless-steel latrine that looked like an airplane toilet. On the wall above the commode, somebody had etched, "Don't look here, the joke is in your hands."

The last time I saw a clock it was eleven p.m., and Buzz was sweating me out in the visitation room just outside my cell. He'd brought the thunder for over an hour, demanding to know where I got the weed and why two of Dalton's dogs were missing. I didn't budge. I straight-up told Buzz I wasn't going to give up that information.

I thought Buzz would have taken it easier on me since we had some history together, but he didn't. He was a total dick. "You know that by not talking, you're going to be even more fucked than you already are, right, sport?" he roared, two inches from my face, pelting me with spit droplets.

"Yes," I said, emotionless.

All I gave him were one-word answers, or no answers at all. If I would have told Buzz anything about the shooter or otherwise, there was a chance he could trace things back to Finn.

I refused to compromise Finn. I would take this on the chin for him.

I didn't even want a lawyer. I'd already confessed to everything and was content with telling a judge the weed was mine, that I was to blame for the dogs, that that's all he needed to know. I'd take full responsibility for this. That's what men do.

Granted, taking responsibility would suck. I recalled when Dalton and I drove by the Western Alaska Correctional Facility, located two blocks down the road, the day I moved to Kusko. He said the place was filled with three hundred of the YK Delta's worst assholes. Now *I* was one of the assholes. Surely I was headed to the big house.

The fact it was Christmas intensified my misery. A year ago, I was sipping virgin eggnog with R.J. and our Chateau Eagle River host parents, eating spiral-cut honey ham with all the fixings, sitting at a long dinner table with a centerpiece of bright red poinsettias. Two years ago, I was at home — ah, home — with my dad and Max, eating Swedish meatballs, opening presents, reminiscing about my mom.

Taylor wasn't an easy pill to swallow, either. She must have been worried about me, unsure of why I didn't show up at her house, maybe angry at me. I couldn't imagine what our next — and likely final — conversation would be like.

I shut my eyes, wanting the world to go away. In my mind I saw red and white dots pulsating gently to the sound of my fingers tapping my stomach. My fingers went still as the dots gave way to rainbow-colored blobs swirling around, slowly, like lava.

\* \* \*

Somebody thump, thump, thumped on my cell door, and I opened my eyes.

"Ashford! Get your ass up!"

My throat was so dry I couldn't speak. I chugged the last bit of water in my jug. "Coming," I replied, putting on my T-shirt and overalls.

Buzz opened the door as I finished fastening the second strap over my shoulder. "What time is it?" I asked.

"Just past eight o'clock."

"Geez, Buzz — is your shift ever going to end?"

"Shut your face, sport," he said, not going for my attempt at friendly small talk. "Someone's here to see you. You've got five minutes."

I walked outside my cell and sat at a black metal table in the center of the visitation area. Five doors surrounded me — four to holding cells like mine, one to an intake room. Through a thick bulletproof window in the door to the intake room I saw the blurry, distorted image of Nicolai waiting to enter.

Buzz opened the door and let him in. Nicolai still wore the navy blue suit and Christmas tie he'd been wearing last night. I wondered about the sermon he'd given. At the end of it, he and the congregation must have prayed for the lost, imbecilic souls of people like me.

Nicolai sat down across from me as Buzz made his way out. "Don't make any physical contact," Buzz warned. "I'll be watching on the monitor."

Nicolai glared at me from beneath raised, worry-filled eyebrows.

"Merry Christmas," I said cheerily, trying to break the ice.

He didn't respond. I could tell what Nicolai was thinking: I'd crossed the threshold of making one bad decision that led to my doing something monumentally stupid.

"Nicolai, I know everything you're about to tell me, so don't bother. I know what I did was wrong. It's the biggest mistake of my life. I'll learn from it and move forward."

"I think what you did was terrible," he said.

"Is that what this is going to be? Come visit Eddie in jail so you can make me feel shittier than I already feel?"

I'd never sworn in front of Nicolai before. It almost felt good, considering I had no comeback to anything he was about to say.

"That's right, Mr. Pastor. I said 'shit.' I also know how to say twat waffle and chode yodeler."

He wasn't amused. "Stop acting like a child."

"Then start treating me like an adult. Like I told you a second ago — I know. Whatever you were going to say, I already know. What I need right now is some positivity. That's supposed to be your forte."

Nicolai sighed in frustration. "Can I finish?"

"Fine," I replied. "Finish."

"What you did was terrible," he said. "But in the end you did the right thing, and I'm proud to know you."

"Oh," I said dumbly.

"You proved who you are when you took ownership of the problem you created. You had the mettle to fess up to what appears to be a fairly messy crime," he said. "Your friend, Finn, could learn something from you. With any luck, he'll come to understand that turning his life around won't happen without making difficult decisions."

I'd never realized Nicolai knew anything about Finn. I'd never seen the two of them talk.

"What do you know about Finn?" I asked.

"I see a lot of cabs pull in and out of his driveway." Nicolai looked at me and raised his eyebrows. "I understand the reason for the coming and going."

"Oh, right," I said.

I told Nicolai that, actually, Finn had been making progress the last few months, that he was probably already a better person than me.

"Not to mention," I continued, "we're probably not friends anymore. Without getting into the details, let's just say that I totally screwed him. I hope he forgives me."

Nicolai perked up. "From your mistake, I believe Finn can learn a valuable lesson in forgiveness."

"What do you mean?"

Buzz opened the intake door. "Time's up!"

Nicolai and I looked at Buzz. Over his shoulder, I saw Finn waiting to come inside.

"But what did you mean about a lesson in forgiveness?" I asked.

Buzz blurted, "I said, time's up!"

Nicolai rose to his feet. "We'll talk later. I have things to tell you."

Nicolai and Finn brushed shoulders in the doorway but didn't acknowledge each other.

Finn sat down across from me but didn't look me in the eye. He wore a black sweatshirt and the same blue jeans as last night. I couldn't read his mood.

"I called Taylor for you," he said.

"What did you say to her?" I asked, wondering if I should be relieved or panicked.

According to Finn, he'd told Taylor I was safe but in some trouble, and when she hounded him for details, he kept his mouth shut.

"Then she got pissed and hung up," Finn said.

At least Taylor knew I was safe. For the first time in twenty-four hours, I felt happy about something.

"I called your dad, too," Finn said, proud to have gone above and beyond.

"Nice, dude," I said, relieved that at least my dad understood why I hadn't called him on Christmas Eve. "But what'd you say?"

Finn said he couldn't help but leak some — but not all — of the details of my predicament.

"I said you were in jail," Finn said. "When your dad asked why, I said you'd have to tell him. I told him not to worry, that you weren't hurt."

"Then what?" I asked.

"Your dad gave me a message for you. He said, 'Figure it out.'"

I nodded.

"Your brother had a message for you too," Finn added.

"Yeah? What'd Max say?"

"He said, 'Dumbass.'"

Finn laughed, but it was halfhearted.

*This is Christmas,* I thought. Christmas behind bars, being visited by my Sucktown friends — a pastor and a pothead. Maybe he was an ex-pothead now. I was relieved to have visitors on Christmas and grateful people still cared about me. I didn't want to think about all the trouble ahead.

"I appreciate your visit," I told Finn.

"No worries," he said. "But I haven't forgiven you yet. How am I supposed to pay rent?"

Excellent question. I told him I didn't know, that I'd try to figure out a way to repay him.

"What I do know," I said, "is that whatever happens, you still need to stop selling weed.

After dealing all summer, I have a clearer picture of where that life will get you."

Finn laughed again, this time sounding resentful. "A moral lesson from you? Look at you, Eddie. You're in jail for — wait for it — selling weed. You're the dumbass, not me. Not to mention, I'm done selling the stuff once I find a job, or move to Anchorage, or whatever the hell happens."

I couldn't argue. Finn sat back in his chair with his arms folded. But I asked him what would happen if he didn't find a job, or if he got a job but was fired again.

"Maybe I'll sell again, maybe I won't," he replied. "I'll do what I have to do. At least I'm not smoking anymore."

"I hope it stays that way," I said, "because you were on your way to becoming your parents."

Finn's face darkened, and he glared at me.

"You don't know shit about my parents," he said.

Buzz opened the door. "Time's up, girls!"

Buzz led Finn to the door to the intake room. As Finn walked through, he raised the backs of his hands to the sides of his head and flashed me the double-finger without turning around.

Just before the door closed behind him, I heard him say, "Suck it, nerd."

# CHAPTER 27

# TOUGH CALL

A rubber band, perhaps dropped and forgotten by a previous occupant, ended up on the floor of my jail cell, and I was happy to spot it in the corner. The entertainment value it provided was significant. For hours I lay on my cot pointing the band at the same mint-green cement block across the room, seeing how many times in a row I could hit it. The record stood at forty-one.

The heat finally got turned down inside my cell, thank God. My situation still bordered on the unbearable. Outside of the rubber band, I had nothing to do. No book to read. No harmonica to play the blues. I napped, snapped the rubber band, and thought.

I suspected it must have been getting close to lunchtime, but I remained spread out on my cot and contemplated everything in my life that had led to me landing in jail. I launched the rubber band. That made thirty-eight.

Between my botched weed delivery and being locked up, I felt like my life had been in shambles for ages. In reality, it'd been less than three days.

Earlier in the morning, on this second full day of jail, I'd finally gotten answers about what my future could hold. Buzz said I might be able to go before a judge on Monday, depending on how many other cases were on the court docket. That list could be long, Buzz added, because a lot of people got hammered on Christmas and caused trouble.

*Forty-one,* I thought as the rubber band smacked the concrete block, dead center.

I retrieved the band, lay back down, and cocked the band, anxious to break my personal best. I rested the band on the tip of my pointer finger and pulled it back, and the band snapped, zipped toward my face, and hit me just below the eye.

Then I wrapped the broken band around my finger, off and on, off and on. Back to having nothing to do. I rested my head on the cot and stared above. By now I had memorized every crack and blemish on the ceiling.

*I couldn't even handle moving to Alaska and going to college,* I thought. *What made me think I could handle Kusko?*

I recalled what my Ethics professor, Dr. Lavin, had said during one of her lectures.

"Look around you," she said, wearing a headset, speaking to a nearly full University of Anchorage auditorium. "Where you are, right now, is the product of all the decisions you have ever made."

That was the only class I almost didn't fail; it was at three o'clock in the afternoon.

I sat up on my cot. Doing so disrupted the air enough that I caught a whiff of myself. I reeked. I hadn't showered since Monday night. My underwear clung to my jock, all sticky and gross.

I wondered what my life would be like in a year. Would I be in jail or a work camp or some damn thing like that? Would I be free? If I were free, would I be living in Alaska or Minnesota?

*Not Alaska,* I thought. *I'm done with this state.*

I recalled some comments Nicolai had made in September while I helped him paint rooms inside his church. As we worked, I'd admitted to him that I'd had problems in Anchorage and that I didn't like Kusko.

"Remember, Eddie, you can't outrun your mind," he said. "Learn to bloom where you're planted."

\* \* \*

I awoke to pounding on my cell door. The deep thumps hung in the room like an echo chamber.

"Hands out of your pants, Ashford!" Buzz said through the door. He opened the door and set a red lunch tray on the floor.

"Whatever," I said, rising from the cot. I walked four steps and picked up the tray.

"Eat fast," Buzz said. "My shift's about to end. I need a damned nap."

I'd found out Buzz worked three sixteen-hour shifts per week, splitting each shift between his patrol car and the jail.

Today's lunch: chicken thighs, green beans, and mashed potatoes, with no eating utensils. For breakfast I'd been served oatmeal, also without utensils. That meal had gotten so messy, dried oats still stuck to the insides of my fingers.

"You were right not to give me a spoon, Buzz. I would have dug my way out of here."

"Watch it, smart ass. Eat your grub now."

Buzz started closing the door. I piped up before he could shut it. "Any chance I could use the phone for a quick minute?"

"Nope, no chance. You already used your call."

I had made a call to Dalton the night I landed in jail, but he didn't answer. I wondered where else he possibly could have been on Christmas Eve.

"Please?" I asked.

"Let me think about it again," Buzz said. "No."

What a prick. I really wanted to call Taylor.

"Hey, Buzz, remember when I helped you bust Bronco?" I asked. "Remember how I risked my life, and how if you had shown up a minute later I might have been killed, and how you always wanted to nail Bronco, and how I'm the only reason you were able to do it?"

Buzz cocked his head sideways.

"Remember when I asked to use the phone a second ago?"

He nodded.

"Can I now?"

He stroked his chin and thought about it. "All right, captain skinny dick. You can make your call. Two minutes."

Buzz led me into the visitation area, next to a black rotary phone mounted to the wall by the door to the intake room. He sat down at the metal table while I dialed. I didn't care if he heard my conversation with Taylor.

Funny, I wasn't even that nervous to call her. I'd been through so much in the last couple days, it's like my emotions had developed calluses. I couldn't feel much of anything, good or bad.

I dialed.

"Oh my gosh!" Taylor said. "What happened? Are you okay?"

"I only have two minutes, so I'll need to boil this down," I said.

I told her I did something really stupid, that I'd be in court a few days from now. I didn't know what the judge would throw at me, but I doubted it'd be good.

When Taylor asked what I did, I said I didn't have enough time to get into it.

"Wrong answer," she said. "Tell me."

I sighed. What could I say other than the truth?

"I, well, the deal is I tried selling some weed, then some stuff happened, then I turned myself in. I was going to put the money toward reenrolling in college."

I held my breath. I knew the idea of my selling weed would be just as shocking to Taylor as it was to Dalton. I feared the next minute of my life.

Taylor gasped. "Where did you get it?"

"Where'd I get the marijuana?"

Buzz joined the conversation. "Yeah, Ashford. Where'd you get the marijuana?"

"Sorry, Taylor," I said, shaking my head at Buzz. "I can't say right now. But think about it."

"Oh right," she said.

I told Taylor there were some things she didn't know about me, things that happened over the summer. But I swore that it was all in the past.

"It's killed me having to hide anything from you," I said. "But I was worried that if I told you, you wouldn't want to be friends anymore."

Buzz pointed at his watch and mouthed, "Thirty seconds."

"Half a minute, Taylor," I said. "Please tell me what you're thinking."

"I'm thinking I don't know who you are."

"Don't say that! This is me, Taylor. It's always *been* me. But I had to make some mistakes in order to understand how to be the person I need to become."

Taylor remained silent. Buzz mouthed, "Fifteen seconds."

I took a deep breath. I had never outright told Taylor how much I liked her. She knew I thought she was hot, but little more. If this was going to be the last time I ever spoke with her, I wanted her to know.

"I would have stayed in Kusko for you," I said.

"What?"

"If you would have become my girlfriend, I'd have stayed. I'd have done anything to be with you. I'd do anything now. I've never liked a girl more."

Buzz tiptoed toward me with his index finger held high, smiling a meddling smile, threatening to hang up the phone.

"Five seconds, Taylor."

"I thought you were a man, Eddie. But a man doesn't — "

The line went dead.

# CHAPTER 28

# JUDGMENT

My sixth day in the clink. I wanted a teardrop tattooed below my eye. Not because I'd killed a person, but because I'd murdered my chances of living any kind of normal life in the foreseeable future. Last I talked to Buzz, he said I could be looking at as much as a couple years for the weed, plus an extra year for the dogs, but since I didn't have any prior offenses, he thought I might get the weed knocked down to six months or so. Still, with the dogs, that could be well over a year in prison.

It was confounding to think I could be locked up that long, and worse knowing Bronco would be one of my peers if the judge hit me with a long sentence. Bronco was inside the big prison down the road. I bet he knew half the inmates and counted them as friends. I'd be a rabbit thrown into a cage of wolves.

Someone rapped on my cell door. I heard Buzz's muffled voice say through the door, "It's go time, Ashford."

I stood up from my cot and put on my shoes. I no longer wore my smelly T-shirt and overalls. Two days prior, I'd traded them for an orange jumpsuit. I didn't mind the disgrace of wearing the jumpsuit because the stink of my other clothes was even more humiliating.

Buzz paraded in. "Turn around, kid. You know the drill."

I placed my hands behind my back. "What time is it?" I asked.

"Noon," Buzz said.

After he cuffed me, he led me outside to his squad car in the frigid December air. I shivered in the back seat, without a jacket.

Just as the vehicle began to warm, we pulled up to the courthouse.

Buzz pushed me in through the front door of the building, where Misty Livermont stood behind the front desk.

"Eddie?" she asked, perplexed. "I saw your name in the police record. I thought it was a misprint."

I was embarrassed, but I did well to mask it. "Long story," I said assuredly, trying to maintain the confidence I'd need in front of the judge. "Will my name print in the police blotter?"

"This week," Misty said.

"What charges?" I asked, walking past her, through the doors to the courtroom.

"Two felonies — drug trafficking and criminal mischief," she replied.

*Wonderful,* I thought. *Soon the entire YK Delta will know.*

I now understood why people would rather hang themselves than see their names in the police blotter. I wanted to dig a hole in the tundra and stick my head inside for a thousand years.

The courtroom was a bland, oversized conference room with maroon carpet and freshly painted walls of off-white. The room smelled like latex. I walked down the center aisle, past three rows of wooden chairs on both sides of me. Three people were seated in the gallery — a young Native couple in the middle row to my right, and an elderly white man in the back row to my left.

The sheriff and I moved through the swinging, waist-high doors separating the observation and hearing areas. Buzz led me to the defendant's table on my left. I sat down as he retreated to a seat right behind me, in the first row of the observation area.

We were early. The judge, clerk, and court reporter were still out to lunch.

Sitting alone in that cold courtroom, wearing prisoner's clothes, awaiting my fate, was surreal. In a weird way, I almost savored the moment because I knew it would never happen again.

I heard the courtroom doors creak open behind me. I turned around and saw Nicolai and Dalton walk through. Both wore suits and ties. They sat down together in the back row. They didn't make eye contact with me.

I couldn't stop looking at them. I wanted them to see me, Dalton especially. His eyes would speak volumes about the level of his anger. He had to know I was staring at him, but he still wouldn't look.

I desperately wanted him to know I tried calling him to apologize and explain myself the night I was arrested. I wanted him to know how sorry I was.

I shifted my eyes to Nicolai. He winked at me but remained straight-faced. I didn't know what the wink meant.

When I heard the door to the judge's chambers open, I swung my head around and faced forward. Buzz got up from his seat, marched to the front of the judge's tall oak bench, and bellowed "All rise!" as Judge Jack Warfield entered the courtroom. He, the clerk, and the court reporter filed in and sat at their posts.

The judge told everyone to be seated, then grabbed his reading glasses. "I've read your case, Mr. Ashford."

His voice sounded deep and ominous. A fat scar, traveling from below his left eye to the corner of his mouth, punctuated his rugged face. He probably got the scar mixing it up with a bear or a knife-wielding drunkard. The old Native radiated justice and authority. Mercy, he did not.

Judge Warfield put on his glasses and flipped the pages of what I assumed was my file. "From what I understand, you're pleading guilty, but you haven't been very cooperative?"

I rose to my feet. "That's correct, sir."

"You'll address me as 'your honor,'" the judge replied sternly, looking up.

When our eyes met, my dink shriveled into my stomach. "No disrespect, your honor. I've never been in this situation before."

"Back to the question, Mr. Ashford."

"Yes, your honor. I haven't been cooperative. The mistakes I've made could get people I care about into trouble."

"'Mistakes' is putting it mildly, Mr. Ashford."

I heard the courtroom doors open again. I turned my head for a split second and saw Bristy and Hope walk through. What were they doing there?

Judge Warfield recited several items from the sheriff's report, which detailed how I tried to sell a large amount of marijuana, and in doing so, two of Mr. Dalton Pace's dogs were killed.

"Why did you do these things?" he asked.

"I needed money to get back into college in Anchorage."

"You should have worked for the money."

"Yes, your honor."

Judge Warfield sighed. "I know your name, Mr. Ashford. You've written about assaults and abuse, all kinds of brutal crimes. All of those tragic events have two foul things in common: drugs and alcohol. If your marijuana delivery would have been successful, your actions would have propagated more of the same garbage. As a reporter, you have an intimate knowledge of the evils that go on in the YK Delta, and still, you chose to contribute to them."

I couldn't muster a response, so I merely nodded. Judge Warfield asked if I had anything to say for myself.

"I think I do," I said nervously.

"Well say it, before I come down on you with the force of an Oregon log splitter."

I heard giggling and turned around to scan the audience. Bristy and Hope, sitting directly behind me in the second row of the observation area, had their hands over their mouths, failing to hold back their laughter. When I made eye contact with Hope, she mouthed, "Oregon log splitter."

I laughed on the inside. It loosened me up before my big moment.

Judge Warfield cleared his throat and glared. "Well, Mr. Ashford?"

I cleared my own throat and began. "Your honor, I came to Kusko a year ago as a boy. Today, I stand before you as a man. If I had committed these crimes even a few months ago, I'd be making excuses to you right now, blaming others, unable to see past myself. Today, I admit that the situation I created is nobody's fault but my own. I've learned that lies lead to more lies. I've learned that the most important thing in my life is the people I love.

"Your honor, I will readily accept whatever judgment you levy, no matter how severe. The harsher your sentence, the stronger I will emerge on the other side."

I could tell Judge Warfield wasn't going for it, even though I sounded sincere and really did believe what I'd said.

"You're not a man," the judge said, smirking, like a war-torn combat veteran talking down to a tenderfoot soldier fresh out of boot camp. "Being a man means more than owning up to your mistakes. It means being proactive with the gifts God has given you, at all hours of every day."

I wanted to tell him that I'd begun to realize that fact, that I had the volunteer hours to prove it. "Yes, your honor."

Judge Warfield took a moment.

"I know this is your first offense, Mr. Ashford," he finally said. "And whether you know it or not, there are people in this courtroom who believe a harsh sentence will do more harm than good as you matriculate into your so-called manhood."

I smelled a trace of hope.

"Because you won't say what happened to Mr. Pace's dogs, I have no choice but to assume you killed them yourself."

I no longer smelled hope.

The judge hesitated, to allow the weight of his words to sink in. I stared into his eyes, afraid. In my head, I saw visions of myself getting pummeled in prison. I saw Bronco leading the beatings, standing above me, opening his dastardly little mouth to call me his bitch. But in the vision, Bronco's words didn't come out like that. Instead, he said, "Mr. Pace has indicated he does not want to press charges against you."

I shook my head and snapped to. Did the judge say what I think he said? Was Dalton going to let me off the hook?

"Which leads us to the marijuana," the judge said. "For that, I sentence you to time served, plus one year of probation."

I shook my head again, this time in disbelief. The judge should have thrown the book at me. Not only because five ounces of weed is a shitload, but because for all he knew, my supplier was still out there, distributing more of the same stuff. The judge should have punished the piss out of me to send a message to Finn, the shooter, and others like them. His decision didn't make sense.

"May this be an earsplitting wakeup call to you, Mr. Ashford. It's clear you have a promising future. People make mistakes. But should you ever make a similar mistake, you can expect to be behind bars for a very, very long time."

I wanted to kiss Judge Warfield on the mouth and hug Dalton so hard his guts exploded onto the wall.

* * *

I looked for Dalton and Nicolai, but they were already out the door. They must have been waiting for me in the entryway. I wanted to thank Dalton as soon as possible, but Bristy and Hope stopped me by the swinging doors.

"What are you two doing here?" I asked.

Bristy said, "We all wanted to see what was going to happen to you."

Hope pointed to my left, where Taylor had taken a spot just in front of where Nicolai and Dalton had been. I rubbed my eyes to make sure they were working properly.

"She snuck in during your lame little speech," Bristy said. "She took a cab here."

Taylor stood up and walked toward us. She wore tight blue jeans and a yellow flannel button-down. Her hair streamed down from beneath an ivory-colored winter hat. She looked like an L.L.Bean model.

I wanted to suck the lip gloss off her mouth.

"Wow, that was intense," Taylor said, smiling a little bit. "Looks like it's your lucky day."

"Seriously," I said, trying to play it cool. "Thanks for coming down for this. All three of you."

"You're welcome," Taylor said as Bristy and Hope nodded.

Hope said, "Now that you're free, are you headed back to Anchorage?"

"No clue," I said, frazzled from the courtroom surprises. "I missed the flight Dalton paid for, and I'm almost positive he didn't ship my truck out. I owe him so much money it's not even funny. Finn, too. I need to talk to both of them. Everything's a mess."

Taylor asked if I needed a ride somewhere.

"Sure," I said. "Let's pick up my stuff at the jail, but I just need to stop in the bathroom first. I might have shit my pants."

The girls laughed, then turned around to leave. I grabbed Taylor's hand before she could go. She told Bristy and Hope to wait for us up front. I couldn't believe she still wanted to know me. Perhaps the speech she'd given me about not giving up on Bristy and Hope applied to me too.

"You don't hate me?" I asked.

"No," she said. "But I'm confused. I want to know which Eddie you are — the one I thought I knew, or the one who did those crazy things."

"I'm the good Eddie," I said. "I promise you. What I did was a stupid, heat-of-the-moment mistake."

"How can I be sure?"

"Because I'm going to prove it to you."

"Maybe so," Taylor said, "but regaining my trust will take a lot of time."

"How long?"

"However long it takes," she said.

\* \* \*

In the men's room, faded blue tiles covered the walls, floor to ceiling. The sink dripped water. The towel dispenser showed its empty mouth. When I pulled up to one of two urinals, I saw shoes underneath the stall. I wondered if they belonged to Dalton or Nicolai. I hadn't seen either of them in the lobby.

I heard the guy zip up and flush as I peed, and after the stall door squeaked open, Judge Warfield and I saw each other in the mirror. He straightened his white oxford shirt at his belt and bellied up to a sink. I'd finished peeing but pretended like I was still going. I didn't want to talk to the judge. I heard him washing his hands, four feet away. I watched him out of the corner of my eye as he wiped his hands on the back of his pants.

"Mr. Ashford," the judge said, turning toward me.

I stopped pretend peeing, zipped up, and faced him. "Judge Warfield."

He looked even more imposing up close. Until him, I'd never met a Native guy taller than me.

"Your flimsy soliloquy in there did not sway my judgment. I should have given you a year or more. Anybody else, and I would have."

I didn't understand. "Anybody else?"

"Two years ago, my youngest brother was killed.

Somebody tied him to a stake and fed him to the bears. My brother was a bootlegger and had his problems. But he didn't deserve to die. Everybody knows who killed him. I suspect you do too."

"I do, your honor."

"I know you helped the sheriff arrest Bronco. Now that Bronco is in custody, new evidence has been gathered that could lead to his being charged with the murder of my brother. In short, Mr. Ashford, we're even."

\* \* \*

Hope shifted her Suburban into reverse as we backed out of a jailhouse parking space. I sat with her in front, with Bristy and Taylor in back.

"You smell like ass," Hope said.

I couldn't argue. After I'd turned in my orange jumpsuit inside the jailhouse, I had no clean clothes to put on — just the T-shirt and overalls I'd worn for days. It killed me that Taylor was smelling the same odor.

"Where to now?" Hope asked.

"My house, I guess," I said, shivering because the rear window of Hope's truck was stuck open. I wore my red hunting coat, but it wasn't enough to keep me warm. "Hopefully Dalton doesn't kill me the moment I walk in the door."

A minute later, we drove past the *Patriot* office, en route to my place, and I saw Dalton's blue truck parked outside.

"Hold up," I told Hope.

She pulled into the space next to Dalton's truck, and Taylor asked if they should wait.

"Nah, this could take a while," I said. "I'll call a cab if I have to. Can someone lend me five bucks?"

When I got out, Taylor got out too and stood close to me.

"I'm taking the front seat," she said. "It's freezing back there. Call me later."

"I will," I said. "Thanks for today. You're hot."

Taylor gave me a five-dollar bill and punched me in the arm.

I entered the Quonset hut as the girls drove away. Big fat Mikey Colosky sat in one of his barber chairs, reading the *Patriot*, waiting for another customer. He lowered the paper from in front of his face.

"I heard what happened," he said, chuckling. "I hope you didn't drop the soap."

"Shut it, Mikey," I said.

In the office, Dalton was seated at his desk, clacking away on his computer. He'd taken off his sport coat and loosened the black tie around the neck of his white shirt. I grabbed the chair at my desk and wheeled it across the room to Dalton's. I sat down.

Dalton still wouldn't look at me. He spoke while staring at his computer screen. "I wanted your head, Eddie."

"Sorry doesn't do my feelings justice," I said.

"You're damned lucky Nicolai talked me down." Dalton finally shifted his eyes to me. "We spoke until sunrise after Buzz arrested you. Nicolai wouldn't shut up about God this, and forgiveness that. The whiskey

I was sipping got me emotional. Normally, I wouldn't have been so sympathetic."

Then we went back to not making eye contact. For as good as I felt about getting my life back, I couldn't show my relief — out of respect for the hurt Dalton felt about Joanie and Lunchbox. I wasn't exactly thrilled about that, either. The image of Joanie's tail sticking above the snow would probably haunt me the rest of my life.

Dalton shuffled in his chair and asked if I got the weed from Finn.

"Finn doesn't smoke anymore," I said, a bit of truth that made my response sound like less of a lie. After all I'd been through, I felt guilty telling another lie. But my vow to protect Finn still stood.

Dalton shifted gears and asked if Joanie and Lunchbox suffered. I told him they died protecting me. In a roundabout way, that was the truth. They and the rest of the dogs ran as fast as they possibly could have when we were trying to outrun the shooter.

"They were excellent dogs," Dalton said, gulping back a lump in his throat. "But you realize, Eddie, that there's no happy ending for me in this. Replacing Joanie and Lunchbox will cost me two or three grand and hundreds of training hours."

Plus, he didn't know if Boris could ever run again. The dog's leg got shot. Replacing him at swing could cost another five hundred and more training hours.

I said, "I know that's a lot of money and time, Dalton. But I'm going to make it up to you. Give me a couple weeks."

Dalton looked at me like I was high on weed. "A couple weeks? What can you possibly accomplish in a couple weeks?"

"Trust me," I said.

CHAPTER 29

# GOODBYE, MY LOVE

Finn wore black athletic pants and a white sleeveless T-shirt. In an hour we'd be playing an evening game of pickup basketball at Kusko Rec Center. Finn grabbed my blanket and pillow from his couch, bunched them up, and set them on the floor. He sat on the couch and flipped on the TV while I was stationed at the kitchen table sipping the only beverage we could afford — water. I'd been trying to explain to him how much I sucked at basketball.

"Just plant yourself under the boards and rebound," Finn said. "You'll be a few inches taller than everybody else."

Finn went into his bedroom and came out carrying a hideous pair of red high-tops and orange short-shorts that looked straight out of the seventies. He set the things on the table.

"I'm supposed to wear *this*?" I asked. "Are we going to a costume party?"

Finn laughed and returned to the couch. He held one additional item of clothing — the red Alaska Grown T-shirt.

"See this?" he asked, balling up the shirt. He chucked it across the room into the garbage bin by the kitchen sink. He raised his arms above his head like he'd just drilled a three-pointer.

"And it's *good*," I said.

I'd been staying with Finn ever since my court date. There was no reason for Dalton and me to spend any more time together than at work; our relationship had been altered. But I'd still been feeding Dalton's dogs and cleaning their shit in the yard. It was the least I could do.

I couldn't believe I still had a job, but then again, considering how difficult it was for Dalton to find reporters willing to work in Kusko, I wasn't totally shocked. Thank you, Kusko. If I'd gotten my boss's dogs killed anywhere else on Earth, I'd have been unemployed.

Finn pointed his remote at the TV and flipped channels. "How's your dad?" he asked.

"Still pissed," I said, then swigged the last of my water. "All he ever says is, 'Figure it out.'"

I knew my dad would have much more to say the next time we talked, but he wouldn't be able to argue with the decision I was about to make. I was doing what needed to be done. I was figuring it out.

The clock above Finn's sink read five o'clock. "I have to go," I said. "I'll put on those stupid clothes when I get back."

After I'd put on my boots, jacket, and mittens, Finn said, "If the guy tries lowballing you, tell him to suck it, nerd."

\* \* \*

Outside Finn's house I walked into the darkness as a heavy snow fell. I started the FJ and grabbed the ice scraper resting on the front seat, then hopped back out and began shaving ice off the windshield and side windows. The two little side windows in the far back were difficult to scrape because the glass was curved, wrapping around the sides and back of the vehicle. The scraper made contact only in half-inch swaths.

I heard somebody else scraping and spotted Nicolai, two houses over, shearing ice from the windows of his red truck. Dalton's vehicle was gone, providing an unobstructed view of Nicolai's driveway.

I hadn't talked to Nicolai since he'd visited me in jail. Twice I tried knocking on his door, but he hadn't been around, so I shuffled through the snow with my scraper in hand. I used it to clean off the big back window of his truck while he continued working on the side windows. He wore a heavy tan hunting coat and bushy red earmuffs that looked like fox fur.

"Thanks for the help, Eddie," he said.

"No, thank you," I replied. I finished scraping and met Nicolai by the driver's side door. "You saved me."

He dropped his scraper to his side and used his other hand to wipe snow from his eyebrows. "In what way?" he asked.

"You talked Dalton down," I said. "I should be behind bars right now. My life would have been ruined."

"Glad to help," Nicolai said. "I know what it's like to need forgiveness."

\* \* \*

I honked the FJ's horn in front of a three-door ambulance garage at Kusko Regional Hospital. The door on the far right of the detached brick building opened. A young doctor named Chase moved one of the ambulances outside, into the snowfall, and I drove the FJ into the open garage stall.

I got out of the FJ as Chase, a Native guy in his early thirties, walked back into the garage and pressed a button on the wall to close the door. He wore a green down parka over blue scrubs. He was lean and clean-shaven, with short dark hair. "What's up, Eddie?" he asked, taking off his coat.

I didn't say anything. I felt like part of me was about to die.

Chase grabbed a spray hose attached to a spigot coming out of the wall near the passenger door of the FJ. He twisted the spigot open and filled a bucket with soapy water. He tossed me a sponge and began spraying the worst of the ice and dirt off the truck.

"When's the last time you washed this?" he asked, aiming the beam of water at clumps of frozen mud stuck inside the wheel wells.

"Last spring, but I only rinsed it," I said, grabbing the bucket of soapy water. "It's been killing me that

Kusko doesn't even have a car wash."

"No problem," the doctor said. "We'll have this baby cleaned up in no time."

For ten minutes I used the sponge and soapy water to scrub the areas Chase hit with water. After I finished, he gave the truck a final rinse.

Then I led Chase around the truck for a body inspection. He had taken the FJ for a test drive over the weekend but had yet to see it clean. I pointed to the passenger-door scratch the FJ had sustained when it first arrived in Kusko. "This should be the only blemish," I said.

Chase handed me a cashier's check in the amount of seven thousand dollars, a painfully low amount, considering the FJ could have fetched north of ten thousand had I sold it on the mainland. Between paying off Finn, Dalton, and my college bill, I was still thousands in the hole, but the FJ made a sizeable dent.

Chase and I stepped back to take in the entirety of the FJ, in all its shiny red beastliness. He gawked at the truck like it was a big rack of boobies. He was practically drooling.

"Damn," Chase said. "I've always wanted one of these sweet things."

At least she'd be going to a good home.

# CHAPTER 30

# SEEiNG iT THROUGH

I propped myself on the edge of Finn's couch on a Saturday afternoon and glanced out the living room window. Outside bright sun beat down on the tundra, which was beginning to look like rocky road ice cream again as winter began to fade.

Finn had taken the spot to my right, and in front of us, bellied up to the coffee table, Taylor sat cross-legged on the floor. She wore baggy jeans and a green University of Anchorage sweatshirt.

"Fifteen for two," Finn said. He advanced his green peg on Taylor's cribbage board, which was made of caribou antler and occupied the center of the table. Taylor and I had taught Finn to play cribbage only a few weeks earlier, and he was already getting good.

"Last card for one," I said, laying down a king of clubs. "Whose crib is it again?"

"Mine," Taylor said. She and Finn were neck and neck. I lagged fifteen spaces behind.

We threw down our four-card hands. I had a three and two fives to go with my king, enough for six lousy points. Finn and Taylor both had double runs, but Taylor's run also included two sevens and an eight, good for four extra points. She pegged out.

Taylor pretend sneezed. "Excuse me, gentlemen," she said. "I'm sick of winning."

"Suck it, Sifsof," Finn replied. He altered his favorite insult only for her because the alliteration sounded funny. I was happy the two of them got along so well. I had always suspected they would.

Finn stood up and said he didn't have time for another game because he needed to get ready for work. Nicolai had hooked Finn up with Willies Jr. and Sr., the construction business owners I'd volunteered with in Napakiak. They hired him full time. It was grunt work, but the job paid better than Finn's former gig at the airport — and even my job at the *Patriot* — and he was learning a viable trade.

Taylor shuffled the cards as Finn walked into his bedroom. "What should we do now?" she asked me.

I got up from the couch, walked closer to the window, and looked outside. I could see Dalton's shed and half of the back dog yard. "Did you wear boots over here?" I asked.

Taylor said yes, her mukluks.

"If Finn lends you a warm coat and snow pants," I said, "would you want to go mushing? We still haven't done that together."

If anything, Dalton trusted me with his dogs more than ever before. He knew I'd rather die than screw anything up again.

Taylor smiled. "Totally."

Finn emerged from his bedroom wearing tan overalls and a tool belt wrapped around his waist. His screwdrivers and wrenches clanked around as he walked to the entryway to put on his leather boots. "I'm helping out on a remodeling project at the hospital," he said. "Be home around midnight. Let's hunt tomorrow morning."

Lately, Finn and I had been hunting rabbit and ptarmigan two or three times a week, and we took turns checking his beaver snares beneath the ice on the Kuskokwim, which needed to be done every other day. The meat we got ourselves saved us each about a hundred bucks a month in grocery bills.

* * *

Taylor rode in front, wearing Finn's green wool hunting coat, clutching the sides of the sled as we bumped along in quiet solitude. The temperature must have been close to forty degrees. Every so often, the sled skated across patches of slush on the four-foot-wide snow trail. In a few weeks, the trail would be gone.

Boris, running at swing, trotted along like his old self again. His former running partner, Aggie, had taken Joanie's spot at lead. Aggie was like a backup quarterback — decent at the job, but not a long-term solution. She was a temporary fix until Dalton could get his new lead dog trained in, which he said could take more than a year. I forked over almost two grand in FJ proceeds for the dog, a tan-colored, six-month-old pup named Spud.

By now we must have been five miles out of town. Taylor and I had barely spoken, and when we did, we half whispered. Mushing out there that day was so epically peaceful, talking out loud would have been like hurling a brick into a placid lake at sunset. On one stretch of smooth trail, we glided right past a small flock of ptarmigan, and the birds didn't even fly away.

Taylor pointed to her left. "There," she said quietly.

Far off, maybe a mile away, little black specs appeared all along the blue horizon. Some of the specs were stationary, some moved slowly, and a few seemed to run and stop in bursts.

It was the Mulchatna herd of caribou. I had written about the herd, but I had never seen it. I jammed my foot on the brake. "Whoa!" I called.

After the dogs stopped, Taylor got out of the sled and handed me the rope and ice hook she'd been holding on her lap. She took my spot on the sled and pressed the brake while I walked ten feet behind her and stomped the ice hook into a snowless patch of tundra. I joined her back by the sled, placed my right hand above my eyebrows to block the sun's glare, and gazed into the distance.

"How many are there?" I asked.

"Hundreds," Taylor said. "Maybe thousands."

I wanted one. Finn and I could eat off it for months. I was sure we had enough scratch to go halfsies on a used chest freezer, because Finn was earning good money now, and I was making headway on my debts. Splitting rent with Finn, it turned out, was slightly cheaper than it had been to keep the FJ going.

"Do you think they'll still be around tomorrow?" I asked, peering at the caribou, as even more of them materialized. The line of animals seemed like it might stretch back to Anchorage.

"Who knows," Taylor replied, standing three feet away. "Tomorrow they could be a hundred miles away. Or two miles. It's anyone's guess."

Taylor shuffled her feet. I could tell she was looking right at me, but I pretended not to notice, kept looking at the caribou. I used the sleeve of my red coat to wipe a drip from my nose.

Taylor cleared her throat and asked, "Will *you* still be around tomorrow?"

I thought for a moment, and then I faced her. She looked beautiful standing there on the vacant tundra, like a flower floating in outer space. A breeze blew strands of her blond hair onto her face, but she didn't push them away.

"I'll be here," I said. "I'll be here for however long it takes."

Taylor didn't blink. Behind her, several dogs barked impatiently. She didn't acknowledge them.

Then she raised an eyebrow and smiled. "Good," she said. "I met this cute guy, but I don't have the guts to ask him out. Maybe you could talk to him for me."

I took off my mitten and started to flick her off, but she swatted my hand before I could finish the job.

**THE END**

# Q&A WITH CRAIG DIRKES

Immense, wild, and in some ways unknowable, Alaska seems a fitting setting for a coming-of-age novel, especially one like Craig Dirkes has written. In his debut, Craig tells the story of a crucial period in the lives of his eighteen-year-old narrator and the handful of friends he makes while living in a desolate region of the state. Throughout their work on this book, Craig and his Switch Press editor, Nick Healy, often talked about Alaska and how it felt like a character as much as a setting in this story.

Here, they discuss *Sucktown, Alaska* and the real places and events that inspired it.

**NICK:** You spent several years in Alaska and lived in a town similar to the fictional Kusko. What drew you there?

**CRAIG:** I had just graduated from college and was determined to spend the rest of my twenties traveling the world. Alaska, I decided, would be a more exciting launching pad than my home state of Minnesota. In Alaska I could have an adventurous life while I saved for all those airplane tickets. I wound up spending close to two years bartending in Anchorage and almost three years working at newspapers in rural towns across Alaska. Later on, I did make those trips to Asia and Africa. But rural Alaska, I came to realize, was as exotic as anywhere on Earth.

**NICK:** Eddie Ashford, your story's narrator, and his friend Finn Wassily are young men living on their own and free to do what they want. Are they ready for it?

**CRAIG:** Well, I wasn't ready. Just like it is for Eddie, my first time being alone in the world came when I moved to Alaska. During my first couple years there I made loads of bad choices. My irresponsibility peaked when, dressed as Jack Daniels, I spent Halloween night locked up in a rural Alaska jail (long story). After that I shaped up quite a bit, much like Eddie and Finn attempt to do. The hope is that you don't make a choice that's so bad it negatively affects the rest of your life or someone else's. This book explores what can happen when people do make those kinds of choices.

**NICK:** Your story doesn't fall into the expected man-versus-nature mold of an Alaska novel. How did you choose to tell this story?

**CRAIG:** In a way, the story chose me. Several key story elements in this book happened to me in real life. Although I never sold marijuana, I did work at a bush newspaper, while living with my boss, who was also a musher. Getting stranded because of my truck happened, too. An Anchorage-based newspaper company I worked for agreed to fly my truck to and from a town called Dillingham, but when it came time for me to leave there fifteen months later, the company refused to fly it back. I would have been stuck there for months had my coworkers not banded together and advocated for me. The more I thought about all of these unusual life events, combined with all of the remarkable things I'd seen and experienced while living in rural Alaska, the more I thought they could be intertwined in a compelling and unexpected story.

**NICK:** Eddie gets himself into some very specific trouble of his own making, but there's something universal in the push and pull between his best and worst impulses. How does he represent the experience of coming of age?

**CRAIG:** We all have a little voice inside our heads telling us the right thing to do, and the younger we are, the harder that voice is to listen to. Through the bad moves Eddie makes and the good people he meets, he eventually figures out something about dealing with those conflicting voices.

**NICK:** Before Eddie leaves Anchorage, someone warns him that Kusko is located in "unromantic" Alaska, the part without towering mountains, rushing rivers, grizzlies snapping at leaping fish, and so on. Is there nothing romantic on the tundra?

**CRAIG:** The delta and bush towns like Kusko do have magic. I wouldn't have lived in rural Alaska for so long if they didn't. But it's easy to understand why some people wouldn't see it that way. Living in a small and isolated community isn't for everybody. Most people can't live without comfortable houses, nice cars, and twenty-four-hour restaurants. Eddie is in that camp when he arrives in Kusko. Gradually, he begins to see what others in rural Alaska already know — creature comforts don't always equate to happiness. The Alaskan lifestyle, in its truest form, does.

**NICK:** Why are Alaska and the YK Delta still on your mind?

**CRAIG:** They will always be on my mind. Once you've lived in Alaska, the place becomes a part of you, and it never stops calling you back. As much as I want to live there again, I probably never will. But that's where this book comes in. In a weird way, I thought that if I could write a book set in Alaska, I'd become part of the state forever, even after I die.

**CRAIG DIRKES** is a public relations writer and professional photographer. He began his career as a journalist in rural Alaska, and currently he lives in Minnesota with his wife and three young children.